ALBERT CAMUS

THE PLAGUE

NEW DELHI (INDIA)

THE PLAGUE

This English Edition Published in India

Published by

MGB®

An Imprint of

MAANU GRAPHICS

MAANU GRAPHICS

(PUBLISHERS OF GENERAL BOOKS)

5FF, Ganpati Bhawan, 21 Ansari Road,
Darya Ganj, New Delhi-110002
Ph: 43755225, 9315898404
E-mail : maanugraphics@yahoo.com
mgbooks.maanu@yahoo.com

Printed at

Satyam Enterprises, Delhi

ABOUT THE AUTHOR

ALBERT CAMUS was born in Mondovi, Algeria, in 1913. After winning a degree in philosophy, he worked at various jobs, ending up in journalism. In the thirties he ran a theatrical company, and during the war was active in the French Resistance, editing an important underground paper, Combat. Among his major works are four widely praised works of fiction, The Stranger (1946), The Plague (1948), The Fall (1957), and Exile and the Kingdom (1958); a volume of plays, Caligula and Three Other Plays (1958); and two books of philosophical essays, The Rebel (1954) and The Myth of Sisyphus (1955), both of which are available in the Vintage series.

Albert Camus was awarded the Nobel Prize for Literature in 1957. He was killed in an automobile accident on January 4, 1960.

It is as reasonable to represent one kind of imprisonment by another, as it is to represent anything that really exists by that which exists not.

DANIEL DEFOE

PART I

The unusual events described in this chronicle occurred in 194- at Oran. Everyone agreed that, considering their somewhat extraordinary character, they were out of place there. For its ordinariness is what strikes one first about the town of Oran, which is merely a large French port on the Algerian coast, headquarters of the Prefect of a French Department.

The town itself, let us admit, is ugly. It has a smug, placid air and you need time to discover what it is that makes it different from so many business centers in other parts of the world. How to conjure up a picture, for instance, of a town without pigeons, without any trees or gardens, where you never hear the beat of wings or the rustle of leaves, a thoroughly negative place, in short?

The seasons are discriminated only in the sky. All that tells you of spring's coming is the feel of the air, or the baskets of flowers brought in from the suburbs by peddlers; it's a spring cried in the marketplaces. During the summer the sun bakes the houses bone-dry, sprinkles our walls with grayish dust, and you have no option but to survive those days of fire indoors, behind closed shutters. In autumn, on the other hand, we have deluges of mud. Only winter brings really pleasant weather.

Perhaps the easiest way of making a town's acquaintance is to ascertain how the people in it work, how they love, and how they die. In our little town (is this, one wonders, an effect of the climate? All three are done on much the same lines, with the same feverish yet casual air. The truth is that everyone is bored, and devotes himself to cultivating habits. Our citizens work hard, but solely with the object of getting rich. Their chief interest is in commerce, and their chief aim in life is, as they call it, "doing business." Naturally they don't eschew such simpler pleasures as love-making, seabathing, going to the pictures. But, very sensibly, they reserve these pastimes for Saturday afternoons and Sundays and employ the rest of the week in making money, as much as possible. In the evening, on leaving the office, they forgather, at an hour that never varies, in the cafes, stroll the same boulevard, or take the air on their balconies. The passions of the young are violent and short-lived; the vices of older men seldom range beyond an addiction to bowling, to banquets and "socials," or clubs where large sums change hands on the fall of a card.

It will be said, no doubt, that these habits are not peculiar to our town; really all our contemporaries are much the same. Certainly nothing is commoner nowadays than to see people working from morn till night and then proceeding to fritter away at card-tables, in cafes and in small-talk what time is left for living. Nevertheless there still exist towns and countries where people have now and then an inkling of something different. In general it doesn't change their lives. Still, they have had an intimation, and that's so much to the good. Oran, however, seems to be a town without intimations; in other words, completely modern. Hence I see no need to dwell on the manner of loving in our town. The men and women consume one another rapidly in what is called "the act of love," or else settle down to a mild habit of conjugality. We seldom find a mean between these extremes. That, too, is not exceptional. At Oran, as elsewhere, for lack of time and thinking, people have to love one another without knowing much about it.

What is more exceptional in our town is the difficulty one may experience there in dying. "Difficulty," perhaps, is not the right word, 'discomfort" would come nearer. Being ill's never agreeable but there are towns that stand by you, so to speak, when you are sick; in which you can, after a fashion, let yourself go.

An invalid needs small attentions, he likes to have something to rely on, and that's natural enough. But at Oran the violent extremes of temperature, the exigencies of business, the uninspiring surroundings, the sudden nightfalls, and the very nature of its pleasures call for good health. An invalid feels out of it there. Think what it must be for a dying man, trapped behind hundreds of walls all sizzling with heat, while the whole population, sitting in cafes or hanging on the telephone, is discussing shipments, bills of lading, discounts! It will then be obvious what discomfort attends death, even modern death, when it waylays you under such conditions in a dry place.

These somewhat haphazard observations may give a fair idea of what our town is like. However, we must not exaggerate. Really, all that was to be conveyed was the banality of the town's appearance and of life in it. But you can get through the days there without trouble, once you have formed habits. And since habits are precisely what our town encourages, all is for the best. Viewed from this angle, its life is not particularly exciting; that must be admitted. But, at least, social unrest is quite unknown among us. And our frank-spoken, amiable, and industrious citizens have always inspired a reasonable esteem in visitors.

Treeless, glamourless, soulless, the town of Oran ends by seeming restful and, after a while, you go complacently to sleep there.

It is only fair to add that Oran is grafted on to a unique landscape, in the center of a bare plateau, ringed with luminous hills and above a perfectly shaped bay. All we may regret is the town's being so disposed that it turns its back on the bay, with the result that it's impossible to see the sea, you always have to go to look for it.

Such being the normal life of Oran, it will be easily understood that our fellow citizens had not the faintest reason to apprehend the incidents that took place in the spring of the year in question and were (as we subsequently realized) premonitory signs of the grave events we are to chronicle. To some, these events will seem quite natural; to others, all but incredible. But, obviously, a narrator cannot take account of these differences of outlook. His business is only to say: "This is what happened," when he knows that it actually did happen, that it closely affected the life of a whole populace, and that there are thousands of eyewitnesses who can appraise in their hearts the truth of what he writes.

In any case the narrator (whose identity will be made known in due course) would have little claim to competence for a task like this, had not chance put him in the way of gathering much information, and had he not been, by the force of things, closely involved in all that he proposes to narrate. This is his justification for playing the part of a historian. Naturally, a historian, even an amateur, always has data, personal or at second hand, to guide him. The present narrator has three kinds of data: first, what he saw himself; secondly, the accounts of other eyewitnesses (thanks to the part he played, he was enabled to learn their personal impressions from all those figuring in this chronicle); and, lastly, documents that subsequently came into his hands. He proposes to draw on these records whenever this seems desirable, and to employ them as he thinks best. He also proposes...

But perhaps the time has come to drop preliminaries and cautionary remarks and to launch into the narrative proper. The account of the first days needs giving in some detail.

When leaving his surgery on the morning of April 16, Dr. Bernard Rieux felt something soft under his foot. It was a dead rat lying in the middle of the landing.

On the spur of the moment he kicked it to one side and, without giving it a further thought, continued on his way downstairs. Only when he was stepping out into the street did it occur to him that a dead rat had no business to be on his landing, and he turned back to ask the concierge of the building to see to its removal. It was not until he noticed old M. Michel's reaction to the news that he realized the peculiar nature of his discovery. Personally, he had thought the presence of the dead rat rather odd, no more than that; the concierge, however, was genuinely outraged. On one point he was categorical: "There weren't no rats here." In vain the doctor assured him that there was a rat, presumably dead, on the second-floor landing; M. Michel's conviction wasn't to be shaken. There "weren't no rats in the building," he repeated, so someone must have brought this one from outside. Some youngster trying to be funny, most likely.

That evening, when Dr. Rieux was standing in the entrance, feeling for the latch-key in his pocket before starting up the stairs to his apartment, he saw a big rat coming toward him from the dark end of the passage. It moved uncertainly, and its fur was sopping wet. The animal stopped and seemed to be trying to get its balance, moved forward again toward the doctor, halted again, then spun round on itself with a little squeal and fell on its side. Its mouth was slightly open and blood was spurting from it. After gazing at it for a moment, the doctor went upstairs.

He wasn't thinking about the rat. That glimpse of spurting blood had switched his thoughts back to something that had been on his mind all day. His wife, who had been ill for a year now, was due to leave next day for a sanatorium in the mountains. He found her lying down in the bedroom, resting, as he had asked her to do, in view of the exhausting journey before her. She gave him a smile.

"Do you know, I'm feeling ever so much better!" she said.

The doctor gazed down at the face that turned toward him in the glow of the bedside lamp. His wife was thirty, and the long illness had left its mark on her face. Yet the thought that came to Rieux's mind as he gazed at her was: "How young she looks, almost like a little girl!" But perhaps that was because of the smile, which effaced all else.

"Now try to sleep," he counseled. "The nurse is coming at eleven, you know, and you have to catch the midday train."

He kissed the slightly moist forehead. The smile escorted him to the door.

Next day, April 17, at eight o'clock the concierge buttonholed the doctor as he was going out. Some young scallywags, he said, had dumped three dead rats in the hall. They'd obviously been caught in traps with very strong springs, as they were bleeding profusely. The concierge had lingered in the doorway for quite a while, holding the rats by their legs and keeping a sharp eye on the passers-by, on the off chance that the miscreants would give themselves away by grinning or by some facetious remark. His watch had been in vain.

"But I'll nab 'em all right," said M. Michel hopefully.

Much puzzled, Rieux decided to begin his round in the outskirts of the town, where his poorer patients lived. The scavenging in these districts was done late in the morning and, as he drove his car along the straight, dusty streets, he cast glances at the garbage cans aligned along the edge of the sidewalk. In one street alone the doctor counted as many as a dozen rats deposited on the vegetable and other refuse in the cans.

He found his first patient, an asthma case of long standing, in bed, in a room that served as both dining-room and bedroom and overlooked the street. The invalid was an old Spaniard with a hard, rugged face. Placed on the coverlet in front of him were two pots containing dried peas. When the doctor entered, the old man was sitting up, bending his neck back, gasping and wheezing in his efforts to recover his breath. His wife brought a bowl of water.

"Well, doctor," he said, while the injection was being made, "they're coming out, have you noticed?"

"The rats, he means," his wife explained. "The man next door found three."

"They're coming out, you can see them in all the trash cans. It's hunger!"

Rieux soon discovered that the rats were the great topic of conversation in that part of the town. After his round of visits he drove home.

"There's a telegram for you, sir, upstairs," M. Michel informed him.

The doctor asked him if he'd seen any more rats.

"No," the concierge replied, "there ain't been any more. I'm keeping a sharp lookout, you know. Those youngsters wouldn't dare when I'm around."

The telegram informed Rieux that his mother would be arriving next day. She was going to keep house for her son during his wife's absence. When the doctor entered his apartment he found the nurse already there. He looked at his wife.

She was in a tailor-made suit, and he noticed that she had used rouge. He smiled to her.

"That's splendid," he said. "You're looking very nice."

A few minutes later he was seeing her into the sleeping-car. She glanced round the compartment.

"It's too expensive for us really, isn't it?"

"It had to be done," Rieux replied.

"What's this story about rats that's going round?"

"I can't explain it. It certainly is queer, but it'll pass."

Then hurriedly he begged her to forgive him; he felt he should have looked after her better, he'd been most remiss. When she shook her head, as if to make him stop, he added: "Anyhow, once you're back everything will be better. We'll make a fresh start."

"That's it!" Her eyes were sparkling. "Let's make a fresh start."

But then she turned her head and seemed to be gazing through the car window at the people on the platform, jostling one another in their haste. The hissing of the locomotive reached their ears. Gently he called his wife's first name; when she looked round he saw her face wet with tears.

"Don't," he murmured.

Behind the tears the smile returned, a little tense. She drew a deep breath.

"Now off you go! Everything will be all right."

He took her in his arms, then stepped back on the platform. Now he could only see her smile through the window.

"Please, dear," he said, "take great care of yourself."

But she could not hear him.

As he was leaving the platform, near the exit he met M. Othon, the police magistrate, holding his small boy by the hand. The doctor asked him if he was going away.

Tall and dark, M. Othon had something of the air of what used to be called a man of the world, and something of an undertaker's assistant.

"No," the magistrate replied, "I've come to meet Madame Othon, who's been to present her respects to my family."

The engine whistled.

"These rats, now?" the magistrate began.

Rieux made a brief movement in the direction of the train, then turned back toward the exit.

"The rats?" he said. "It's nothing."

The only impression of that moment which, afterwards, he could recall was the passing of a railroadman with a box full of dead rats under his arm.

Early in the afternoon of that day, when his consultations were beginning, a young man called on Rieux. The doctor gathered that he had called before, in the morning, and was a journalist by profession. His name was Raymond Rambert.

Short, square-shouldered, with a determined-looking face and keen, intelligent eyes, he gave the impression of someone who could keep his end up in any circumstances. He wore a sports type of clothes. He came straight to the point.

His newspaper, one of the leading Paris dailies, had commissioned him to make a report on the living-conditions prevailing among the Arab population, and especially on the sanitary conditions.

Rieux replied that these conditions were not good. But, before he said any more, he wanted to know if the journalist would be allowed to tell the truth.

"Certainly," Rambert replied.

"I mean," Rieux explained, "would you be allowed to publish an unqualified condemnation of the present state of things?"

"Unqualified? Well, no, I couldn't go that far. But surely things aren't quite so bad as that?"

"No," Rieux said quietly, they weren't so bad as that. He had put the question solely to find out if Rambert could or couldn't state the facts without paltering with the truth. "I've no use for statements in which something is kept back," he added. "That is why I shall not furnish information in support of yours."

The journalist smiled. "You talk the language of Saint-Just."

Without raising his voice Rieux said he knew nothing about that. The language he used was that of a man who was sick and tired of the world he lived in, though he had much liking for his fellow men and had resolved, for his part, to have no truck with injustice and compromises with the truth.

His shoulders hunched, Rambert gazed at the doctor for some moments without speaking. Then, "I think I understand you," he said, getting up from his chair.

The doctor accompanied him to the door.

"It's good of you to take it like that," he said.

"Yes, yes, I understand," Rambert repeated, with what seemed a hint of impatience in his voice. "Sorry to have troubled you."

When shaking hands with him, Rieux suggested that if he was out for curious stories for his paper, he might say something about the extraordinary number of dead rats that were being found in the town just now.

"Ah!" Rambert exclaimed. "That certainly interests me."

On his way out at five for another round of visits, the doctor passed on the stairway a stocky, youngish man, with a big, deeply furrowed face and bushy eyebrows. He had met him once or twice in the top-floor apartment, which was occupied by some male Spanish dancers. Puffing a cigarette, Jean Tarrou was gazing down at the convulsions of a rat dying on the step in front of him. He looked up, and his gray eyes remained fixed on the doctor for some moments; then, after wishing him good day, he remarked that it was rather odd, the way all these rats were coming out of their holes to die.

"Very odd," Rieux agreed, "and it ends by getting on one's nerves."

"In a way, doctor, only in a way. We've not seen anything of the sort before, that's all. Personally I find it interesting, yes, definitely interesting."

Tarrou ran his fingers through his hair to brush it off his forehead, looked again at the rat, which had now stopped moving, then smiled toward Rieux.

"But really, doctor, it's the concierge's headache, isn't it?"

As it so happened, the concierge was the next person Rieux encountered. He was leaning against the wall beside the street door; he was looking tired and his normally rubicund face had lost its color.

"Yes, I know," the old man told Rieux, who had informed him of the latest casualty among the rats. "I keep finding 'em by twos and threes. But it's the same thing in the other houses in the street."

He seemed depressed and worried, and was scratching his neck absentmindedly.

Rieux asked him how he felt. The concierge wouldn't go so far as to say he was feeling ill. Still he wasn't quite up to the mark. In his opinion it was just due to worry; these damned rats had given him "a shock, like." It would be a relief when they stopped coming out and dying all over the place.

Next morning, it was April 18, when the doctor was bringing back his mother from the station, he found M. Michel looking still more out of sorts. The stairway from the cellar to the attics was strewn with dead rats, ten or a dozen of them.

The garbage cans of all the houses in the street were full of rats.

The doctor's mother took it quite calmly.

"It's like that sometimes," she said vaguely. She was a small woman with silver hair and dark, gentle eyes. "I'm so glad to be with you again, Bernard," she added. "The rats can't change that, anyhow."

He nodded. It was a fact that everything seemed easy when she was there.

However, he rang up the Municipal Office. He knew the man in charge of the department concerned with the extermination of vermin and he asked him if he'd heard about all the rats that were coming out to die in the open. Yes, Mercier knew all about it; in fact, fifty rats had been found in his offices, which were near the wharves. To tell the truth, he was rather perturbed; did the doctor think it meant anything serious? Rieux couldn't give a definite opinion, but he thought the sanitary service should take action of some kind.

Mercier agreed. "And, if you think it's really worth the trouble, I'll get an order issued as well."

"It certainly is worth the trouble," Rieux replied.

His charwoman had just told him that several hundred dead rats had been collected in the big factory where her husband worked.

It was about this time that our townsfolk began to show signs of uneasiness.

For, from April 18 onwards, quantities of dead or dying rats were found in factories and warehouses. In some cases the animals were killed to put an end to their agony. From the outer suburbs to the center of the town, in all the byways where the doctor's duties took him, in every thoroughfare, rats were piled up in garbage cans or lying in long lines in the gutters. The evening papers that day took up the matter and inquired whether or not the city fathers were going to take steps, and what emergency measures were contemplated, to abate this particularly disgusting nuisance. Actually the municipality had not contemplated doing anything at all, but now a meeting was convened to discuss the situation.

An order was transmitted to the sanitary service to collect the dead rats at daybreak every morning. When the rats had been collected, two municipal trucks were to take them to be burned in the town incinerator.

But the situation worsened in the following days. There were more and more dead vermin in the streets, and the collectors had bigger truckloads every morning.

On the fourth day the rats began to come out and die in batches. From basements, cellars, and sewers they emerged in long wavering files into the light of day, swayed helplessly, then did a sort of pirouette and fell dead at the feet of the horrified onlookers. At night, in passages and alleys, their shrill little death-cries could be clearly heard. In the mornings the bodies were found lining the gutters, each with a gout of blood, like a red flower, on its tapering muzzle; some were bloated and already beginning to rot, others rigid, with their whiskers still erect. Even in the busy heart of the town you found them piled in little heaps on landings and in backyards. Some stole forth to die singly in the halls of public offices, in school playgrounds, and even on cafe terraces. Our townsfolk were amazed to find such busy centers as the Place d'Armes, the boulevards, the promenade along the waterfront, dotted with repulsive little corpses. After the daily clean-up of the town, which took place at sunrise, there was a brief respite; then gradually the rats began to appear again in numbers that went on increasing throughout the day. People out at night would often feel underfoot the squelchy roundness of a still warm body. It was as if the earth on which our houses stood were being purged of its secreted humors; thrusting up to the surface the abscesses and pus-clots that had been forming in its entrails. You must picture the consternation of our little town, hitherto so tranquil, and now, out of the blue, shaken to its core, like a quite healthy man who all of a sudden feels his temperature shoot up and the blood seething like wildfire in his veins.

Things went so far that the Ransdoc Information Bureau (inquiries on all subjects promptly and accurately answered), which ran a free-information talk on the radio, by way of publicity, began its talk by announcing that no less than 6,231 rats had been collected and burned in a single day, April 25. Giving as it did an ampler and more precise view of the scene daily enacted before our eyes, this amazing figure administered a jolt to the public nerves. Hitherto people had merely grumbled at a stupid, rather obnoxious visitation; they now realized that this strange phenomenon, whose scope could not be measured and whose origins escaped detection, had something vaguely menacing about it. Only the old Spaniard whom Dr. Rieux was treating for asthma went on rubbing his hands and chuckling: "They're coming out, they're coming out," with senile glee.

On April 28, when the Ransdoc Bureau announced that 8,000 rats had been collected, a wave of something like panic swept the town.

There was a demand for drastic measures, the authorities were accused of slackness, and people who had houses on the coast spoke of moving there, early in the year though it was. But next day the bureau informed them that the phenomenon had abruptly ended and the sanitary service had collected only a trifling number of rats. Everyone breathed more freely.

It was, however, on this same day, at noon, that Dr. Rieux, when parking his car in front of the apartment house where he lived, noticed the concierge coming toward him from the end of the street. He was dragging himself along, his head bent, arms and legs curiously splayed out, with the jerky movements of a clockwork doll. The old man was leaning on the arm of a priest whom the doctor knew. It was Father Paneloux, a learned and militant Jesuit, whom he had met occasionally and who was very highly thought of in our town, even in circles quite indifferent to religion. Rieux waited for the two men to draw up to him.

M. Michel's eyes were fever-bright and he was breathing wheezily. The old man explained that, feeling "a bit off color," he had gone out to take the air. But he had started feeling pains in all sorts of places, in his neck, armpits, and groin, and had been obliged to turn back and ask Father Paneloux to give him an arm.

"It's just swellings," he said. "I must have strained myself somehow."

Leaning out of the window of the car, the doctor ran his hand over the base of Michel's neck; a hard lump, like a knot in wood, had formed there.

"Go to bed at once, and take your temperature. I'll come to see you this afternoon."

When the old man had gone, Rieux asked Father Paneloux what he made of this queer business about the rats.

"Oh, I suppose it's an epidemic they've been having." The Father's eyes were smiling behind his big round glasses.

After lunch, while Rieux was reading for the second time the telegram his wife had sent him from the sanatorium, announcing her arrival, the phone rang. It was one of his former patients, a clerk in the Municipal Office, ringing him up. He had suffered for a long time from a constriction of the aorta, and, as he was poor, Rieux had charged no fee.

"Thanks, doctor, for remembering me. But this time it's somebody else. The man next door has had an accident. Please come at once." He sounded out of breath.

Rieux thought quickly; yes, he could see the concierge afterwards. A few minutes later he was entering a small house in the rue Faidherbe, on the outskirts of the town. Halfway up the drafty, foul-smelling stairs, he saw Joseph Grand, the clerk, hurrying down to meet him. He was a man of about fifty years of age, tall and drooping, with narrow shoulders, thin limbs, and a yellowish mustache.

"He looks better now," he told Rieux, "but I really thought his number was up."

He blew his nose vigorously.

On the top floor, the third, Rieux noticed something scrawled in red chalk on a door on the left: Come in, I've hanged myself.

They entered the room. A rope dangled from a hanging lamp above a chair lying on its side. The dining-room table had been pushed into a corner. But the rope hung empty.

"I got him down just in time." Grand seemed always to have trouble in finding his words, though he expressed himself in the simplest possible way. "I was going out and I heard a noise. When I saw that writing on the door, I thought it was a a prank. Only, then I heard a funny sort of groan; it made my blood run cold, as they say." He scratched his head. "That must be a painful way of of doing it, I should think. Naturally I went in."

Grand had opened a door and they were standing on the threshold of a bright but scantily furnished bedroom. There was a brass bedstead against one of the walls, and a plump little man was lying there, breathing heavily. He gazed at them with bloodshot eyes.

Rieux stopped short. In the intervals of the man's breathing he seemed to hear the little squeals of rats. But he couldn't see anything moving in the corners of the room. Then he went to the bedside. Evidently the man had not fallen from a sufficient height, or very suddenly, for the collar-bone had held.

Naturally there was some asphyxia. An X-ray photograph would be needed.

Meanwhile the doctor gave him a camphor injection and assured him he would be all right in a few days.

"Thanks, doctor," the man mumbled.

When Rieux asked Grand if he had notified the police, he hung his head.

"Well, as a matter of fact, I haven't. The first thing, I thought, was to?"

"Quite so," Rieux cut in. "I'll see to it."

But the invalid made a fretful gesture and sat up in bed. He felt much better, he explained; really it wasn't worth the trouble.

"Don't feel alarmed," Rieux said. "It's little more than a formality. Anyhow, I have to report this to the police."

"Oh!" The man slumped back on the bed and started sobbing weakly.

Grand, who had been twiddling his mustache while they were speaking, went up to the bed.

"Come, Monsieur Cottard," he said. "Try to understand. People could say the doctor was to blame, if you took it into your head to have another shot at it."

Cottard assured him tearfully that there wasn't the least risk of that; he'd had a sort of crazy fit, but it had passed and all he wanted now was to be left in peace. Rieux was writing a prescription.

"Very well," he said. "We'll say no more about it for the present. I'll come and see you again in a day or two. But don't do anything silly."

On the landing he told Grand that he was obliged to make a report, but would ask the police inspector to hold up the inquiry for a couple of days.

"But somebody should watch Cottard tonight," he added. "Has he any relations?"

"Not that I know of. But I can very well stay with him. I can't say I really know him, but one's got to help a neighbor, hasn't one?"

As he walked down the stairs Rieux caught himself glancing into the darker corners, and he asked Grand if the rats had quite disappeared in his part of the town.

Grand had no idea. True, he'd heard some talk about rats, but he never paid much attention to gossip like that. "I've other things to think about," he added.

Rieux, who was in a hurry to get away, was already shaking his hand. There was a letter to write to his wife, and he wanted to see the concierge first.

News-venders were shouting the latest news that the rats had disappeared. But Rieux found his patient leaning over the edge of the bed, one hand pressed to his belly and the other to his neck, vomiting pinkish bile into a slop-pail.

After retching for some moments, the man lay back again, gasping. His temperature was 103, the ganglia of his neck and limbs were swollen, and two black patches were developing on his thighs. He now complained of internal pains.

"It's like fire," he whimpered. "The bastard's burning me inside."

He could hardly get the words through his fever-crusted lips and he gazed at the doctor with bulging eyes that his headache had suffused with tears. His wife cast an anxious look at Rieux, who said nothing.

"Please, doctor," she said, "what is it?"

"It might be almost anything. There's nothing definite as yet. Keep him on a light diet and give him plenty to drink."

The sick man had been complaining of a raging thirst.

On returning to his apartment Rieux rang up his colleague Richard, one of the leading practitioners in the town.

"No," Richard said, "I can't say I've noticed anything exceptional."

"No cases of fever with local inflammation?"

"Wait a bit! I have two cases with inflamed ganglia."

"Abnormally so?"

"Well," Richard said, "that depends on what you mean by 'normal.'"

Anyhow, that night the porter was running a temperature of 104 and in delirium, always babbling about "them rats." Rieux tried a fixation abscess. When he felt the sting of the turpentine, the old man yelled: "The bastards!"

The ganglia had become still larger and felt like lumps of solid fibrous matter embedded in the flesh. Mme Michel had completely broken down.

"Sit up with him," the doctor said, "and call me if necessary."

Next day, April 30, the sky was blue and slightly misty. A warm, gentle breeze was blowing, bringing with it a smell of flowers from the outlying suburbs. The morning noises of the streets sounded louder, gayer than usual. For everyone in our little town this day brought the promise of a new lease of life, now that the shadow of fear under which they had been living for a week had lifted.

Rieux, too, was in an optimistic mood when he went down to see the concierge; he had been cheered up by a letter from his wife that had come with the first mail.

Old M. Michel's temperature had gone down to 99 and, though he still looked very weak, he was smiling. "He's better, doctor, isn't he?" his wife inquired. "Well, it's a bit too early to say."

At noon the sick man's temperature shot up abruptly to 104, he was in constant delirium and had started vomiting again. The ganglia in the neck were painful to the touch, and the old man seemed to be straining to hold his head as far as possible from his body. His wife sat at the foot of the bed, her hands on the counterpane, gently clasping his feet. She gazed at Rieux imploringly.

"Listen," he said, "we'll have to move him to a hospital and try a special treatment. I'll ring up for the ambulance."

Two hours later the doctor and Mme Michel were in the ambulance bending over the sick man. Rambling words were issuing from the gaping mouth, thickly coated now with sores. He kept on repeating: "Them rats! Them damned rats!" His face had gone livid, a grayish green, his lips were bloodless, his breath came in sudden gasps. His limbs spread out by the ganglia, embedded in the berth as if he were trying to bury himself in it or a voice from the depths of the earth were summoning him below, the unhappy man seemed to be stifling under some unseen pressure. His wife was sobbing.

"Isn't there any hope left, doctor?"

"He's dead," said Rieux.

Michel's death marked, one might say, the end of the first period, that of bewildering portents, and the beginning of another, relatively more trying, in which the perplexity of the early days gradually gave place to panic. Reviewing that first phase in the light of subsequent events, our townsfolk realized that they had never dreamed it possible that our little town should be chosen out for the scene of such grotesque happenings as the wholesale death of rats in broad daylight or the decease of concierges through exotic maladies. In this respect they were wrong, and their views obviously called for revision. Still, if things had gone thus far and no farther, force of habit would doubtless have gained the day, as usual. But other members of our community, not all menials or poor people, were to follow the path down which M. Michel had led the way. And it was then that fear, and with fear serious reflection, began.

However, before entering on a detailed account of the next phase, the narrator proposes to give the opinion of another witness on the period that has been described.

Jean Tarrou, whose acquaintance we have already made at the beginning of this narrative, had come to Oran some weeks before and was staying in a big hotel in the center of the town. Apparently he had private means and was not engaged in business. But though he gradually became a familiar figure in our midst, no one knew where he hailed from or what had brought him to Oran. He was often to be seen in public and at the beginning of spring was seen on one or other of the beaches almost every day; obviously he was fond of swimming. Good-humored, always ready with a smile, he seemed an addict of all normal pleasures without being their slave. In fact, the only habit he was known to have was that of cultivating the society of the Spanish dancers and musicians who abound in our town.

His notebooks comprise a sort of chronicle of those strange early days we all lived through. But an unusual type of chronicle, since the writer seems to make a point of understatement, and at first sight we might almost imagine that Tarrou had a habit of observing events and people through the wrong end of a telescope. In those chaotic times he set himself to recording the history of what the normal historian passes over. Obviously we may deplore this curious kink in his character and suspect in him a lack of proper feeling. All the same, it is undeniable that these notebooks, which form a sort of discursive diary, supply the chronicler of the period with a host of seeming-trivial details which yet have their importance, and whose very oddity should be enough to prevent the reader from passing hasty judgment on this singular man.

The earliest entries made by Jean Tarrou synchronize with his coming to Oran.

From the outset they reveal a paradoxical satisfaction at the discovery of a town so intrinsically ugly. We find in them a minute description of the two bronze lions adorning the Municipal Office, and appropriate comments on the lack of trees, the hideousness of the houses, and the absurd lay-out of the town.

Tarrou sprinkles his descriptions with bits of conversation overheard in streetcars and in the streets, never adding a comment on them except, this comes somewhat later' in the report of a dialogue concerning a man named Camps. It was a chat between two streetcar conductors.

"You knew Camps, didn't you?" asked one of them. "Camps? A tall chap with a black mustache?"

"That's him. A switchman." "Ah yes, I remember now." "Well, he's dead." "Oh? When did he die?" "After that business about the rats." "You don't say so! What did he die of?" "I couldn't say exactly. Some kind of fever.

Of course, he never was what you might call fit. He got abscesses under the arms, and they did him in, it seems."

"Still, he didn't look that different from other people." "I wouldn't say that. He had a weak chest and he used to play the trombone in the town band. It's hard on the lungs, blowing a trombone."

"Ah, if you've got weak lungs, it don't do you any good, blowing down a big instrument like that."

After jotting down this dialogue Tarrou went on to speculate why Camps had joined a band when it was so clearly inadvisable, and what obscure motive had led him to risk his life for the sake of parading the streets on Sunday mornings.

We gather that Tarrou was agreeably impressed by a little scene that took place daily on the balcony of a house facing his window. His room at the hotel looked on to a

small side street and there were always several cats sleeping in the shadow of the walls. Every day, soon after lunch, at a time when most people stayed indoors, enjoying a siesta, a dapper little old man stepped out on the balcony on the other side of the street. He had a soldierly bearing, very erect, and affected a military style of dressing; his snow-white hair was always brushed to perfect smoothness. Leaning over the balcony he would call: "Pussy!

Pussy!" in a voice at once haughty and endearing. The cats blinked up at him with sleep-pale eyes, but made no move as yet. He then proceeded to tear some paper into scraps and let them fall into the street; interested by the fluttering shower of white butterflies, the cats came forward, lifting tentative paws toward the last scraps of paper. Then, taking careful aim, the old man would spit vigorously at the cats and, whenever a liquid missile hit the quarry, would beam with delight.

Lastly, Tarrou seemed to have been quite fascinated by the commercial character of the town, whose aspect, activities, and even pleasures all seemed to be dictated by considerations of business. This idiosyncrasy, the term he uses in his diary?was warmly approved of by Tarrou; indeed, one of his appreciative comments ends on the exclamation: "At last!"

These are the only passages in which our visitor's record, at this period, strikes a seemingly personal note. Its significance and the earnestness behind it might escape the reader on a casual perusal. For example, after describing how the discovery of a dead rat led the hotel cashier to make an error in his bill, Tarrou added: "Query: How contrive not to waste one's time? Answer: By being fully aware of it all the while. Ways in which this can be done: By spending one's days on an uneasy chair in a dentist's waiting-room; by remaining on one's balcony all a Sunday afternoon; by listening to lectures in a language one doesn't know; by traveling by the longest and least-convenient train routes, and of course standing all the way; by lining up at the box-office of theaters and then not buying a seat; and so forth."

Then, immediately following these eccentricities of thought and expression, we come on a detailed description of the streetcar service in the town, the structure of the cars, their indeterminate color, their unvarying dirtiness, and he concludes his observations with a "Very odd," which explains -nothing.

So much by way of introduction to Tarrou's comments on the phenomenon of the rats.

"The little old fellow opposite is quite disconsolate today. There are no more cats. The sight of all those dead rats strewn about the street may have excited their hunting instinct; anyhow, they all have vanished. To my thinking, there's no question of their eating the dead rats. Mine, I remember, turned up their noses at dead things. All the same, they're probably busy hunting in the cellars, hence the old boy's plight. His hair isn't as well brushed as usual, and he looks less alert, less military. You can see he is worried. After a few moments he went back into the room. But first he spat once on emptiness.

"In town today a streetcar was stopped because a dead rat had been found in it.

(Query: How did it get there?) Two or three women promptly alighted. The rat was thrown out. The car went on.

"The night watchman at the hotel, a level-headed man, assured me that all these rats meant trouble coming. 'When the rat leave a ship...' I replied that this held good for ships, but for towns it hadn't yet been demonstrated. But he stuck to his point. I asked

what sort of 'trouble' we might expect. That he couldn't say; disasters always come out of the blue. But he wouldn't be surprised if there were an earthquake brewing. I admitted that was possible, and then he asked if the prospect didn't alarm me.

" 'The only thing I'm interested in,' I told him, 'is acquiring peace of mind.'

"He understood me perfectly.

"I find a family that has its meals in this hotel quite interesting. The father is a tall, thin man, always dressed in black and wearing a starched collar. The top of his head is bald, with two tufts of gray hair on each side. His small, beady eyes, narrow nose, and hard, straight mouth make him look like a well-brought-up owl. He is always first at the door of the restaurant, stands aside to let his wife, a tiny woman, like a black mouse, go in, and then comes in himself with a small boy and girl, dressed like performing poodles, at his heels. When they are at the table he remains standing till his wife is seated and only then the two poodles can perch themselves on their chairs. He uses no terms of endearment to his family, addresses politely spiteful remarks to his wife, and bluntly tells the kids what he thinks of them.

" 'Nicole, you're behaving quite disgracefully.'

"The little girl is on the brink of tears, which is as it should be.

"This morning the small boy was all excitement about the rats, and started saying something on the subject.

" 'Philippe, one doesn't talk of rats at table. For the future I forbid you to use the word.'

" 'Your father's right,' approved the mouse.

"The two poodles buried their noses in their plates, and the owl acknowledged thanks by a curt, perfunctory nod.

"This excellent example notwithstanding, everybody in town is talking about the rats, and the local newspaper has taken a hand. The town-topics column, usually very varied, is now devoted exclusively to a campaign against the local authorities. 'Are our city fathers aware that the decaying bodies of these rodents constitute a grave danger to the population?' The manager of the hotel can talk of nothing else. But he has a personal grievance, too; that dead rats should be found in the elevator of a three-star hotel seems to him the end of all things. To console him, I said: 'But, you know, everybody's in the same boat.'

" 'That's just it,' he replied. 'Now we're like everybody else.'

"He was the first to tell me about the outbreak of this queer kind of fever which is causing much alarm. One of his chambermaids has got it.

" 'But I feel sure it's not contagious,' he hastened to assure me.

"I told him it was all the same to me.

" 'Ah, I understand, sir. You're like me, you're a fatalist.'

"I had said nothing of the kind and, what's more, am not a fatalist. I told him so...."

From this point onwards Tarrou's entries deal in some detail with the curious fever that was causing much anxiety among the public. When noting that the little old man, now that the rats had ceased appearing, had regained his cats and was studiously perfecting his shooting, Tarrou adds that a dozen or so cases of this fever were known to have occurred, and most had ended fatally.

For the light it may throw on the narrative that follows, Tarrou's description of Dr. Rieux may be suitably inserted here. So far as the narrator can judge, it is fairly accurate.

"Looks about thirty-five. Moderate height. Broad shoulders. Almost rectangular face. Dark, steady eyes, but prominent jaws. A biggish, well-modeled nose. Black hair, cropped very close. A curving mouth with thick, usually tight-set lips.

With his tanned skin, the black down on his hands and arms, the dark but becoming suits he always wears, he reminds one of a Sicilian peasant.

"He walks quickly. When crossing a street, he steps off the sidewalk without changing his pace, but two out of three times makes a little hop when he steps on to the sidewalk on the other side. He is absentminded and, when driving his car, often leaves his side-signals on after he has turned a corner. Always bareheaded. Looks knowledgeable."

Tarrou's figures were correct. Dr. Rieux was only too well aware of the serious turn things had taken. After seeing to the isolation of the concierge's body, he had rung up Richard and asked what he made of these inguinal-fever cases.

"I can make nothing of them," Richard confessed. "There have been two deaths, one in forty-eight hours, the other in three days. And the second patient showed all the signs of convalescence when I visited him on the second day."

"Please let me know if you have other cases," Rieux said.

He rang up some other colleagues. As a result of these inquiries he gathered that there had been some twenty cases of the same type within the last few days.

Almost all had ended fatally. He then advised Richard, who was chairman of the local Medical Association, to have any fresh cases put into isolation wards.

"Sorry," Richard said, "but I can't do anything about it. An order to that effect can be issued only by the Prefect. Anyhow, what grounds have you for supposing there's danger of contagion?"

"No definite grounds. But the symptoms are definitely alarming."

Richard, however, repeated that "such measures were outside his province." The most he could do was to put the matter up to the Prefect.

But while these talks were going on, the weather changed for the worse. On the day following old Michel's death the sky clouded up and there were brief torrential downpours, each of which was followed by some hours of muggy heat. The aspect of the sea, too, changed; its dark-blue translucency had gone and, under the lowering sky, it had steely or silvery glints that hurt the eyes to look at. The damp heat of the spring made everyone long for the coming of the dry, clean summer heat. On the town, humped snail-wise on its plateau and shut off almost everywhere from the sea, a mood of listlessness descended. Hemmed in by lines and lines of whitewashed walls, walking between rows of dusty shops, or riding in the dingy yellow streetcars, you felt, as it were, trapped by the climate. This, however, was not the case with Rieux's old Spanish patient, who welcomed this weather with enthusiasm.

"It cooks you," he said. "Just the thing for asthma."

Certainly it "cooked you," but exactly like a fever. Indeed, "the whole town was running a temperature; such anyhow was the impression Dr. Rieux could not shake off as he drove to the rue Faidherbe for the inquiry into Cottard's attempted suicide. That this impression was unreasonable he knew, and he attributed it to nervous exhaustion; he had certainly his full share of worries just at present.

In fact, it was high time to put the brakes on and try to get his nerves into some sort of order.

On reaching his destination he found that the police inspector hadn't turned up yet. Grand, who met him on the landing, suggested they should wait in his place, leaving the door open. The municipal clerk had two rooms, both very sparsely furnished. The only objects to catch the eye were a bookshelf on which lay two or three dictionaries, and a small blackboard on which one could just read two half-obliterated words: "flowery avenues."

Grand announced that Cottard had had a good night. But he'd waked up this morning with pains in his head and feeling very low.

Grand, too, looked tired and overwrought; he kept pacing up and down the room, opening and closing a portfolio crammed with sheets of manuscript that lay on the table.

Meanwhile, however, he informed the doctor that he really knew very little about Cottard, but believed him to have private means in a small way. Cottard was a queer bird. For a long while their relations went no farther than wishing each other good-day when they met on the stairs.

"I've only had two conversations with him. Some days ago I upset a box of colored chalks I was bringing home, on the landing. They were red and blue chalks. Just then Cottard came out of his room and he helped me pick them up. He asked me what I wanted colored chalks for."

Grand had then explained to him that he was trying to brush up his Latin. He'd learned it at school, of course, but his memories had grown blurred.

"You see, doctor, I've been told that a knowledge of Latin gives one a better understanding of the real meanings of French words."

So he wrote Latin words on his blackboard, then copied out again in blue chalk the part of each word that changed in conjugation or declension, and in red chalk the part of the word that never varied.

"I'm not sure if Cottard followed this very clearly, but he seemed interested and asked me for a red chalk. That rather surprised me, but after all? Of course I couldn't guess the use he'd put it to."

Rieux asked what was the subject of their second conversation. But just then the inspector came, accompanied by a clerk, and said he wished to begin by hearing Grand's statement. The doctor noticed that Grand, when referring to Cottard, always called him "the unfortunate man," and at one moment used even the expression "his grim resolve." When discussing the possible motives for the attempted suicide, Grand showed an almost finical anxiety over his choice of words. Finally he elected for the expression "a secret grief." The inspector asked if there had been anything in Cottard's manner that suggested what he called his "intent to felo-de-se."

"He knocked at my door yesterday," Grand said, "and asked me for a match. I gave him a box. He said he was sorry to disturb me but that, as we were neighbors, he hoped I wouldn't mind. He assured me he'd bring back my box, but I told him to keep it."

The inspector asked Grand if he'd noticed anything queer about Cottard.

"What struck me as queer was that he always seemed to want to start a conversation. But he should have seen I was busy with my work." Grand turned to Rieux and added rather shyly: "Some private work."

The inspector now said that he must see the invalid and hear what he had to say.

Rieux thought it would be wiser to prepare Cottard for the visit. When he entered the bedroom he found Cottard, who was wearing a gray flannel nightshirt, sitting up in bed and gazing at the door with a scared expression on his face.

"It's the police, isn't it?"

"Yes," Rieux said, "but don't get flustered. There are only some formalities to be gone through, and then you'll be left in peace."

Cottard replied that all this was quite needless, to his thinking, and anyhow he didn't like the police.

Rieux showed some irritation.

"I don't love them either. It's only a matter of answering a few questions as briefly and correctly as you can, and then you'll be through with it."

Cottard said nothing and Rieux began to move to the door. He had hardly taken a step when the little man called him back and, as soon as he was at the bedside, gripped his hands.

"They can't be rough with an invalid, a man who's hanged himself, can they, doctor?"

Rieux gazed down at him for a moment, then assured him that there was no question of anything like that, and in any case he was here to protect his patient. This seemed to relieve Cottard, and Rieux went out to get the inspector.

After Grand's deposition had been read out, Cottard was asked to state the exact motive of his act. He merely replied, without looking at the police officer, that "a secret grief" described it well enough. The inspector then asked him peremptorily if he intended to "have another go at it." Showing more animation, Cottard said certainly not, his one wish was to be left in peace.

"Allow me to point out, my man," the police officer rejoined with asperity, "that just now it's you who're troubling the peace of others." Rieux signed to him not to continue, and he left it at that.

"A good hour wasted!" the inspector sighed when the door closed behind them. "As you can guess, we've other things to think about, what with this fever everybody's talking of."

He then asked the doctor if there was any serious danger to the town; Rieux answered that he couldn't say.

"It must be the weather," the police officer decided. "That's what it is."

No doubt it was the weather. As the day wore on, everything grew sticky to the touch, and Rieux felt his anxiety increasing after each visit. That evening a neighbor of his old patient in the suburbs started vomiting, pressing his hand to his groin, and running a high fever accompanied by delirium. The ganglia were much bigger than M. Michel's. One of them was beginning to suppurate, and presently split open like an overripe fruit. On returning to his apartment, Rieux rang up the medical-stores depot for the district. In his professional diary for the day the only entry was: "Negative reply." Already he was receiving calls for similar cases from various parts of the town. Obviously the abscesses had to be lanced. Two crisscross strokes, and the ganglion disgorged a mixture of blood and pus. Their limbs stretched out as far as they could manage, the sick man went on bleeding. Dark patches appeared on their legs and stomachs; sometimes a ganglion would stop suppurating, then suddenly swell again. Usually the sick man died, in a stench of corruption.

The local press, so lavish of news about the rats, now had nothing to say. For rats died in the street; men in their homes. And newspapers are concerned only with the street. Meanwhile, government and municipal officials were putting their heads together. So long as each individual doctor had come across only two or three cases, no one had thought of taking action. But it was merely a matter of adding up the figures and, once this had been done, the total was startling.

In a very few days the number of cases had risen by leaps and bounds, and it became evident to all observers of this strange malady that a real epidemic had set in. This was the state of affairs when Castel, one of Rieux's colleagues and a much older man than he, came to see him.

"Naturally," he said to Rieux, "you know what it is."

"I'm waiting for the result of the post-mortems."

"Well, I know. And I don't need any post-mortems. I was in China for a good part of my career, and I saw some cases in Paris twenty years ago. Only no one dared to call them by their name on that occasion. The usual taboo, of course; the public mustn't be alarmed, that wouldn't do at all. And then, as one of my colleagues said, 'It's unthinkable. Everyone knows it's ceased to appear in western Europe.' Yes, everyone knew that, except the dead men. Come now, Rieux, you know as well as I do what it is."

Rieux pondered. He was looking out of the window of his surgery, at the tall cliff that closed the half-circle of the bay on the far horizon. Though blue, the sky had a dull sheen that was softening as the light declined.

"Yes, Castel," he replied. "It's hardly credible. But everything points to its being plague."

Castel got up and began walking toward the door.

"You know," the old doctor said, "what they're going to tell us? That it vanished from temperate countries long ago."

"'Vanished'? What does that word really mean?" Rieux shrugged his shoulders.

"Yes. And don't forget. Just under twenty years ago, in Paris too."

"Right. Let's hope it won't prove any worse this time than it did then. But really it's incredible."

The word "plague" had just been uttered for the first time. At this stage of the narrative, with Dr. Bernard Rieux standing at his window, the narrator may, perhaps, be allowed to justify the doctor's uncertainty and surprise, since, with very slight differences, his reaction was the same as that of the great majority of our townsfolk. Everybody knows that pestilences have a way of recurring in the world; yet somehow we find it hard to believe in ones that crash down on our heads from a blue sky. There have been as many plagues as wars in history; yet always plagues and wars take people equally by surprise.

In fact, like our fellow citizens, Rieux was caught off his guard, and we should understand his hesitations in the light of this fact; and similarly understand how he was torn between conflicting fears and confidence. When a war breaks out, people say: "It's too stupid; it can't last long." But though a war may well be "too stupid," that doesn't prevent its lasting. Stupidity has a knack of getting its way; as we should see if we were not always so much wrapped up in ourselves.

In this respect our townsfolk were like everybody else, wrapped up in themselves; in other words they were humanists: they disbelieved in pestilences.

A pestilence isn't a thing made to man's measure; therefore we tell ourselves that pestilence is a mere bogy of the mind, a bad dream that will pass away. But it doesn't always pass away and, from one bad dream to another, it is men who pass away, and the humanists first of all, because they haven't taken their precautions.

Our townsfolk were not more to blame than others; they forgot to be modest, that was all, and thought that everything still was possible for them; which presupposed that pestilences were impossible. They went on doing business, arranged for journeys, and formed views. How should they have given a thought to anything like plague, which rules out any future, cancels journeys, silences the exchange of views. They fancied themselves free, and no one will ever be free so long as there are pestilences.

Indeed, even after Dr. Rieux had admitted in his friend's company that a handful of persons, scattered about the town, had without warning died of plague, the danger still remained fantastically unreal. For the simple reason that, when a man is a doctor, he comes to have his own ideas of physical suffering, and to acquire somewhat more imagination than the average. Looking from his window at the town, outwardly quite unchanged, the doctor felt little more than a faint qualm for the future, a vague unease.

He tried to recall what he had read about the disease. Figures floated across his memory, and he recalled that some thirty or so great plagues known to history had accounted for nearly a hundred million deaths. But what are a hundred million deaths? When one has served in a war, one hardly knows what a dead man is, after a while. And since a dead man has no substance unless one has actually seen him dead, a hundred million corpses broadcast through history are no more than a puff of smoke in the imagination. The doctor remembered the plague at Constantinople that, according to Procopius, caused ten thousand deaths in a single day. Ten thousand dead made about five times the audience in a biggish cinema. Yes, that was how it should be done. You should collect the people at the exits of five picture-houses, you should lead them to a city square and make them die in heaps if you wanted to get a clear notion of what it means. Then at least you could add some familiar faces to the anonymous mass. But naturally that was impossible to put into practice; moreover, what man knows ten thousand faces? In any case the figures of those old historians, like Procopius, weren't to be relied on; that was common knowledge. Seventy years ago, at Canton, forty thousand rats died of plague before the disease spread to the inhabitants. But, again, in the Canton epidemic there was no reliable way of counting up the rats. A very rough estimate was all that could be made, with, obviously, a wide margin for error.

"Let's see," the doctor murmured to himself, "supposing the length of a rat to be ten inches, forty thousand rats placed end to end would make a line of..."

He pulled himself up sharply. He was letting his imagination play pranks, the last thing wanted just now. A few cases, he told himself, don't make an epidemic; they merely call for serious precautions. He must fix his mind, first of all, on the observed facts: stupor and extreme prostration, buboes, intense thirst, delirium, dark blotches on the body, internal dilatation, and, in conclusion... In conclusion, some words came back to the doctor's mind; aptly enough, the concluding sentence of the description of the symptoms given in his medical handbook: "The pulse becomes fluttering, dicrotic, and intermittent, and death ensues as the result of the slightest movement." Yes, in conclusion, the patient's life hung on a thread, and three people out of four (he remembered the exact figures) were too impatient not to make the very slight movement that snapped the thread.

The doctor was still looking out of the window. Beyond it lay the tranquil radiance of a cool spring sky; inside the room a word was echoing still, the word "plague." A word that conjured up in the doctor's mind not only what science chose to put into it, but a whole series of fantastic possibilities utterly out of keeping with that gray and yellow town under his eyes, from which were rising the sounds of mild activity characteristic of the hour; a drone rather than a bustling, the noises of a happy town, in short, if it's possible to be at once so dull and happy. A tranquillity so casual and thoughtless seemed almost effortlessly to give the lie to those old pictures of the plague: Athens, a charnel-house reeking to heaven and deserted even by the birds; Chinese towns cluttered up with victims silent in their agony; the convicts at Marseille piling rotting corpses into pits; the building of the Great Wall in Provence to fend off the furious plague-wind; the damp, putrefying pallets stuck to the mud floor at the Constantinople lazar-house, where the patients were hauled up from their beds with hooks; the carnival of masked doctors at the Black Death; men and women copulating in the cemeteries of Milan; cartloads of dead bodies rumbling through London's ghoul-haunted darkness, nights and days filled always, everywhere, with the eternal cry of human pain. No, all those horrors were not near enough as yet even to ruffle the equanimity of that spring afternoon. The clang of an unseen streetcar came through the window, briskly refuting cruelty and pain. Only the sea, murmurous behind the dingy checkerboard of houses, told of the unrest, the precariousness, of all things in this world. And, gazing in the direction of the bay, Dr. Rieux called to mind the plague-fires of which Lucretius tells, which the Athenians kindled on the seashore. The dead were brought there after nightfall, but there was not room enough, and the living fought one another with torches for a space where to lay those who had been dear to them; for they had rather engage in bloody conflicts than abandon their dead to the waves. A picture rose before him of the red glow of the pyres mirrored on a wine-dark, slumbrous sea, battling torches whirling sparks across the darkness, and thick, fetid smoke rising toward the watchful sky. Yes, it was not beyond the bounds of possibility....

But these extravagant forebodings dwindled in the light of reason. True, the word "plague" had been uttered; true, at this very moment one or two victims were being seized and laid low by the disease. Still, that could stop, or be stopped. It was only a matter of lucidly recognizing what had to be recognized; of dispelling extraneous shadows and doing what needed to be done. Then the plague would come to an end, because it was unthinkable, or, rather, because one thought of it on misleading lines. If, as was most likely, it died out, all would be well. If not, one would know it anyhow for what it was and what steps should be taken for coping with and finally overcoming it.

The doctor opened the window, and at once the noises of the town grew louder.

The brief, intermittent sibilance of a machine-saw came from a near-by workshop.

Rieux pulled himself together. There lay certitude; there, in the daily round.

All the rest hung on mere threads and trivial contingencies; you couldn't waste your time on it. The thing was to do your job as it should be done.

The doctor's musings had reached this point when the visit of Joseph Grand was announced. Grand's duties as clerk in the Municipal Office were varied, and he was sometimes employed in the statistical department on compiling the figures of births,

marriages, and deaths. Thus it had fallen to him to add up the number of deaths during the last few days, and, being of an obliging disposition, he had volunteered to bring a copy of the latest figures to the doctor.

Grand, who was waving a sheet of paper, was accompanied by his neighbor, Cottard.

"The figures are going up, doctor. Eleven deaths in forty-eight hours."

Rieux shook hands with Cottard and asked him how he was feeling. Grand put in a word explaining that Cottard was bent on thanking the doctor and apologizing for the trouble he had given. But Rieux was gazing frowningly at the figures on the sheet of paper.

"Well," he said, "perhaps we'd better make up our minds to call this disease by its name. So far we've been only shillyshallying. Look here, I'm off to the laboratory; like to come with me?"

"Quite so, quite so," Grand said as he went down the stairs at the doctor's heels. "I, too, believe in calling things by their name. But what's the name in this case?"

"That I shan't say, and anyhow you wouldn't gain, anything by knowing."

"You see," Grand smiled. "It's not so easy after all!"

They started off toward the Place d'Armes. Cottard still kept silent. The streets were beginning to fill up. The brief dusk of our town was already giving place to night, and the first stars glimmered above the still clearly marked horizon. A few moments later all the street-lamps went on, dimming the sky, and the voices in the street seemed to rise a tone.

"Excuse me," Grand said at the corner of the Place d'Armes, "but I must catch my car now. My evenings are sacred. As we say in my part of the world: 'Never put off to tomorrow?'"

Rieux had already noticed Grand's trick of professing to quote some turn of speech from "his part of the world" (he hailed from Montélimar), and following up with some such hackneyed expression as "lost in dreams," or "pretty as a picture."

"That's so," Cottard put in. "You can never budge him from his den after dinner."

Rieux asked Grand if he was doing extra work for the municipality. Grand said no, he was working on his own account.

"Really?" Rieux said, to keep the conversation going. "And are you getting on well with it?"

"Considering I've been at it for years, it would be surprising if I wasn't.

Though in one sense there hasn't been much progress."

"May one know", the doctor halted, "what it is that you're engaged on?"

Grand put a hand up to his hat and tugged it down upon his big, protruding ears, then murmured some half-inaudible remark from which Rieux seemed to gather that Grand's work was connected with "the growth of a personality." Then he turned rather hastily and a moment later was hurrying, with short, quick steps, under the fig trees lining the boulevard de la Marne.

When they were at the laboratory gate, Cottard told the doctor that he would greatly like to see him and ask his advice about something. Rieux, who was fingering in his pocket the sheet of paper with the figures on it, said he'd better call during his consulting-hours; then, changing his mind, told him he would be in his part of the town next day and would drop in to see him at the end of the afternoon.

On leaving Cottard the doctor noticed that he was thinking of Grand, trying to picture him in the midst of an outbreak of plague, not an outbreak like the present one, which would probably not prove serious, but like one of the great visitations of the past. "He's the kind of man who always escapes in such cases." Rieux remembered having read somewhere that the plague spared weak constitutions and chose its victims chiefly among the robust. Still thinking of Grand, he decided that he was something of a "mystery man" in his small way.

True, at first sight, Grand manifested both the outward signs and typical manner of a humble employee in the local administration. Tall and thin, he seemed lost in the garments that he always chose a size too large, under the illusion that they would wear longer. Though he still had most of the teeth in his lower jaw, all the upper ones were gone, with the result that when he smiled, raising his upper lip, the lower scarcely moved, his mouth looked like a small black hole let into his face. Also he had the walk of a shy young priest, sidling along walls and slipping mouse-like into doorways, and he exuded a faint odor of smoke and basement rooms; in short, he had all the attributes of insignificance. Indeed, it cost an effort to picture him otherwise than bent over a desk, studiously revising the tariff of the town baths or gathering for a junior secretary the materials of a report on the new garbage-collection tax. Even before you knew what his employment was, you had a feeling that he'd been brought into the world for the sole purpose of performing the discreet but needful duties of a temporary assistant municipal clerk on a salary of sixty-two francs, thirty centimes a day.

This was, in fact, the entry that he made each month in the staff register at the Municipal Office, in the column Post in Which Employed. When twenty-two years previously, after obtaining a matriculation certificate beyond which, for lack of money, he was unable to progress, he was given this temporary post, he had been led to expect, or so he said, speedy "confirmation" in it. It was only a matter of proving his ability to cope with the delicate problems raised by the administration of our city. Once confirmed, they had assured him, he couldn't fail to be promoted to a grade that would enable him to live quite comfortably.

Ambition, certainly, was not the spur that activated Joseph Grand; that he would swear to, wryly smiling. All he desired was the prospect of a life suitably insured on the material side by honest work, enabling him to devote his leisure to his hobbies. If he'd accepted the post offered him, it was from honorable motives and, if he might say so, loyalty to an ideal.

But this "temporary" state of things had gone on and on, the cost of living rose by leaps and bounds, and Grand's pay, in spite of some statutory rises, was still a mere pittance. He had confided this to Rieux, but nobody else seemed aware of his position. And here lies Grand's originality, or anyhow an indication of it. He could certainly have brought to official notice, if not his rights, of which he wasn't sure, at least the promises given him. But, for one thing, the departmental head who had made them had been dead for some time and, furthermore, Grand no longer remembered their exact terms. And lastly, this was the real trouble, Joseph Grand couldn't find his words.

This peculiarity, as Rieux had noticed, was really the key to the personality of our worthy fellow citizen. And this it was which always prevented him from writing the mildly protesting letter he had in mind, or taking the steps the situation called for. According to him, he felt a particular aversion from talking about his "rights", the word

was one that gave him pause, and likewise from mentioning a "promise", which would have implied that he was claiming his due and thus bespoken an audacity incompatible with the humble post he filled.

On the other hand, he refused to use expressions such as "your kindness," "gratitude," or even "solicit," which, to his thinking, were incompatible with his personal dignity. Thus, owing to his inability to find the right words, he had gone on performing his obscure, ill-paid duties until a somewhat advanced age. Also this, anyhow, was what he told Dr. Rieux he had come, after long experience, to realize that he could always count on living within his means; all he had to do was to scale down his needs to his income. Thus he confirmed the wisdom of an opinion often voiced by our mayor, a business magnate of the town, when he insisted vehemently that in the last analysis (he emphasized this choice expression, which indeed clinched his argument, there was no reason to believe that anyone had ever died of hunger in the town. In any case, the austere, not to say ascetic life of Joseph Grand was, in the last analysis, a guarantee against any anxiety in this respect. He went on looking for his words.

In a certain sense it might well be said that his was an exemplary life. He was one of those rare people, rare in our town as elsewhere, who have the courage of their good feelings. What little he told of his personal life vouched for acts of kindness and a capacity for affection that no one in our times dares own to. Without a blush he confessed to dearly loving his nephews and sister, his only surviving near relation, whom he went to France to visit every other year.

He admitted that the thought of his parents, whom he lost when he was very young, often gave him a pang. He did not conceal the fact that he had a special affection for a church bell in his part of the town which started pealing very melodiously at about five every afternoon. Yet to express such emotions, simple as they were, the least word cost him a terrible effort. And this difficulty in finding his words had come to be the bane of his life. "Oh, doctor," he would exclaim, "how I'd like to learn to express myself!" He brought the subject up each time he met Rieux.

That evening, as he watched Grand's receding form, it flashed on the doctor what it was that Grand was trying to convey; he was evidently writing a book or something of the sort. And quaintly enough, as he made his way to the laboratory, this thought reassured him. He realized how absurd it was, but he simply couldn't believe that a pestilence on the great scale could befall a town where people like Grand were to be found, obscure functionaries cultivating harmless eccentricities. To be precise, he couldn't picture such eccentricities existing in a plague-stricken community, and he concluded that the chances were all against the plague's making any headway among our fellow citizens.

NEXT day, by dint of a persistence that many thought ill-advised, Rieux persuaded the authorities to convene a health committee at the Prefect's office.

"People in town are getting nervous, that's a fact," Dr. Richard admitted. "And of course all sorts of wild rumors are going round. The Prefect said to me, 'Take prompt action if you like, but don't attract attention.' He personally is convinced that it's a false alarm."

Rieux gave Castel a lift to the Prefect's office.

"Do you know," Castel said when they were in the car, "that we haven't a gram of serum in the whole district?"

"I know. I rang up the depot. The director seemed quite startled. It'll have to be sent from Paris."

"Let's hope they're quick about it."

"I sent a wire yesterday," Rieux said.

The Prefect greeted them amiably enough, but one could see his nerves were on edge.

"Let's make a start, gentlemen," he said. "Need I review the situation?"

Richard thought that wasn't necessary. He and his colleagues were acquainted with the facts. The only question was what measures should be adopted.

"The question," old Castel cut in almost rudely, "is to know whether it's plague or not."

Two or three of the doctors present protested. The others seemed to hesitate.

The Prefect gave a start and hurriedly glanced toward the door to make sure it had prevented this outrageous remark from being overheard in the corridor Richard said that in his opinion the great thing was not to take an alarmist view. All that could be said at present was that we had to deal with a special type of fever, with inguinal complications; in medical science, as in daily life, it was unwise to jump to conclusions. Old Castel, who was placidly chewing his draggled yellow mustache, raised his pale, bright eyes and gazed at Rieux.

Then, after sweeping the other members of the committee with a friendly glance, he said that he knew quite well that it was plague and, needless to say, he also knew that, were this to be officially admitted, the authorities would be compelled to take very drastic steps. This was, of course, the explanation of his colleagues' reluctance to face the facts and, if it would ease their minds, he was quite prepared to say it wasn't plague. The Prefect seemed ruffled and remarked that, in any case, this line of argument seemed to him unsound.

"The important thing," Castel replied, "isn't the soundness or otherwise of the argument, but for it to make you think." Rieux, who had said nothing so far, was asked for his opinion.

"We are dealing," he said, "with a fever of a typhoidal nature, accompanied by vomiting and buboes. I have incised these buboes and had the pus analyzed; our laboratory analyst believes he has identified the plague bacillus. But I am bound to add that there are specific modifications that don't quite tally with the classical description of the plague bacillus."

Richard pointed out that this justified a policy of wait-and-see; anyhow, it would be wise to await the statistical report on the series of analyses that had been going on for several days.

"When a microbe," Rieux said, "after a short intermission can quadruple in three days' time the volume of the spleen, can swell the mesenteric ganglia to the size of an orange and give them the consistency of gruel, a policy of wait-and-see is, to say the least of it, unwise. The foci of infection are steadily extending. Judging by the rapidity with which the disease is spreading, it may well, unless we can stop it, kill off half the town before two months are out. That being so, it has small importance whether you call it plague or some rare kind of fever. The important thing is to prevent its killing off half the population of this town."

Richard said it was a mistake to paint too gloomy a picture, and, moreover, the disease hadn't been proved to be contagious; indeed, relatives of his patients, living under the same roof, had escaped it.

"But others have died," Rieux observed. "And obviously contagion is never absolute; otherwise you'd have a constant mathematical progression and the death-rate would rocket up catastrophically. It's not a question of painting too black a picture. It's a question of taking precautions."

Richard, however, summing up the situation as he saw it, pointed out that, if the epidemic did not cease spontaneously, it would be necessary to apply the rigorous prophylactic measures laid down in the Code. And, to do this, it would be necessary to admit officially that plague had broken out. But of this there was no absolute certainty; therefore any hasty action was to be deprecated.

Rieux stuck to his guns. "The point isn't whether the measures provided for in the Code are rigorous, but whether they are needful to prevent the death of half the population. All the rest is a matter of administrative action, and I needn't remind you that our constitution has provided for such emergencies by empowering prefects to issue the necessary orders."

"Quite true," the Prefect assented, "but I shall need your professional declaration that the epidemic is one of plague."

"If we don't make that declaration," Rieux said, "there's a risk that half the population may be wiped out."

Richard cut in with some impatience.

"The truth is that our colleague is convinced it's plague; his description of the syndrome proved it."

Rieux replied that he had not described a "syndrome," but merely what he'd seen with his own eyes. And what he'd seen was buboes, and high fever accompanied by delirium, ending fatally within forty-eight hours. Could Dr. Richard take the responsibility of declaring that the epidemic would die out without the imposition of rigorous prophylactic measures?

Richard hesitated, then fixed his eyes on Rieux.

"Please answer me quite frankly. Are you absolutely convinced it's plague?"

"You're stating the problem wrongly. It's not a question of the term I use; it's a question of time."

"Your view, I take it," the Prefect put in, "is this. Even if it isn't plague, the prophylactic measures enjoined by law for coping with a state of plague should be put into force immediately?"

"If you insist on my having a 'View,' that conveys it accurately enough."

The doctors confabulated. Richard was their spokesman:

"It comes to this. We are to take the responsibility of acting as though the epidemic were plague."

This way of putting it met with general approval.

"It doesn't matter to me," Rieux said, "how you phrase it. My point is that we should not act as if there were no likelihood that half the population would be wiped out; for then it would be."

Followed by scowls and protestations, Rieux left the committee-room. Some minutes later, as he was driving down a back street redolent of fried fish and urine, a woman screaming in agony, her groin dripping blood, stretched out her arms toward him.

ON the day after the committee meeting the fever notched another small advance.

It even found its way into the papers, but discreetly; only a few brief references to it were made. On the following day, however, Rieux observed that small official notices had been just put up about the town, though in places where they would not attract much attention. It was hard to find in these notices any indication that the authorities were facing the situation squarely.

The measures enjoined were far from Draconian and one had the feeling that many concessions had been made to a desire not to alarm the public. The instructions began with a bald statement that a few cases of a malignant fever had been reported in Oran; it was not possible as yet to say if this fever was contagious. The symptoms were not so marked as to be really perturbing and the authorities felt sure they could rely on the townspeople to treat the situation with composure. None the less, guided by a spirit of prudence that all would appreciate, the Prefect was putting into force some precautionary measures. If these measures were carefully studied and properly applied, they would obviate any risk of an epidemic. This being so, the Prefect felt no doubt that everybody in his jurisdiction would wholeheartedly second his personal efforts.

The notice outlined the general program that the authorities had drawn up. It included a systematic extermination of the rat population by injecting poison gas into the sewers, and a strict supervision of the water-supply. The townspeople were advised to practice extreme cleanliness, and any who found fleas on their persons were directed to call at the municipal dispensaries. Also heads of households were ordered promptly to report any fever case diagnosed by their doctors and to permit the isolation of sick members of their families in special wards at the hospital. These wards, it was explained, were equipped to provide patients with immediate treatment and ensure the maximum prospect of recovery. Some supplementary regulations enjoined compulsory disinfection of the sickroom and of the vehicle in which the patient traveled.

For the rest, the Prefect confined himself to advising all who had been in contact with the patient to consult the sanitary inspector and strictly to follow his advice.

Dr. Rieux swung round brusquely from the poster and started back to his surgery.

Grand, who was awaiting him there, raised his arms dramatically when the doctor entered.

"Yes," Rieux said, "I know. The figures are rising."

On the previous day ten deaths had been reported. The doctor told Grand that he might be seeing him in the evening, as he had promised to visit Cottard.

"An excellent idea," Grand said. "You'll do him good. As a matter of fact, I find him greatly changed."

"In what way?"

"He's become amiable."

"Wasn't he amiable before?"

Grand seemed at a loss. He couldn't say that Cottard used to be unamiable; the term wouldn't have been correct. But Cottard was a silent, secretive man, with something

about him that made Grand think of a wild boar. His bedroom, meals at a cheap restaurant, some rather mysterious comings and goings, these were the sum of Cottard's days. He described himself as a traveling salesman in wines and spirits. Now and then he was visited by two or three men, presumably customers.

Sometimes in the evening he would go to a movie across the way. In this connection Grand mentioned a detail he had noticed, that Cottard seemed to have a preference for gangster films. But the thing that had struck him most about the man was his aloofness, not to say his mistrust of everyone he met.

And now, so Grand said, there had been a complete change.

"I don't quite know how to put it, but I must say I've an impression that he is trying to make himself agreeable to all and sundry, to be in everybody's good books. Nowadays he often talks to me, he suggests we should go out together, and I can't bring myself to refuse. What's more, he interests me, and of course I saved his life."

Since his attempt at suicide Cottard had had no more visitors. In the streets, in shops, he was always trying to strike up friendships. To the grocer he was all affability; no one could take more pains than he to show his interest in the tobacconist's gossip.

"This particular tobacconist, a woman, by the way," Grand explained, "is a holy terror. I told Cottard so, but he replied that I was prejudiced and she had plenty of good points, only one had to find them out."

On two or three occasions Cottard had invited Grand to come with him to the luxury restaurants and cafes of the town, which he had recently taken to patronizing.

"There's a pleasant atmosphere in them," he explained, "and then one's in good company."

Grand noticed that the staff made much of Cottard and he soon discovered why, when he saw the lavish tips his companion gave.

The traveling salesman seemed greatly to appreciate the amiability shown him in return for his largesse. One day when the head waiter had escorted him to the door and helped him into his overcoat, Cottard said to Grand:

"He's a nice fellow, and he'd make a good witness."

"A witness? I don't follow."

Cottard hesitated before answering.

"Well, he could say I'm not really a bad kind of man."

But his humor had its ups and downs. One day when the grocer had shown less affability, he came home in a tearing rage.

"He's siding with the others, the swine!"

"With what others?"

"The whole damned lot of them."

Grand had personally witnessed an odd scene that took place at the tobacconist's. An animated conversation was in progress and the woman behind the counter started airing her views about a murder case that had created some stir in Algiers. A young commercial employee had killed an Algerian on a beach.

"I always say," the woman began, "if they clapped all that scum in jail, decent folks could breathe more freely."

She was too much startled by Cottard's reaction, he dashed out of the shop without a word of excuse, to continue. Grand and the woman gazed after him, dumbfounded.

Subsequently Grand reported to the doctor other changes in Cottard's character.

Cottard had always professed very liberal ideas, as his pet dictum on economic questions, "Big fish eat little fish," implied. But now the only Oran newspaper he bought was the conservative organ, and one could hardly help suspecting that he made a point of reading it in public places. Somewhat of the same order was a request he made to Grand shortly before he left his sick-bed; Grand mentioned he was going to the post office and Cottard asked him to be kind enough to dispatch a money order for a hundred francs to a sister living at a distance, mentioning that he sent her this sum every month. Then, just when Grand was leaving the room, he called him back.

"No, send her two hundred francs. That'll be a nice surprise for her. She believes I never give her a thought. But actually I'm devoted to her."

Not long after this he made some curious remarks to Grand in the course of conversation. He had badgered Grand into telling him about the somewhat mysterious "private work" to which Grand gave his evenings.

"I know!" Cottard exclaimed. "You're writing a book, aren't you?"

"Something of the kind. But it's not so simple as that."

"Ah!" Cottard sighed. "I only wish I had a knack for writing."

When Grand showed his surprise, Cottard explained with some embarrassment that being a literary man must make things easier in lots of ways.

"Why?" Grand asked.

"Why, because an author has more rights than ordinary people, as everybody knows. People will stand much more from him."

"It looks," said Rieux to Grand on the morning when the official notices were posted, "as if this business of the rats had addled his brain, as it has done for so many other people. That's all it is. Or perhaps he's scared of the 'fever.'"

"I doubt it, doctor. If you want to know my opinion, he?"

He paused; with a machine-gun rattle from its exhaust the "deratization" van was clattering by. Rieux kept silent until it was possible to make himself audible, then asked, without much interest, what Grand's opinion was.

"He's a man with something pretty serious on his conscience," Grand said gravely.

The doctor shrugged his shoulders. As the inspector had said, he'd other fish to fry.

That afternoon Rieux had another talk with Castel. The serum had not yet come.

"In any case," Rieux said, "I wonder if it will be much use. This bacillus is such a queer one."

"There," Castel said, "I don't agree with you. These little brutes always have an air of originality. But, at bottom, it's always the same thing."

"That's your theory, anyhow. Actually, of course, we know next to nothing on the subject."

"I grant you, it's only my theory. Still, in a sense, that goes for everybody."

Throughout the day the doctor was conscious that the slightly dazed feeling that came over him whenever he thought about the plague was growing more pronounced.

Finally he realized that he was afraid! On two occasions he entered crowded cafes. Like Cottard he felt a need for friendly contacts, human warmth. A stupid instinct, Rieux told himself; still, it served to remind him that he'd promised to visit the traveling salesman.

Cottard was standing beside the dining-table when the doctor entered his room that evening. A detective story lay open on the tablecloth. But the night was closing in and it would have been difficult to read in the growing darkness.

Most likely Cottard had been sitting musing in the twilight until he heard the ring at his door. Rieux asked how he was feeling. Cottard sat down and replied rather grumpily that he was feeling tolerably well, adding that he'd feel still better if only he could be sure of being left in peace. Rieux remarked that one couldn't always be alone.

"That's not what I meant. I was thinking of people who take an interest in you only to make trouble for you." When Rieux said nothing, he went on: "Mind you, that's not my case. Only I've been reading that detective story. It's about a poor devil who's arrested one fine morning, all of a sudden. People had been taking an interest in him and he knew nothing about it. They were talking about him in offices, entering his name on card indexes. Now, do you think that's fair? Do you think people have a right to treat a man like that?"

"Well," Rieux said, "that depends. In one sense I agree, nobody has the right.

But all that's beside the mark. What's important is for you to go out a bit.

It's a mistake staying indoors too much."

Cottard seemed vexed and said that on the contrary he was always going out, and, if need arose, all the people in the street could vouch for him. What's more, he knew lots of people in other parts of the town.

"Do you know Monsieur Rigaud, the architect? He's a friend of mine."

The room was in almost complete darkness. Outside, the street was growing noisier and a sort of murmur of relief greeted the moment when all the street-lamps lit up, all together. Rieux went out on the balcony, and Cottard followed him.

From the outlying districts, as happens every evening in our town, a gentle breeze wafted a murmur of voices, smells of roasting meat, a gay, perfumed tide of freedom sounding on its way, as the streets filled up with noisy young people released from shops and offices. Nightfall, with its deep, remote baying of unseen ships, the rumor rising from the sea, and the happy tumult of the crowd, that first hour of darkness which in the past had always had a special charm for Rieux, seemed today charged with menace, because of all he knew.

"How about turning on the lights?" he suggested when they went back into the room.

After this had been done, the little man gazed at him, blinking his eyes.

"Tell me, doctor. Suppose I fell ill, would you put me in your ward at the hospital?"

"Why not?"

Cottard then inquired if it ever happened that a person in a hospital or a nursing home was arrested. Rieux said it had been known to happen, but all depended on the invalid's condition.

"You know, doctor," Cottard said, "I've confidence in you." Then he asked the doctor if he'd be kind enough to give him a lift, as he was going into town.

In the center of the town the streets were already growing less crowded and the lights fewer. Children were playing in front of the doorways. At Cottard's request the doctor stopped his car beside one of the groups of children. They were playing hopscotch

and making a great deal of noise. One of them, a boy with sleek, neatly parted hair and a grubby face, stared hard at Rieux with bright, bold eyes. The doctor looked away.

Standing on the sidewalk Cottard shook his head. He then said in a hoarse, rather labored voice, casting uneasy glances over his shoulder:

"Everybody's talking about an epidemic. Is there anything in it, doctor?"

"People always talk," Rieux replied. "That's only to be expected."

"You're right. And if we have ten deaths they'll think it's the end of the world. But it's not that we need here."

The engine was ticking over. Rieux had his hand on the clutch. But he was looking again at the boy who was still watching him with an oddly grave intentness. Suddenly, unexpectedly, the child smiled, showing all his teeth.

"Yes? And what do we need here?" Rieux asked, returning the child's smile.

Abruptly Cottard gripped the door of the car and, as he turned to go, almost shouted in a rageful, passionate voice:

"An earthquake! A big one!"

There was no earthquake, and the whole of the following day was spent, so far as Rieux was concerned, in long drives to every corner of the town, in parleyings with the families of the sick and arguments with the invalids themselves. Never had Rieux known his profession to weigh on him so heavily. Hitherto his patients had helped to lighten his task; they gladly put themselves into his hands. For the first time the doctor felt they were keeping aloof, wrapping themselves up in their malady with a sort of bemused hostility. It was a struggle to which he wasn't yet accustomed. And when, at ten that evening, he parked his car outside the home of his old asthma patient, his last visit of the day, it was an effort for Rieux to drag himself from his seat. For some moments he lingered, gazing up the dark street, watching the stars appear and disappear in the blackness of the sky.

When Rieux entered the room, the old man was sitting up in bed, at his usual occupation, counting out dried peas from one pan to another. On seeing his visitor he looked up, beaming with delight.

"Well, doctor? It's cholera, isn't it?"

"Where on earth did you get that idea from?"

"It's in the paper, and the radio said it, too."

"No, it's not cholera."

"Anyhow," the old man chuckled excitedly, "the big bugs are laying it on thick.

Got the jitters, haven't they?"

"Don't you believe a word of it," the doctor said.

He had examined the old man and now was sitting in the middle of the dingy little dining-room. Yes, despite what he had said, he was afraid. He knew that in this suburb alone eight or ten unhappy people, cowering over their buboes, would be awaiting his visit next morning. In only two or three cases had incision of the buboes caused any improvement. For most of them it would mean going to the hospital, and he knew how poor people feel about hospitals.

"I don't want them trying their experiments on him," had said the wife one of his patients. But he wouldn't be experimented on; he would die, that was all. That the regulations now in force were inadequate was lamentably clear. As for the "specially equipped" wards, he knew what they amounted to: two outbuildings from which the other patients had been hastily evacuated, whose windows had been hermetically sealed, and round which a sanitary cordon had been set. The only hope was
that the outbreak would die a natural death; it certainly wouldn't be arrested by the measures the authorities had so far devised.

Nevertheless, that night the official communique was still optimistic. On the following day Ransdoc announced that the rules laid down by the local administration had won general approval and already thirty sick persons had reported. Castel rang up Rieux.

"How many beds are there in the special wards?"

"Eighty."

"Surely there are far more than thirty cases in the town?"

"Don't forget there are two sorts of cases: those who take fright, and those, they're the majority, who don't have time to do so."

"I see. Are they checking up on the burials?"

"No. I told Richard over the phone that energetic measures were needed, not just words; we'd got to set up a real barrier against the disease, otherwise we might just as well do nothing."

"Yes? And what did he say?"

"Nothing doing. He hadn't the powers. In my opinion, it's going to get worse."

That was so. Within three days both wards were full. According to Richard, there was talk of requisitioning a school and opening an auxiliary hospital. Meanwhile Rieux continued incising buboes and waiting for the anti-plague serum. Castel went back to his old books and spent long hours in the public library.

"Those rats died of plague," was his conclusion, "or of something extremely like it. And they've loosed on the town tens of thousands of fleas, which will spread the infection in geometrical progression unless it's checked in time."

Rieux said nothing.

About this time the weather appeared set fair, and the sun had drawn up the last puddles left by the recent rain. There was a serene blue sky flooded with golden light each morning, with sometimes a drone of planes in the rising heat, all seemed well with the world. And yet within four days the fever had made four startling strides: sixteen deaths, twenty-four, twenty-eight, and thirty-two. On the fourth day the opening of the auxiliary hospital in the premises of a primary school was officially announced. The local population, who so far had made a point of masking their anxiety by facetious comments, now seemed tongue-tied and went their ways with gloomy faces.

Rieux decided to ring up the Prefect.

"The regulations don't go anywhere near far enough."

"Yes," the Prefect replied. "I've seen the statistics and, as you say, they're most perturbing."

"They're more than perturbing; they're conclusive."

"I'll ask government for orders."

When Rieux next met Castel, the Prefect's remark was still rankling.

"Orders!" he said scornfully. "When what's needed is imagination."

"Any news of the serum?"

"It'll come this week."

The Prefect sent instructions to Rieux, through Richard, asking him to draw up a minute to be transmitted for orders to the central administration of the colony.

Rieux included in it a clinical diagnosis and statistics of the epidemic. On that day forty deaths were reported. The Prefect took the responsibility, as he put it, of tightening up the new regulations. Compulsory declaration of all cases of fever and their isolation were to be strictly enforced. The residences of sick people were to be shut up and disinfected; persons living in the same house were to go into quarantine; burials were to be supervised by the local authorities in a manner which will be described later on. Next day the serum arrived by plane. There was enough for immediate requirements, but not enough if the epidemic were to spread. In reply to his telegram Rieux was informed that the emergency reserve stock was exhausted, but that a new supply was in preparation.

Meanwhile, from all the outlying districts, spring was making its progress into the town. Thousands of roses wilted in the flower-venders' baskets in the market-places and along the streets, and the air was heavy with their cloying perfume. Outwardly, indeed, this spring was like any other. The streetcars were always packed at the rush hours, empty and untidy during the rest of the day. Tarrou watched the little old man, and the little old man spat on the cats. Grand hurried home every evening to his mysterious literary activities. Cottard went his usual desultory ways, and M. Othon, the magistrate, continued to parade his menagerie.

The old Spaniard decanted his dried peas from pan to pan, and sometimes you encountered Rambert, the journalist, looking interested as ever in all he saw.

In the evening the usual crowd thronged the streets and the lines lengthened outside the picture-houses. Moreover, the epidemic seemed to be on the wane; on some days only ten or so deaths were notified. Then, all of a sudden, the figure shot up again, vertically. On the day when the death-roll touched thirty, Dr. Rieux read an official telegram that the Prefect had just handed him, remarking:

"So they've got alarmed at last." The telegram ran: Proclaim a state of plague stop close the town.

PART II

From now on, it can be said that plague was the concern of all of us. Hitherto, surprised as he may have been by the strange things happening around him, each individual citizen had gone about his business as usual, so far as this was possible. And no doubt he would have continued doing so. But once the town gates were shut, every one of us realized that all, the narrator included, were, so to speak, in the same boat, and each would have to adapt himself to the new conditions of life. Thus, for example, a feeling normally as individual as the ache of separation from those one loves suddenly became a feeling in which all shared alike and, together with fear, the greatest affliction of the long period of exile that lay ahead.

One of the most striking consequences of the closing of the gates was, in fact, this sudden deprivation befalling people who were completely unprepared for it.

Mothers and children, lovers, husbands and wives, who had a few days previously taken it for granted that their parting would be a short one, who had kissed one another good-by on the platform and exchanged a few trivial remarks, sure as they were of seeing one another again after a few days or, at most, a few weeks, duped by our blind human faith in the near future and little if at all diverted from their normal interests by this leave-

taking, all these people found themselves, without the least warning, hopelessly cut off, prevented from seeing one another again, or even communicating with one another. For actually the closing of the gates took place some hours before the official order was made known to the public, and, naturally enough, it was impossible to take individual cases of hardship into account. It might indeed be said that the first effect of this brutal visitation was to compel our townspeople to act as if they had no feelings as individuals.

During the first part of the day on which the prohibition to leave the town came into force the Prefect's office was besieged by a crowd of applicants advancing pleas of equal cogency but equally impossible to take into consideration.

Indeed, it needed several days for us to realize that we were completely cornered; that words like "special arrangements," "favor," and "priority" had lost all effective meaning.

Even the small satisfaction of writing letters was denied us. It came to this: not only had the town ceased to be in touch with the rest of the world by normal means of communication, but also, according to a second notification, all correspondence was forbidden, to obviate the risk of letters carrying infection outside the town. In the early days a favored few managed to persuade the sentries at the gates to allow them to get messages through to the outside world. But that was only at the beginning of the epidemic, when the sentries found it natural to obey their feelings of humanity. Later on, when these same sentries had had the gravity of the situation drummed into them, they flatly refused to take responsibilities whose possible after-effects they could not foresee. At first, telephone calls to other towns were allowed, but this led to such crowding of the telephone booths and delays on the lines that for some days they also were prohibited, and thereafter limited to what were called "urgent cases," such as deaths, marriages, and births. So we had to fall back on telegrams.

People linked together by friendship, affection, or physical love found themselves reduced to hunting for tokens of their past communion within the compass of a ten-word telegram. And since, in practice, the phrases one can use in a telegram are quickly exhausted, long lives passed side by side, or passionate yearnings, soon declined to the exchange of such trite formulas as: "Am well. Always thinking of you. Love."

Some few of us, however, persisted in writing letters and gave much time to hatching plans for corresponding with the outside world; but almost always these plans came to nothing. Even on the rare occasions when they succeeded, we could not know this, since we received no answer. For weeks on end we were reduced to starting the same letter over and over again recopying the same scraps of news and the same personal appeals, with the result that after a certain time the living words, into which we had as it were transfused our hearts' blood, were drained of any meaning. Thereafter we went on copying them mechanically, trying, through the dead phrases, to convey some notion of our ordeal. And in the long run, to these sterile, reiterated monologues, these futile colloquies with a blank wall, even the banal formulas of a telegram came to seem preferable.

Also, after some days, when it was clear that no one had the least hope of being able to leave our town, inquiries began to be made whether the return of people who had gone away before the outbreak would be permitted. After some days' consideration of the matter the authorities replied affirmatively. They pointed out, however, that in no case would persons who returned be allowed to leave the town again; once here, they would

have to stay, whatever happened. Some families, actually very few, refused to take the position seriously and in their eagerness to have the absent members of the family with them again, cast prudence to the winds and wired to them to take this opportunity of returning. But very soon those who were prisoners of the plague realized the terrible danger to which this would expose their relatives, and sadly resigned themselves to their absence. At the height of the epidemic we saw only one case in which natural emotions overcame the fear of death in a particularly painful form. It was not, as might be expected, the case of two young people, whose passion made them yearn for each other's nearness at whatever cost of pain. The two were old Dr. Castel and his wife, and they had been married for very many years. Mme Castel had gone on a visit to a neighboring town some days before the epidemic started. They weren't one of those exemplary married couples of the Darby-and-Joan pattern; on the contrary, the narrator has grounds for saying that, in all probability, neither partner felt quite sure the marriage was all that could have been desired. But this ruthless, protracted separation enabled them to realize that they could not live apart, and in the sudden glow of this discovery the risk of plague seemed insignificant.

That was an exception. For most people it was obvious that the separation must last until the end of the epidemic. And for every one of us the ruling emotion of his life, which he had imagined he knew through and through (the people of Oran, as has been said, have simple passions), took on a new aspect. Husbands who had had complete faith in their wives found, to their surprise, that they were jealous; and lovers had the same experience. Men who had pictured themselves as Don Juans became models of fidelity. Sons who had lived beside their mothers hardly giving them a glance fell to picturing with poignant regret each wrinkle in the absent face that memory cast upon the screen. This drastic, clean-cut deprivation and our complete ignorance of what the future held in store had taken us unawares; we were unable to react against the mute appeal of presences, still so near and already so far, which haunted us daylong. In fact, our suffering was twofold; our own to start with, and then the imagined suffering of the absent one, son, mother, wife, or mistress.

Under other circumstances our townsfolk would probably have found an outlet in increased activity, a more sociable life. But the plague forced inactivity on them, limiting their movements to the same dull round inside the town, and throwing them, day after day, on the illusive solace of their memories. For in their aimless walks they kept on coming back to the same streets and usually, owing to the smallness of the town, these were streets in which, in happier days, they had walked with those who now were absent.

Thus the first thing that plague brought to our town was exile. And the narrator is convinced that he can set down here, as holding good for all, the feeling he personally had and to which many of his friends confessed. It was undoubtedly the feeling of exile, that sensation of a void within which never left us, that irrational longing to hark back to the past or else to speed up the march of time, and those keen shafts of memory that stung like fire. Sometimes we toyed with our imagination, composing ourselves to wait for a ring at the bell announcing somebody's return, or for the sound of a familiar footstep on the stairs; but, though we might deliberately stay at home at the hour when a traveler coming by the evening train would normally have arrived, and though we might contrive to forget for the moment that no trains were running, that game of make-believe, for obvious reasons, could not last. Always a moment came when we had to face the fact that no trains were coming in. And then we realized that the separation was destined to continue, we had no choice but to come to terms with the days ahead. In short, we returned to our prison-house, we had nothing left us but the past, and even if some were tempted to live in the future, they had speedily to abandon the idea anyhow, as soon as could be, once they felt the wounds that the imagination inflicts on those who yield themselves to it.

It is noteworthy that our townspeople very quickly desisted, even in public, from a habit one might have expected them to form, that of trying to figure out the probable duration of their exile. The reason was this: when the most pessimistic had fixed it at, say, six months; when they had drunk in advance the dregs of bitterness of those six black months, and painfully screwed up their courage to the sticking-place, straining all their remaining energy to endure valiantly the long ordeal of all those weeks and days, when they had done this, some friend they met, an article in a newspaper, a vague suspicion, or a flash of foresight would suggest that, after all, there was no reason why the epidemic shouldn't last more than six months; why not a year, or even more?

At such moments the collapse of their courage, willpower, and endurance was so abrupt that they felt they could never drag themselves out of the pit of despond into which they had fallen. Therefore they forced themselves never to think about the problematic day of escape, to cease looking to the future, and always to keep, so to speak, their eyes fixed on the ground at their feet. But, naturally enough, this prudence, this habit of feinting with their predicament and refusing to put up a fight, was ill rewarded. For, while averting that revulsion which they found so unbearable, they also deprived themselves of those redeeming moments, frequent enough when all is told, when by conjuring up pictures of a reunion to be, they could forget about the plague. Thus, in a middle course between these heights and depths, they drifted through life rather than lived, the prey of aimless days and sterile memories, like wandering shadows that could have acquired substance only by consenting to root themselves in the solid earth of their distress.

Thus, too, they came to know the incorrigible sorrow of all prisoners and exiles, which is to live in company with a memory that serves no purpose. Even the past, of which they thought incessantly, had a savor only of regret. For they would have wished to add to it all that they regretted having left undone, while they might yet have done it, with the man or woman whose return they now awaited; just as in all the activities, even the relatively happy ones, of their life as prisoners they kept vainly trying to include the absent one. And thus there was always something missing in their lives. Hostile to the past, impatient of the present, and cheated of the future, we were much like those whom men's justice, or hatred, forces to live behind prison bars. Thus the only way of escaping from that intolerable leisure was to set the trains running again in one's imagination and in filling the silence with the fancied tinkle of a doorbell, in practice obstinately mute.

Still, if it was an exile, it was, for most of us, exile in one's own home. And though the narrator experienced only the common form of exile, he cannot forget the case of those who, like Rambert the journalist and a good many others, had to endure an aggravated deprivation, since, being travelers caught by the plague and forced to stay where they were, they were cut off both from the person with whom they wanted to be and from their homes as well. In the general exile they were the most exiled; since while time gave rise for them, as for us all, to the suffering appropriate to it, there was also for

them the space factor; they were obsessed by it and at every moment knocked their heads against the walls of this huge and alien lazar-house secluding them from their lost homes. These were the people, no doubt, whom one often saw wandering forlornly in the dusty town at all hours of the day, silently invoking nightfalls known to them alone and the daysprings of their happier land. And they fed their despondency with fleeting intimations, messages as disconcerting as a flight of swallows, a dew-fall at sundown, or those queer glints the sun sometimes dapples on empty streets. As for that outside world, which can always offer an escape from everything, they shut their eyes to it, bent as they were on cherishing the all-too-real phantoms of their imagination and conjuring up with all their might pictures of a land where a special play of light, two or three hills, a favorite tree, a woman's smile, composed for them a world that nothing could replace.

To come at last, and more specifically, to the case of parted lovers, who present the greatest interest and of whom the narrator is, perhaps, better qualified to speak, their minds were the prey of different emotions, notably remorse. For their present position enabled them to take stock of their feelings with a sort of feverish objectivity. And, in these conditions, it was rare for them not to detect their own shortcomings. What first brought these home to them was the trouble they experienced in summoning up any clear picture of what the absent one was doing. They came to deplore their ignorance of the way in which that person used to spend his or her days, and reproached themselves for having troubled too little about this in the past, and for having affected to think that, for a lover, the occupations of the loved one when they are not together could be a matter of indifference and not a source of joy. Once this had been brought home to them, they could retrace the course of their love and see where it had fallen short. In normal times all of us know, whether consciously or not, that there is no love which can't be bettered; nevertheless, we reconcile ourselves more or less easily to the fact that ours has never risen above the average. But memory is less disposed to compromise. And, in a very definite way, this misfortune which had come from outside and befallen a whole town did more than inflict on us an unmerited distress with which we might well be indignant.

It also incited us to create our own suffering and thus to accept frustration as a natural state. This was one of the tricks the pestilence had of diverting attention and confounding issues.

Thus each of us had to be content to live only for the day, alone under the vast indifference of the sky. This sense of being abandoned, which might in time have given characters a finer temper, began, however, by sapping them to the point of futility. For instance, some of our fellow citizens became subject to a curious kind of servitude, which put them at the mercy of the sun and the rain.

Looking at them, you had an impression that for the first time in their lives they were becoming, as some would say, weather-conscious. A burst of sunshine was enough to make them seem delighted with the world, while rainy days gave a dark cast to their faces and their mood. A few weeks before, they had been free of this absurd subservience to the weather, because they had not to face life alone; the person they were living with held, to some extent, the foreground of their little world. But from now on it was different; they seemed at the mercy of the sky's caprices, in other words, suffered and hoped irrationally.

Moreover, in this extremity of solitude none could count on any help from his neighbor; each had to bear the load of his troubles alone. If, by some chance, one of us

tried to unburden himself or to say something about his feelings, the reply he got, whatever it might be, usually wounded him. And then it dawned on him that he and the man with him weren't talking about the same thing. For while he himself spoke from the depths of long days of brooding upon his personal distress, and the image he had tried to impart had been slowly shaped and proved in the fires of passion and regret, this meant nothing to the man to whom he was speaking, who pictured a conventional emotion, a grief that is traded on the market-place, mass-produced. Whether friendly or hostile, the reply always missed fire, and the attempt to communicate had to be given up. This was true of those at least for whom silence was unbearable, and since the others could not find the truly expressive word, they resigned themselves to using the current coin of language, the commonplaces of plain narrative, of anecdote, and of their daily paper. So in these cases, too, even the sincerest grief had to make do with the set phrases of ordinary conversation. Only on these terms could the prisoners of the plague ensure the sympathy of their concierge and the interest of their hearers.

Nevertheless, and this point is most important, however bitter their distress and however heavy their hearts, for all their emptiness, it can be truly said of these exiles that in the early period of the plague they could account themselves privileged. For at the precise moment when the residents of the town began to panic, their thoughts were wholly fixed on the person whom they longed to meet again. The egoism of love made them immune to the general distress and, if they thought of the plague, it was only in so far as it might threaten to make their separation eternal. Thus in the very heart of the epidemic they maintained a saving indifference, which one was tempted to take for composure.

Their despair saved them from panic, thus their misfortune had a good side. For instance, if it happened that one of them was carried off by the disease, it was almost always without his having had time to realize it. Snatched suddenly from his long, silent communion with a wraith of memory, he was plunged straightway into the densest silence of all. He'd had no time for anything.

WHILE our townspeople were trying to come to terms with their sudden isolation, the plague was posting sentries at the gates and turning away ships bound for Oran. No vehicle had entered the town since the gates were closed. From that day onwards one had the impression that all cars were moving in circles.

The harbor, too, presented a strange appearance to those who looked down on it from the top of the boulevards. The commercial activity that hitherto made it one of the chief ports on the coast had ceased abruptly. Only a few ships, detained in quarantine, were anchored in the bay. But the gaunt, idle cranes on the wharves, tip-carts lying on their sides, neglected heaps of sacks and barrels, all testified that commerce, too, had died of plague.

In spite of such unusual sights our townsfolk apparently found it hard to grasp what was happening to them. There were feelings all could share, such as fear and separation, but personal interests, too, continued to occupy the foreground of their thoughts. Nobody as yet had really acknowledged to himself what the disease connoted. Most people were chiefly aware of what ruffled the normal tenor of their lives or affected their interests. They were worried and irritated, but these are not feelings with which to

confront plague. Their first reaction, for instance, was to abuse the authorities. The Prefect's riposte to criticisms echoed by the press. Could not the regulations be modified and made less stringent? was somewhat unexpected. Hitherto neither the newspapers nor the Ransdoc Information Bureau had been given any official statistics relating to the epidemic. Now the Prefect supplied them daily to the bureau, with the request that they should be broadcast once a week.

In this, too, the reaction of the public was slower than might have been expected. Thus the bare statement that three hundred and two deaths had taken place in the third week of plague failed to strike their imagination. For one thing, all the three hundred and two deaths might not have been due to plague.

Also, no one in the town had any idea of the average weekly death-rate in ordinary times. The population of the town was about two hundred thousand. There was no knowing if the present death-rate were really so abnormal. This is, in fact, the kind of statistics that nobody ever troubles much about, notwithstanding that its interest is obvious. The public lacked, in short, standards of comparison. It was only as time passed and the steady rise in the death-rate could not be ignored that public opinion became alive to the truth. For in the fifth week there were three hundred and twenty-one deaths, and three hundred and forty-five in the sixth. These figures, anyhow, spoke for themselves. Yet they were still not sensational enough to prevent our townsfolk, perturbed though they were, from persisting in the idea that what was happening was a sort of accident, disagreeable enough, but certainly of a temporary order.

So they went on strolling about the town as usual and sitting at the tables on cafe terraces. Generally speaking, they did not lack courage, bandied more jokes than lamentations, and made a show of accepting cheerfully unpleasantnesses that obviously could be only passing. In short, they kept up appearances. However, toward the end of the month, about the time of the Week of Prayer which will be described later on, there were more serious developments, altering the whole aspect of the town. To begin with, the Prefect took measures controlling the traffic and the food-supply. Gasoline was rationed and restrictions were placed on the sale of foodstuffs. Reductions were ordered in the use of electricity.

Only necessaries were brought by road or air to Oran. Thus the traffic thinned out progressively until hardly any private cars were on the roads; luxury shops closed overnight, and others began to put up "Sold Out" notices, while crowds of buyers stood waiting at their doors.

Oran assumed a novel appearance. You saw more pedestrians, and in the slack hours numbers of people, reduced to idleness because shops and a good many offices were closed, crowded the streets and cafes. For the present they were not unemployed; merely on holiday. So it was that on fine days, toward three in the afternoon, Oran brought to mind a city where public rejoicings are in progress, shops are shut, and traffic is stopped to give a merry-making populace the freedom of the streets.

Naturally the picture-houses benefited by the situation and made money hand over fist. They had one difficulty, however, to provide a change of program, since the circulation of films in the region had been suspended. After a fortnight the various cinemas were obliged to exchange films and, after a further lapse of time, to show always the same program. In spite of this their takings did not fall off.

The cafes, thanks to the big stocks accumulated in a town where the wine-and-liquor trade holds pride of place, were equally able to cater for their patrons. And, to tell the truth, there was much heavy drinking. One of the cafes had the brilliant idea of putting up a slogan: "The best protection against infection is a bottle of good wine," which confirmed an already prevalent opinion that alcohol is a safeguard against infectious disease. Every night, toward two a.m., quite a number of drunken men, ejected from the cafes, staggered down the streets, vociferating optimism.

Yet all these changes were, in one sense, so fantastic and had been made so precipitately that it wasn't easy to regard them as likely to have any permanence. With the result that we went on focusing our attention on our personal feelings.

When leaving the hospital two days after the gates were closed, Dr. Rieux met Cottard in the street. The little man was beaming with satisfaction. Rieux congratulated him on his appearance.

"Yes," Cottard said, "I'm feeling very fit. Never was fitter in my life. But tell me, doctor. This blasted plague, what about it? Getting to look mighty serious, isn't it?" When the doctor nodded, he continued exuberantly: "And there's no reason for it to stop now. This town's going to be in an unholy mess, by the look of things."

They walked a little way together. Cottard told the story of a grocer in his street who had laid by masses of canned provisions with the idea of selling them later on at a big profit. When the ambulance men came to fetch him he had several dozen cans of meat under his bed.

"He died in the hospital. There's no money in plague, that's sure." Cottard was a mine of stories of this kind, true or false, about the epidemic. One of them was about a man with all the symptoms and running a high fever who dashed out into the street, flung himself on the first woman he met, and embraced her, yelling that he'd "got it."

"Good for him!" was Cottard's comment. But his next remark seemed to belie his gleeful exclamation. "Anyhow, we'll all be nuts before long, unless I'm much mistaken."

It was on the afternoon of the same day that Grand at last unburdened himself to Rieux. Noticing Mme Rieux's photograph on the desk, he looked at the doctor inquiringly. Rieux told him that his wife was under treatment in a sanatorium some distance from the town. "In one way," Grand said, "that's lucky." The doctor agreed that it was lucky in a sense; but, he added, the great thing was that his wife should recover.

"Yes," Grand said, "I understand."

And then, for the first time since Rieux had made his acquaintance, he became quite voluble. Though he still had trouble over his words he succeeded nearly always in finding them; indeed, it was as if for years he'd been thinking over what he now said.

When in his teens, he had married a very young girl, one of a poor family living near by. It was, in fact, in order to marry that he'd abandoned his studies and taken up his present job. Neither he nor Jeanne ever stirred from their part of the town. In his courting days he used to go to see her at her home, and the family were inclined to make fun of her bashful, silent admirer. Her father was a railroadman. When off duty, he spent most of the time seated in a corner beside the window gazing meditatively at the passers-by, his enormous hands splayed out on his thighs. His wife was always busy with domestic duties, in which Jeanne gave her a hand. Jeanne was so tiny that it always made Grand nervous to see her crossing a street, the vehicles bearing down on her looked so gigantic. Then one day shortly before Christmas they went out for a short walk together and

stopped to admire a gaily decorated shop-window. After gazing ecstatically at it for some moments, Jeanne turned to him. "Oh, isn't it lovely!" He squeezed her wrist. It was thus that the marriage had come about.

The rest of the story, to Grand's thinking, was very simple. The common lot of married couples. You get married, you go on loving a bit longer, you work. And you work so hard that it makes you forget to love. As the head of the office where Grand was employed hadn't kept his promise, Jeanne, too, had to work outside. At this point a little imagination was needed to grasp what Grand was trying to convey. Owing largely to fatigue, he gradually lost grip of himself, had less and less to say, and failed to keep alive the feeling in his wife that she was loved. An overworked husband, poverty, the gradual loss of hope in a better future, silent evenings at home, what chance had any passion of surviving such conditions? Probably Jeanne had suffered. And yet she'd stayed; of course one may often suffer a long time without knowing it. Thus years went by. Then, one day, she left him. Naturally she hadn't gone alone. "I was very fond of you, but now I'm so tired. I'm not happy to go, but one needn't be happy to make another start." That, more or less, was what she'd said in her letter.

Grand, too, had suffered. And he, too, might, as Rieux pointed out, have made a fresh start. But no, he had lost faith. Only, he couldn't stop thinking about her. What he'd have liked to do was to write her a letter justifying himself.

"But it's not easy," he told Rieux. "I've been thinking it over for years. While we loved each other we didn't need words to make ourselves understood. But people don't love forever. A time came when I should have found the words to keep her with me, only I couldn't." Grand produced from his pocket something that looked like a check duster and blew his nose noisily. Then he wiped his mustache. Rieux gazed at him in silence. "Forgive me, doctor," Grand added hastily, "but how shall I put it? I feel you're to be trusted. That's why I can talk to you about these things. And then, you see, I get all worked up."

Obviously Grand's thoughts were leagues away from the plague.

That evening Rieux sent a telegram to his wife telling her that the town was closed, that she must go on taking great care of herself, and that she was in his thoughts.

One evening when he was leaving the hospital, it was about three weeks after the closing of the gates, Rieux found a young man waiting for him in the street.

"You remember me, don't you?"

Rieux believed he did, but couldn't quite place him.

"I called on you just before this trouble started," the young man said, "for information about the living-conditions in the Arab quarter. My name is Raymond Rambert."

"Ah yes, of course. Well, you've now the makings of a good story for your paper."

Rambert, who gave the impression of being much less self-assured than he had seemed on the first occasion when they met, said it wasn't that he'd come about.

He wanted to know if the doctor would kindly give him some help.

"I must apologize," he continued, "but really I don't know a soul here, and the local representative of my paper is a complete dud."

Rieux said he had to go to a dispensary in the center of the town and suggested they should walk there together. Their way lay through the narrow streets of the Negro district. Evening was coming on, but the town, once so noisy at this hour, was strangely

still. The only sounds were some bugle-calls echoing through the air, still golden with the end of daylight; the army, anyhow, was making a show of carrying on as usual. Meanwhile, as they walked down the steep little streets flanked by blue, mauve, and saffron-yellow walls, Rambert talked incessantly, as if his nerves were out of hand.

He had left his wife in Paris, he said. Well, she wasn't actually his wife, but it came to the same thing. The moment the town was put into quarantine he had sent her a wire. His impression then was that this state of things was quite temporary, and all he'd tried to do was to get a letter through to her. But the post-office officials had vetoed this, his colleagues of the local press said they could do nothing for him, and a clerk in the Prefect's office had laughed in his face. It was only after waiting in line for a couple of hours that he had managed to get a telegram accepted: All goes well. Hope to see you soon.

But next morning, when he woke up, it had dawned on him that, after all, there was absolutely no knowing how long this business was going to last. So he'd decided to leave the town at once. Being able, thanks to his professional status, to pull some strings, he had secured an interview with a high official in the Prefect's office. He had explained that his presence in Oran was purely accidental, he had no connection with the town and no reasons for staying in it; that being so, he surely was entitled to leave, even if, once outside the town, he had to undergo a spell of quarantine. The official told him he quite appreciated his position, but no exceptions could be made. He would, however, see if anything could be done, though he could hold out little hope of a quick decision, as the authorities were taking a very serious view of the situation.

"But, confound it," Rambert exclaimed, "I don't belong here!"

"Quite so. Anyhow, let's hope the epidemic will soon be over." Finally, he had tried to console Rambert by pointing out that, as a journalist, he had an excellent subject to his hand in Oran; indeed, when one came to think of it, no event, however disagreeable in some ways, but had its bright side. Whereat Rambert had shrugged his shoulders petulantly and walked out.

They had come to the center of the town.

"It's so damn silly, doctor, isn't it? The truth is I wasn't brought into the world to write newspaper articles. But it's quite likely I was brought into the world to live with a woman. That's reasonable enough, isn't it?"

Rieux replied cautiously that there might be something in what he said.

The central boulevards were not so crowded as usual. The few people about were hurrying to distant homes. Not a smile was to be seen on any face. Rieux guessed that this was a result of the latest Ransdoc announcement. After twenty-four hours our townspeople would begin to hope again. But on the days when they were announced, the statistics were too fresh in everybody's memory.

"The truth," Rambert remarked abruptly, "is that she and I have been together only a short time, and we suit each other perfectly." When Rieux said nothing, he continued: "I can see I'm boring you. Sorry. All I wanted to know was whether you couldn't possibly give me a certificate stating that I haven't got this damned disease. It might make things easier, I think."

Rieux nodded. A small boy had just run against his legs and fallen; he set him on his feet again. Walking on, they came to the Place d'Armes. Gray with dust, the palms and fig trees drooped despondently around a statue of the Republic, which too was coated with grime and dust. They stopped beside the statue. Rieux stamped his feet on the flagstones to shake off the coat of white dust that had gathered on them. His hat pushed slightly back, his shirt-collar gaping under a loosely knotted tie, his cheeks ill-shaven, the journalist had the sulky, stubborn look of a young man who feels himself deeply injured.

"Please don't doubt I understand you," Rieux said, "but you must see your argument doesn't hold water. I can't give you that certificate because I don't know whether you have the disease or not, and even if I did, how could I certify that between the moment of leaving my consulting-room and your arrival at the Prefect's office you wouldn't be infected? And even if I did?"

"And even if you did?"

"Even if I gave you a certificate, it wouldn't help."

"Why not?"

"Because there are thousands of people placed as you are in this town, and there can't be any question of allowing them to leave it."

"Even supposing they haven't got plague?"

"That's not a sufficient reason. Oh, I know it's an absurd situation, but we're all involved in it, and we've got to accept it as it is."

"But I don't belong here."

"Unfortunately, from now on you'll belong here, like everybody else."

Rambert raised his voice a little.

"But, damn it, doctor, can't you see it's a matter of common human feeling? Or don't you realize what this sort of separation means to people who are fond of each other?"

Rieux was silent for a moment, then said he understood it perfectly. He wished nothing better than that Rambert should be allowed to return to his wife and that all who loved one another and were parted should come together again. Only the law was the law, plague had broken out, and he could only do what had to be done.

"No," Rambert said bitterly, "you can't understand. You're using the language of reason, not of the heart; you live in a world of abstractions."

The doctor glanced up at the statue of the Republic, then said he did not know if he was using the language of reason, but he knew he was using the language of the facts as everybody could see them, which wasn't necessarily the same thing.

The journalist tugged at his tie to straighten it.

"So, I take it, I can't count on help from you. Very good. But" his tone was challenging "leave this town I shall."

The doctor repeated that he quite understood, but all that was none of his business.

"Excuse me, but it is your business." Rambert raised his voice again. "I approached you because I'd been told you played a large part in drawing up the orders that have been issued. So I thought that in one case anyhow you could unmake what you'd helped to make. But you don't care; you never gave a thought to anybody, you didn't take the case of people who are separated into account."

Rieux admitted this was true up to a point; he'd preferred not to take such cases into account.

"Ah, I see now!" Rambert exclaimed. "You'll soon be talking about the interests of the general public. But public welfare is merely the sum total of the private welfares of each of us."

The doctor seemed abruptly to come out of a dream.

"Oh, come!" he said. "There's that, but there's much more to it than that. It doesn't do to rush to conclusions, you know. But you've no reason to feel angered. I assure you that if you find a way out of your quandary, I shall be extremely pleased. Only, there are things that my official position debars me from doing."

Rambert tossed his head petulantly.

"Yes, yes, I was wrong to show annoyance. And I've taken up too much of your time already."

Rieux asked him to let him know how he got on with his project, and not to bear him a grudge for not having been more amenable. He was sure, he added, that there was some common ground on which they could meet. Rambert looked perplexed.

Then, "Yes," he said after a short silence, "I rather think so, too, in spite of myself, and of all you've just been saying." He paused. "Still, I can't agree with you."

Pulling down his hat over his eyes, he walked quickly away. Rieux saw him enter the hotel where Tarrou was staying.

After a moment the doctor gave a slight nod, as if approving of some thought that had crossed his mind. Yes, the journalist was right in refusing to be balked of happiness. But was he right in reproaching him, Rieux, with living in a world of abstractions? Could that term "abstraction" really apply to these days he spent in his hospital while the plague was battening on the town, raising its death-toll to five hundred victims a week? Yes, an element of abstraction, of a divorce from reality, entered into such calamities. Still when abstraction sets to killing you, you've got to get busy with it. And so much Rieux knew: that this wasn't the easiest course. Running this auxiliary hospital, for instance, of which he was in charge' there were now three such hospitals, was no light task.

He had had an anteroom, leading into his surgery, installed, equipped for dealing with patients on arrival. The floor had been excavated and replaced by a shallow lake of water and cresylic acid, in the center of which was a sort of island made of bricks. The patient was carried to the island, rapidly undressed, and his clothes dropped into the disinfectant water. After being washed, dried, and dressed in one of the coarse hospital nightshirts, he was taken to Rieux for examination, then carried to one of the wards. This hospital, a requisitioned schoolhouse, now contained five hundred beds, almost all of which were occupied.

After the reception of the patients, which he personally supervised, Rieux injected serum, lanced buboes, checked the statistics again, and returned for his afternoon consultations. Only when night was setting in did he start on his round of visits, and he never got home till a very late hour. On the previous night his mother, when handing him a telegram from his wife, had remarked that his hands were shaking.

"Yes," he said. "But it's only a matter of sticking to it, and my nerves will steady down, you'll see."

He had a robust constitution and, as yet, wasn't really tired. Still his visits, for one thing, were beginning to put a great strain on his endurance. Once the epidemic was diagnosed, the patient had to be evacuated forthwith. Then indeed began "abstraction" and a tussle with the family, who knew they would not see the sick man again until he

was dead or cured. "Have some pity, doctor!" It was Mme Loret, mother of the chambermaid at Tarrou's hotel, who made the appeal. An unnecessary appeal; of course he had pity. But what purpose could it serve? He had to telephone, and soon the ambulance could be heard clanging down the street. (At first the neighbors used to open windows and watch. Later they promptly shut them.) Then came a second phase of conflict, tears and pleadings, abstraction, in a word. In those fever-hot, nerve-ridden sickrooms crazy scenes took place.

But the issue was always the same. The patient was removed. Then Rieux, too, could leave.

In the early days he had merely telephoned, then rushed off to see other patients, without waiting for the ambulance. But no sooner was he gone than the family locked and barred their doors, preferring contact with the plague to a parting whose issue they now knew only too well. There followed objurgations, screams, batterings on the door, action by the police, and later armed force; the patient was taken by storm. Thus during the first few weeks Rieux was compelled to stay with the patient till the ambulance came. Later, when each doctor was accompanied by a volunteer police officer, Rieux could hurry away to the next patient. But, to begin with, every evening was like that evening when he was called in for Mme Loret's daughter. He was shown into a small apartment decorated with fans and artificial flowers. The mother greeted him with a faltering smile.

"Oh, I do hope it's not the fever everyone's talking about."

Lifting the coverlet and chemise, he gazed in silence at the red blotches on the girl's thighs and stomach, the swollen ganglia. After one glance the mother broke into shrill, uncontrollable cries of grief. And every evening mothers wailed thus, with a distraught abstraction, as their eyes fell on those fatal stigmata on limbs and bellies; every evening hands gripped Rieux's arms, there was a rush of useless words, promises, and tears; every evening the nearing tocsin of the ambulance provoked scenes as vain as every form of grief. Rieux had nothing to look forward to but a long sequence of such scenes, renewed again and again. Yes, plague, like abstraction, was monotonous; perhaps only one factor changed, and that was Rieux himself. Standing at the foot of the statue of the Republic that evening, he felt it; all he was conscious of was a bleak indifference steadily gaining on him as he gazed at the door of the hotel Rambert had just entered.

After these wearing weeks, after all those nightfalls when the townsfolk poured into the streets to roam them aimlessly, Rieux had learned that he need no longer steel himself against pity. One grows out of pity when it's useless. And in this feeling that his heart had slowly closed in on itself, the doctor found a solace, his only solace, for the almost unendurable burden of his days. This, he knew, would make his task easier, and therefore he was glad of it. When he came home at two in the morning and his mother was shocked at the blank look he gave her, she was deploring precisely the sole alleviation Rieux could then experience. To fight abstraction you must have something of it in your own make-up.

But how could Rambert be expected to grasp that? Abstraction for him was all that stood in the way of his happiness. Indeed, Rieux had to admit the journalist was right, in one sense. But he knew, too, that abstraction sometimes proves itself stronger than happiness; and then, if only then, it has to be taken into account. And this was what was going to happen to Rambert, as the doctor was to learn when, much later, Rambert told him more about himself. Thus he was enabled to follow, and on a different plane, the dreary struggle in progress between each man's happiness and the abstractions of the plague, which constituted the whole life of our town over a long period of time.

BUT where some saw abstraction others saw the truth. The first month of the plague ended gloomily, with a violent recrudescence of the epidemic and a dramatic sermon preached by Father Paneloux, the Jesuit priest who had given an arm to old Michel when he was tottering home at the start of his illness. Father Paneloux had already made his mark with frequent contributions to the Oran Geographical Society; these dealt chiefly with ancient inscriptions, on which he was an authority. But he had also reached a wider, non-specialist public with a series of lectures on present-day individualism. In these he had shown himself a stalwart champion of Christian doctrine at its most precise and purest, equally remote from modern laxity and the obscurantism of the past. On these occasions he had not shrunk from trouncing his hearers with some vigorous home-truths.

Hence his local celebrity.

Toward the end of the month the ecclesiastical authorities in our town resolved to do battle against the plague with the weapons appropriate to them, and organized a Week of Prayer. These manifestations of public piety were to be concluded on Sunday by a High Mass celebrated under the auspices of St. Roch, the plague-stricken saint, and Father Paneloux was asked to preach the sermon. For a fortnight he desisted from the research work on St. Augustine and the African Church that had won for him a high place in his Order. A man of a passionate, fiery temperament, he flung himself wholeheartedly into the task assigned him. The sermon was a topic of conversation long before it was delivered and, in its way, it marks an important date in the history of the period.

There were large attendances at the services of the Week of Prayer. It must not, however, be assumed that in normal times the townsfolk of Oran are particularly devout. On Sunday mornings, for instance, sea-bathing competes seriously with churchgoing. Nor must it be thought that they had seen a great light and had a sudden change of heart. But, for one thing, now that the town was closed and the harbor out of bounds, there was no question of bathing; moreover, they were in a quite exceptional frame of mind and, though in their heart of hearts they were far from recognizing the enormity of what had come on them, they couldn't help feeling, for obvious reasons, that decidedly something had changed.

Nevertheless, many continued hoping that the epidemic would soon die out and they and their families be spared. Thus they felt under no obligation to make any change in their habits as yet. Plague was for them an unwelcome visitant, bound to take its leave one day as unexpectedly as it had come. Alarmed, but far from desperate, they hadn't yet reached the phase when plague would seem to them the very tissue of their existence; when they forgot the lives that until now it had been given them to lead. In short, they were waiting for the turn of events.

With regard to religion, as to many other problems, plague had induced in them a curious frame of mind, as remote from indifference as from fervor; the best name to give it, perhaps, might be "objectivity." Most of those who took part in the Week of Prayer would have echoed a remark made by one of the churchgoers in Dr. Rieux's hearing: "Anyhow, it can't do any harm." Even Tarrou, after recording in his notebook that in such cases the Chinese fall to playing tambourines before the Genius of Plague, observed that there was no means of telling whether, in practice, tambourines proved more efficacious than prophylactic measures. He merely added that, to decide the point, we should need first to ascertain if a Genius of Plague actually existed, and our ignorance on this point nullified any opinions we might form.

In any case the Cathedral was practically always full of worshippers throughout the Week of Prayer. For the first two or three days many stayed outside, under the palms and pomegranate trees in the garden in front of the porch, and listened from a distance to the swelling tide of prayers and invocations whose backwash filled the neighboring streets. But once an example had been given, they began to enter the Cathedral and join timidly in the responses. And on the Sunday of the sermon a huge congregation filled the nave, overflowing on to the steps and precincts. The sky had clouded up on the previous day, and now it was raining heavily. Those in the open unfurled umbrellas. The air inside the Cathedral was heavy with fumes of incense and the smell of wet clothes when Father Paneloux stepped into the pulpit.

He was a stockily built man, of medium height. When he leaned on the edge of the pulpit, grasping the woodwork with his big hands, all one saw was a black, massive torso and, above it, two rosy cheeks overhung by steel-rimmed spectacles. He had a powerful, rather emotional delivery, which carried to a great distance, and when he launched at the congregation his opening phrase in clear, emphatic tones: "Calamity has come on you, my brethren, and, my brethren, you deserved it" there was a flutter that extended to the crowd massed in the rain outside the porch.

In strict logic what came next did not seem to follow from this dramatic opening. Only as the sermon proceeded did it become apparent to the congregation that, by a skillful oratorical device, Father Paneloux had launched at them, like a fisticuff, the gist of his whole discourse. After launching it he went on at once to quote a text from Exodus relating to the plague of Egypt, and said:

"The first time this scourge appears in history, it was wielded to strike down the enemies of God. Pharaoh set himself up against the divine will, and the plague beat him to his knees. Thus from the dawn of recorded history the scourge of God has humbled the proud of heart and laid low those who hardened themselves against Him. Ponder this well, my friends, and fall on your knees."

The downpour had increased in violence, and these words, striking through a silence intensified by the drumming of raindrops on the chancel windows, carried such conviction that, after a momentary hesitation, some of the worshippers slipped forward from their seats on to their knees. Others felt it right to follow their example, and the movement gradually spread until presently everyone was kneeling, from end to end of the cathedral. No sound, except an occasional creak of chairs, accompanied the movement. Then Paneloux drew himself up to his full height, took a deep breath, and continued his sermon in a voice that gathered strength as it proceeded.

"If today the plague is in your midst, that is because the hour has struck for taking thought. The just man need have no fear, but the evildoer has good cause to tremble. For plague is the flail of God and the world His threshing-floor, and implacably He will thresh out His harvest until the wheat is separated from the chaff. There will be more chaff than wheat, few chosen of the many called.

Yet this calamity was not willed by God. Too long this world of ours has connived at evil, too long has it counted on the divine mercy, on God's forgiveness.

Repentance was enough, men thought; nothing was forbidden. Everyone felt comfortably assured; when the day came, he would surely turn from his sins and repent. Pending that day, the easiest course was to surrender all along the line; divine compassion would do the rest. For a long while God gazed down on this town with eyes of compassion; but He grew weary of waiting, His eternal hope was too long deferred, and now He has turned His face away from us. And so, God's light withdrawn, we walk in darkness, in the thick darkness of this plague."

Someone in the congregation gave a little snort, like that of a restive horse.

After a short silence the preacher continued in a lower tone.

"We read in the Golden Legend that in the time of King Umberto Italy was swept by plague and its greatest ravages took place in Rome and Pavia. So dreadful were these that the living hardly sufficed to bury the dead. And a good angel was made visible to human eyes, giving his orders to an evil angel who bore a great hunting-spear, and bidding him strike the houses; and as many strokes as he dealt a house, so many dead were carried out of it."

Here Paneloux stretched forth his two short arms toward the open porch, as if pointing to something behind the tumbling curtain of the rain.

"My brothers," he cried, "that fatal hunt is up, and harrying our streets today.

See him there, that angel of the pestilence, comely as Lucifer, shining like Evil's very self! He is hovering above your roofs with his great spear in his right hand, poised to strike, while his left hand is stretched toward one or other of your houses. Maybe at this very moment his finger is pointing to your door, the red spear crashing on its panels, and even now the plague is entering your home and settling down in your bedroom to await your return. Patient and watchful, ineluctable as the order of the scheme of things, it bides its time. No earthly power, nay, not even, mark me well, the vaunted might of human science can avail you to avert that hand once it is stretched toward you. And winnowed like corn on the blood-stained threshing-floor of suffering, you will be cast away with the chaff."

At this point the Father reverted with heightened eloquence to the symbol of the flail. He bade his hearers picture a huge wooden bar whirling above the town, striking at random, swinging up again in a shower of drops of blood, and spreading carnage and suffering on earth, "for the seedtime that shall prepare the harvest of the truth."

At the end of his long phrase Father Paneloux paused; his hair was straggling over his forehead, his body shaken by tremors that his hands communicated to the pulpit. When he spoke again, his voice was lower, but vibrant with accusation.

"Yes, the hour has come for serious thought. You fondly imagined it was enough to visit God on Sundays, and thus you could make free of your weekdays. You believed some brief formalities, some bendings of the knee, would recompense Him well enough for your criminal indifference. But God is not mocked. These brief encounters could not sate the fierce hunger of His love. He wished to see you longer and more often; that is His manner of loving and, indeed, it is the only manner of loving. And this is why, wearied of waiting for you to come to Him, He loosed on you this visitation; as He has visited all the cities that offended against Him since the dawn of history. Now you are learning your lesson, the lesson that was learned by Cain and his offspring, by the people of Sodom and Gomorrah, by Job and Pharaoh, by all that hardened their hearts against Him. And like them you have been beholding mankind and all creation with new eyes,

since the gates of this city closed on you and on the pestilence. Now, at last, you know the hour has struck to bend your thoughts to first and last things."

A wet wind was sweeping up the nave, making the candle-flames bend and flicker.

The pungency of burning wax, coughs, a stifled sneeze, rose toward Father Paneloux, who, reverting to his exordium with a subtlety that was much appreciated, went on in a calm, almost matter-of-fact voice: "Many of you are wondering, I know, what I am leading up to. I wish to lead you to the truth and teach you to rejoice, yes, rejoice, in spite of all that I have been telling you.

For the time is past when a helping hand or mere words of good advice could set you on the right path. Today the truth is a command. It is a red spear sternly pointing to the narrow path, the one way of salvation. And thus, my brothers, at last it is revealed to you, the divine compassion which has ordained good and evil in everything; wrath and pity; the plague and your salvation. This same pestilence which is slaying you works for your good and points your path.

"Many centuries ago the Christians of Abyssinia saw in the plague a sure and God-sent means of winning eternal life. Those who were not yet stricken wrapped round them sheets in which men had died of plague, so as to make sure of their death. I grant you such a frenzied quest of salvation was not to be commended.

It shows an overhaste, indeed, a presumptuousness, which we can but deplore. No man should seek to force God's hand or to hurry on the appointed hour, and from a practice that aims at speeding up the order of events which God has ordained unalterably from all time, it is but a step to heresy. Yet we can learn a salutary lesson from the zeal, excessive though it was, of those Abyssinian Christians. Much of it is alien to our more enlightened spirits, and yet it gives us a glimpse of that radiant eternal light which glows, a small still flame, in the dark core of human suffering. And this light, too, illuminates the shadowed paths that lead towards deliverance. It reveals the will of God in action, unfailingly transforming evil into good. And once again today it is leading us through the dark valley of fears and groans towards the holy silence, the wellspring of all life. This, my friends, is the vast consolation I would hold out to you, so that when you leave this house of God you will carry away with you not only words of wrath, but a message, too, of comfort for your hearts."

Everyone supposed that the sermon had ended. Outside, the rain had ceased and watery sunshine was yellowing the Cathedral square. Vague sounds of voices came from the streets, and a low hum of traffic, the speech of an awakening town.

Discreetly, with a subdued rustling, the congregation gathered together their belongings. However, the Father had a few more words to say. He told them that after having made it clear that this plague came from God for the punishment of their sins, he would not have recourse, in concluding, to an eloquence that, considering the tragic nature of the occasion, would be out of keeping. He hoped and believed that all of them now saw their position in its true light. But, before leaving the pulpit, he would like to tell them of something he had been reading in an old chronicle of the Black Death at Marseille. In it Mathieu Marais, the chronicler, laments his lot; he says he has been cast into hell to languish without succor and without hope. Well, Mathieu Marais was blind! Never more intensely than today had he, Father Paneloux, felt the immanence of divine succor and Christian hope granted to all alike. He hoped against hope that, despite all the

horrors of these dark days, despite the groans of men and women in agony, our fellow citizens would offer up to heaven that one prayer which is truly Christian, a prayer of love. And God would see to the rest.

IT is hard to say if this sermon had any effect on our townsfolk. M. Othon, the magistrate, assured Dr. Rieux that he had found the preacher's arguments "absolutely irrefutable." But not everyone took so unqualified a view. To some the sermon simply brought home the fact that they had been sentenced, for an unknown crime, to an indeterminate period of punishment. And while a good many people adapted themselves to confinement and carried on their humdrum lives as before, there were others who rebelled and whose one idea now was to break loose from the prison-house.

At first the fact of being cut off from the outside world was accepted with a more or less good grace, much as people would have put up with any other temporary inconvenience that interfered with only a few of their habits. But, now they had abruptly become aware that they were undergoing a sort of incarceration under that blue dome of sky, already beginning to sizzle in the fires of summer, they had a vague sensation that their whole lives were threatened by the present turn of events, and in the evening, when the cooler air revived their energy, this feeling of being locked in like criminals prompted them sometimes to foolhardy acts.

It is noteworthy, this may or may not have been due to mere coincidence, that this Sunday of the sermon marked the beginning of something like a widespread panic in the town, and it took so deep a hold as to lead one to suspect that only now had the true nature of their situation dawned on our townspeople. Seen from this angle, the atmosphere of the town was somewhat changed. But, actually, it was a problem whether the change was in the atmosphere or in their hearts.

A few days after the sermon, when Rieux, on his way to one of the outlying districts of the town, was discussing the change with Grand, he collided in the darkness with a man who was standing in the middle of the pavement swaying from side to side without trying to advance. At the same moment the street-lamps, which were being lit later and later in the evening, went on suddenly, and a lamp just behind Rieux and his companion threw its light full on the man's face.

His eyes were shut and he was laughing soundlessly. Big drops of sweat were rolling down the face convulsed with silent merriment.

"A lunatic at large," Grand observed.

Rieux took his arm and was shepherding him on when he noticed that Grand was trembling violently.

"If things go on as they are going," Rieux remarked, "the whole town will be a madhouse." He felt exhausted, his throat was parched. "Let's have a drink."

They turned into a small cafe. The only light came from a lamp over the bar, the heavy air had a curious reddish tinge, and for no apparent reason everyone was speaking in undertones.

To the doctor's surprise Grand asked for a small glass of straight liquor, which he drank off at a gulp. "Fiery stuff!" he observed; then, a moment later, suggested making a move.

Out in the street it seemed to Rieux that the night was full of whispers.

Somewhere in the black depths above the street-lamps there was a low soughing that brought to his mind that unseen flail threshing incessantly the languid air of which Paneloux had spoken.

"Happily, happily," Grand muttered, then paused.

Rieux asked him what he had been going to say.

"Happily, I've my work."

"Ah yes," Rieux said. "That's something, anyhow." Then, so as not to hear that eerie whistling in the air, he asked Grand if he was getting good results.

"Well, yes, I think I'm making headway."

"Have you much more to do?"

Grand began to show an animation unlike his usual self, and his voice took ardor from the liquor he had drunk.

"I don't know. But that's not the point, doctor; yes, I can assure you that's not the point."

It was too dark to see clearly, but Rieux had the impression that he was waving his arms. He seemed to be working himself up to say something, and when he spoke, the words came with a rush.

"What I really want, doctor, is this. On the day when the manuscript reaches the publisher, I want him to stand up? after he's read it through, of course, and say to his staff: 'Gentlemen, hats off!'"

Rieux was dumbfounded, and, to add to his amazement, he saw, or seemed to see, the man beside him making as if to take off his hat with a sweeping gesture, bringing his hand to his head, then holding his arm out straight in front of him. That queer whistling overhead seemed to gather force.

"So you see," Grand added, "it's got to be flawless."

Though he knew little of the literary world, Rieux had a suspicion that things didn't happen in it quite so picturesquely, that, for instance, publishers do not keep their hats on in their offices. But, of course, one never can tell, and Rieux preferred to hold his peace. Try as he might to shut his ears to it, he still was listening to that eerie sound above, the whispering of the plague.

They had reached the part of the town where Grand lived and, as it was on a slight eminence, they felt the cool night breeze fanning their cheeks and at the same time carrying away from them the noises of the town.

Grand went on talking, but Rieux failed to follow all the worthy man was saying.

All he gathered was that the work he was engaged on ran to a great many pages, and he was at almost excruciating pains to bring it to perfection. "Evenings, whole weeks, spent on one word, just think! Sometimes on a mere conjunction!"

Grand stopped abruptly and seized the doctor by a button of his coat. The words came stumbling out of his almost toothless mouth.

"I'd like you to understand, doctor. I grant you it's easy enough to choose between a 'but' and an 'and.' It's a bit more difficult to decide between 'and' and 'then.' But definitely the hardest thing may be to know whether one should put an 'and' or leave it out."

"Yes," Rieux said, "I see your point."

He started walking again. Grand looked abashed, then stepped forward and drew level.

"Sorry," he said awkwardly. "I don't know what's come over me this evening."

Rieux patted his shoulder encouragingly, saying he'd been much interested in what Grand had said and would like to help him. This seemed to reassure Grand, and when they reached his place he suggested, after some slight hesitation, that the doctor should come in for a moment. Rieux agreed.

They entered the dining-room and Grand gave him a chair beside a table strewn with sheets of paper covered with writing in a microscopic hand, criscrossed with corrections.

"Yes, that's it," he said in answer to the doctor's questioning glance. "But won't you drink something? I've some wine."

Rieux declined. He was bending over the manuscript.

"No, don't look," Grand said. "It's my opening phrase, and it's giving trouble, no end of trouble."

He too was gazing at the sheets of paper on the table, and his hand seemed irresistibly drawn to one of them. Finally he picked it up and held it to the shadeless electric bulb so that the light shone through. The paper shook in his hand and Rieux noticed that his forehead was moist with sweat.

"Sit down," he said, "and read it to me."

"Yes." There was a timid gratitude in Grand's eyes and smile. "I think I'd like you to hear it."

He waited for a while, still gazing at the writing, then sat down. Meanwhile Rieux was listening to the curious buzzing sound that was rising from the streets as if in answer to the soughings of the plague. At that moment he had a preternaturally vivid awareness of the town stretched out below, a victim world secluded and apart, and of the groans of agony stifled in its darkness. Then, pitched low but clear, Grand's voice came to his ears.

"One fine morning in the month of May an elegant young horsewoman might have been seen riding a handsome sorrel mare along the flowery avenues of the Bois de Boulogne."

Silence returned, and with it the vague murmur of the prostrate town. Grand had put down the sheet and was still staring at it. After a while he looked up.

"What do you think of it?"

Rieux replied that this opening phrase had whetted his curiosity; he'd like to hear what followed. Whereat Grand told him he'd got it all wrong. He seemed excited and slapped the papers on the table with the flat of his hand.

"That's only a rough draft. Once I've succeeded in rendering perfectly the picture in my mind's eye, once my words have the exact tempo of this ride, the horse is trotting, one-two-three, one-two-three, see what I mean? the rest will come more easily and, what's even more important, the illusion will be such that from the very first words it will be possible to say: 'Hats off!'.

But before that, he admitted, there was lots of hard work to be done. He'd never dream of handing that sentence to the printer in its present form. For though it sometimes satisfied him, he was fully aware it didn't quite hit the mark as yet, and also that to some extent it had a facility of tone approximating, remotely perhaps, but recognizably, to the commonplace. That was more or less what he was saying when they heard the sound of people running in the street below the window.

Rieux stood up.

"Just wait and see what I make of it," Grand said, and, glancing toward the window, added: "When all this is over."

But then the sound of hurried footsteps came again. Rieux was already halfway down the stairs, and when he stepped out into the street two men brushed past him. They seemed to be on their way to one of the town gates. In fact, what with the heat and the plague, some of our fellow citizens were losing their heads; there had already been some scenes of violence and nightly attempts were made to elude the sentries and escape to the outside world.

OTHERS, too, Rambert for example, were trying to escape from this atmosphere of growing panic, but with more skill and persistence, if not with greater success.

For a while Rambert had gone on struggling with officialdom. If he was to be believed, he had always thought that perseverance would win through, inevitably, and, as he pointed out, resourcefulness in emergency was up his street, in a manner of speaking. So he plodded away, calling on all sorts of officials and others whose influence would have had weight in normal conditions. But, as things were, such influence was unavailing. For the most part they were men with well-defined and sound ideas on everything concerning exports, banking, the fruit or wine trade; men of proved ability in handling problems relating to insurance, the interpretation of ill-drawn contracts, and the like; of high qualifications and evident good intentions. That, in fact, was what struck one most, the excellence of their intentions. But as regards plague their competence was practically nil.

However, whenever opportunity arose, Rambert had tackled each of them and pleaded his cause. The gist of his argument was always the same: that he was a stranger to our town and, that being so, his case deserved special consideration.

Mostly the men he talked to conceded this point readily enough. But usually they added that a good number of other people were in a like case, and thus his position was not so exceptional as he seemed to suppose. To this Rambert could reply that this did not affect the substance of his argument in any way. He was then told that it did affect the position, already difficult, of the authorities, who were against showing any favoritism and thus running the risk of creating what, with obvious repugnance, they called "a precedent."

In conversation with Dr. Rieux, Rambert classified the people whom he had approached in various categories. Those who used the arguments mentioned above he called the sticklers. Besides these there were the consolers, who assured him that the present state of things couldn't possibly last and, when asked for definite suggestions, fobbed him off by telling him he was making too much fuss about a passing inconvenience. Then there were the very important persons who asked the visitor to leave a brief note of his case and informed him they would decide on it in due course; the triflers, who offered him billeting warrants or gave the addresses of lodgings; the red-tape merchants, who made him fill up a form and promptly interred it in a file; overworked officials, who raised their arms to heaven, and much-harassed officials who simply looked away; and, finally, the traditionalists, these were by far the greatest number, who referred Rambert to another office or recommended some new method of approach.

These fruitless interviews had thoroughly worn out the journalist; on the credit side he had obtained much insight into the inner workings of a municipal office and a Prefect's headquarters, by dint of sitting for hours on imitation-leather sofas, confronted by posters urging him to invest in savings bonds exempt from income-tax, or to enlist in the colonial army; and by dint of entering offices where human faces were as blank as the filing-cabinets and the dusty records on the shelves behind them.

The only thing gained by all this expenditure of energy, Rambert told Rieux with a hint of bitterness, was that it served to keep his mind off his predicament.

In fact, the rapid progress of the plague practically escaped his notice. Also, it made the days pass more quickly and, given the situation in which the whole town was placed, it might be said that every day lived through brought everyone, provided he survived, twenty-four hours nearer the end of his ordeal. Rieux could but admit the truth of this reasoning, but to his mind its truth was of rather too general an order.

At one moment Rambert had a gleam of hope. A form was sent him from the Prefect's office with instructions that he was to fill in carefully all the blanks. It included questions concerning his identity, his family, his present and former sources of income; in fact, he was to give what is known as a curriculum vitae. He got an impression that inquiries were on foot with a view to drawing up a list of persons who might be instructed to leave the town and return to their homes. Some vague information gleaned from an employee in one of the offices confirmed this impression. But on going further into the matter and finally discovering the office from which the form had emanated, he was told that this information was being collected with a view to certain contingencies.

"What contingencies?" he asked.

He then learned that the contingency was the possibility of his falling ill and dying of plague; the data supplied would enable the authorities to notify his family and also to decide if the hospital expenses should be borne by the municipality or if, in due course, they could be recovered from his relatives. On the face of it this implied that he was not completely cut off from the woman who was awaiting his return, since the powers that be were obviously giving heed to both of them. But that was no consolation. The really remarkable thing, and Rambert was greatly struck by this, was the way in which, in the very midst of catastrophe, offices could go on functioning serenely and take initiatives of no immediate relevance, and often unknown to the highest authority, purely and simply because they had been created originally for this purpose.

The next phase was at once the easiest and the hardest for Rambert. It was a period of sheer lethargy. He had gone the round of offices, taken every step that could be taken, and realized that for the present all avenues of that kind were closed to him. So now he drifted aimlessly from cafe to cafe. In the mornings he would sit on the terrace of one of them and read a newspaper in the hope of finding some indication that the epidemic was on the wane. He would gaze at the faces of the passers-by, often turning away disgustedly from their look of unrelieved gloom, and after reading for the nth time the shopsigns on the other side of the street, the advertisements of popular drinks that were no longer procurable, would rise and walk again at random in the yellow streets.

Thus he killed time till nightfall, moving about the town and stopping now and then at a cafe or restaurant. One evening Rieux noticed him hovering round the door of a cafe, unable to make up his mind to enter. At last he decided to go in and sat down at a table at the back of the room. It was the time when, acting under orders, cafe-proprietors

deferred as long as possible turning on their lights. Gray dusk was seeping into the room, the pink of sunset glowed in the wall mirrors, and the marble-topped tables glimmered white in the gathering darkness. Seated in the empty cafe, Rambert looked pathetically lost, a mere shade among the shadows, and Rieux guessed this was the hour when he felt most derelict. It was, indeed, the hour of day when all the prisoners of the town realized their dereliction and each was thinking that something, no matter what, must be done to hasten their deliverance. Rieux turned hurriedly away.

Rambert also spent a certain amount of time at the railroad station. No one was allowed on the platforms. But the waiting-rooms, which could be entered from outside, remained open and, being cool and dark, were often patronized by beggars on very hot days. Rambert spent much time studying the timetables, reading the prohibitions against spitting, and the passengers' regulations.

After that he sat down in a corner. An old cast-iron stove, which had been stone-cold for months, rose like a sort of landmark in the middle of the room, surrounded by figure-of-eight patterns on the floor, the traceries of long-past sprinklings. Posters on the walls gaily invited tourists to a carefree holiday at Cannes or Bandol. And in his corner Rambert savored that bitter sense of freedom which comes of total deprivation. The evocations which at that time he found most poignant were, anyhow according to what he told Rieux, those of Paris.

There rose before his eyes, unsummoned, vistas of old stones and riverbanks, the pigeons of the Palais-Royal, the Gare du Nord, quiet old streets round the Pantheon, and many another scene of the city he'd never known he loved so much, and these mental pictures killed all desire for any form of action. Rieux felt fairly sure he was identifying these scenes with memories of his love. And when one day Rambert told him that he liked waking up at four in the morning and thinking of his beloved Paris, the doctor guessed easily enough, basing this on his own experience, that that was his favorite time for conjuring up pictures of the woman from whom he now was parted. This was, indeed, the hour when he could feel surest she was wholly his. Till four in the morning one is seldom doing anything and at that hour, even if the night has been a night of betrayal, one is asleep. Yes, everyone sleeps at that hour, and this is reassuring, since the great longing of an unquiet heart is to possess constantly and consciously the loved one, or, failing that, to be able to plunge the loved one, when a time of absence intervenes, into a dreamless sleep timed to last unbroken until the day they meet again.

Shortly after Father Paneloux's sermon the hot weather set in with a vengeance.

On the day following the unseasonable downpour of that Sunday, summer blazed out above the housetops. First a strong, scorching wind blew steadily for a whole day, drying up the walls. And then the sun took charge, incessant waves of heat and light swept the town daylong, and but for arcaded streets and the interiors of houses, everything lay naked to the dazzling impact of the light. The sun stalked our townsfolk along every byway, into every nook; and when they paused, it struck.

Since this first onslaught of the heat synchronized with a startling increase in the number of victims, there were now nearly seven hundred deaths a week, a mood of profound discouragement settled on the town. In the suburbs little was left of the wonted animation between the long flat streets and the terraced houses; ordinarily people living in these districts used to spend the best part of the day on their doorsteps, but now every door was shut, nobody was to be seen, even the Venetian blinds stayed down, and there was no knowing if it was the heat or the plague that they were trying to shut out. In some houses groans could be heard. At first, when that happened, people often gathered outside and listened, prompted by curiosity or compassion. But under the prolonged strain it seemed that hearts had toughened; people lived beside those groans or walked past them as though they had become the normal speech of men.

As a result of the fighting at the gates, in the course of which the police had had to use their revolvers, a spirit of lawlessness was abroad. Some had certainly been wounded in these brushes with the police, but in the town, where, owing to the combined influences of heat and terror, everything was exaggerated, there was talk of deaths. One thing, anyhow, was certain; discontent was on the increase and, fearing worse to come, the local officials debated lengthily on the measures to be taken if the populace, goaded to frenzy by the epidemic, got completely out of hand. The newspapers published new regulations reiterating the orders against attempting to leave the town and warning those who infringed them that they were liable to long terms of imprisonment.

A system of patrols was instituted and often in the empty, sweltering streets, heralded by a clatter of horse hoofs on the cobbles, a detachment of mounted police would make its way between the parallel lines of close-shut windows. Now and again a gunshot was heard; the special brigade recently detailed to destroy cats and dogs, as possible carriers of infection, was at work. And these whipcrack sounds startling the silence increased the nervous tension already existing in the town.

For in the heat and stillness, and for the troubled hearts of our townsfolk, anything, even the least sound, had a heightened significance. The varying aspects of the sky, the very smells rising from the soil that mark each change of season, were taken notice of for the first time. Everyone realized with dismay that hot weather would favor the epidemic, and it was clear that summer was setting in. The cries of swifts in the evening air above the housetops were growing shriller. And the sky, too, had lost the spaciousness of those June twilights when our horizons seem infinitely remote. In the markets the flowers no longer came in buds; they were already in full bloom, and after the morning's marketing the dusty pavements were littered with trampled petals. It was plain to see that spring had spent itself, lavished its ardor on the myriads of flowers that were bursting everywhere into bloom, and now was being crushed out by the twofold onslaught of heat and plague. For our fellow citizens that summer sky, and the streets thick in dust, gray as their present lives, had the same ominous import as the hundred deaths now weighing daily on the town. That incessant sunlight and those bright hours associated with siesta or with holidays no longer invited, as in the past, to frolics and flirtation on the beaches. Now they rang hollow in the silence of the closed town, they had lost the golden spell of happier summers. Plague had killed all colors, vetoed pleasure.

That, indeed, was one of the great changes brought by the epidemic. Hitherto all of us welcomed summer in with pleasant anticipation. The town was open to the sea and its young folk made free of the beaches. But this summer, for all its nearness, the sea was out of bounds; young limbs had no longer the run of its delights. What could we do under these conditions? It is Tarrou once again who paints the most faithful picture of our life in those days. Needless to say, he outlines the progress of the plague and he, too, notes that a new phase of the epidemic was ushered in when the radio announced no longer weekly totals, but ninety-two, a hundred and seven, and a hundred and thirty deaths in a day.

"The newspapers and the authorities are playing ball with the plague. They fancy they're scoring off it because a hundred and thirty is a smaller figure than nine hundred and ten." He also records such striking or moving incidents of the epidemic as came under his notice; that, for instance, of the woman in a lonely street who abruptly opened a shuttered window just above his head and gave two loud shrieks before closing the shutters again on the dark interior of a bedroom. But he also noted that peppermint lozenges had vanished from the drugstores, because there was a popular belief that when sucking them you were proof against contagion.

He went on watching his pet specimen on the opposite balcony. It seemed that tragedy had come to the ancient small-game hunter as well. One morning there had been gunshots in the street and, as Tarrou put it, "some gobs of lead" had killed off most of the cats and scared away the others; anyhow they were no longer about. That day the little old man went on to his balcony at the usual hour, showed some surprise, and, leaning on the rail, closely scanned the corners of the street. Then he settled down to wait, fretfully tapping the balustrade with his right hand. After staying there for some time he tore up a few sheets of paper, went back into his room, and came out again. After another longish wait he retreated again into the room, slamming the french windows behind him. He followed the same procedure daily during the rest of the week, and the sadness and bewilderment on the old face deepened as the days went by.

On the eighth day Tarrou waited in vain for his appearance; the windows stayed resolutely closed on all too comprehensible distress. This entry ends with Tarrou's summing up. "It is forbidden to spit on cats in plague-time."

In another context Tarrou notes that, on coming home in the evenings, he invariably saw the night watchman pacing the hall, like a sentry on his beat.

The man never failed to remind everyone he met that he'd foreseen what was happening.

Tarrou agreed that he'd predicted a disaster, but reminded him that the event predicted by him was an earthquake. To which the old fellow replied: "Ah, if only it had been an earthquake! A good bad shock, and there you are! You count the dead and living, and that's an end of it. But this here damned disease, even them who haven't got it can't think of anything else."

The manager of the hotel was equally downhearted. In the early days travelers, unable to leave the town, had kept on their rooms. But one by one, seeing that the epidemic showed no sign of abating, they moved out to stay with friends. And the same cause that had led to all the rooms' being occupied now kept them empty, since there were no newcomers to the town. Tarrou was one of the very few remaining guests, and the manager never lost an opportunity of informing him that, were he not reluctant to put these gentlemen to inconvenience, he would have closed the hotel long ago. He often asked Tarrou to say how long he thought the epidemic would last. "They say," Tarrou informed him, "that cold weather stamps out diseases of this type." The manager looked aghast. "But, my dear sir, it's never really cold in these parts. And, anyhow, that would mean it's going to last many months more." Moreover, he was sure that for a long while to come travelers would give the town a wide berth. This epidemic spelt the ruin of the tourist trade, in fact.

After a short absence M. Othon, the owlish paterfamilias, made a reappearance in the restaurant, but accompanied only by the two "performing poodles," his offspring. On inquiry it came out that Mme Othon was in quarantine; she had been nursing her mother, who had succumbed to plague.

"I don't like it a bit," the manager told Tarrou. "Quarantine or not, she's under suspicion, which means that they are, too."

Tarrou pointed out that, if it came to that, everyone was "under suspicion." But the manager had his own ideas and was not to be shaken out of them.

"No, sir. You and I, we're not under suspicion. But they certainly are."

However, M. Othon was impervious to such considerations and would not let the plague change his habits. He entered the restaurant with his wonted dignity, sat down in front of his children, and addressed to them at intervals the same nicely worded, unamiable remarks. Only the small boy looked somewhat different; dressed in black like his sister, a little more shrunken than before, he now seemed a miniature replica of his father. The night watchman, who had no liking for M. Othon, had said of him to Tarrou:

"That fine gentleman will pass out with his clothes on. All dressed up and ready to go. So he won't need no laying-out."

Tarrou has some comments on the sermon preached by Paneloux: "I can understand that type of fervor and find it not displeasing. At the beginning of a pestilence and when it ends, there's always a propensity for rhetoric. In the first case, habits have not yet been lost; in the second, they're returning. It is in the thick of a calamity that one gets hardened to the truth, in other words, to silence. So let's wait."

Tarrou also records that he had a long talk with Dr. Rieux; all he remembered was that it had "good results." In this connection he notes the color of Mme Rieux's, the doctor's mother's, eyes, a limpid brown, and makes the odd observation that a gaze revealing so much goodness of heart would always triumph over plague.

He has also a good deal to say about Rieux's asthma patient. He went with the doctor to see him, immediately after their conversation. The old man greeted Tarrou with a chuckle and rubbed his hands cheerfully. He was sitting up in bed with the usual two pans of dried peas in front of him. "Ah, here's another of 'em!" he exclaimed when he saw Tarrou. "It's a topsy-turvy world all right, more doctors than patients. Because it's mowing them down, ain't it, more and more.

That priest's right; we were asking for it." Next day Tarrou came to see him without warning.

From Tarrou's notes we gather that the old man, a dry-goods dealer by occupation, decided at the age of fifty that he'd done enough work for a lifetime. He took to his bed and never left it again, but not because of his asthma, which would not have prevented his getting about. A small fixed income had seen him through to his present age, seventyfive, and the years had not damped his cheerfulness. He couldn't bear the sight of a watch, and indeed there wasn't one in the whole house. "Watches," he said, "are silly gadgets, and dear at that." He worked out the time, that is to say, the time for meals, with his two saucepans, one of which was always full of peas when he woke in the morning. He filled the other, pea by pea, at a constant, carefully regulated speed. Thus time for him was reckoned by these pans and he could take his bearings in it at any moment of the day. "Every fifteen pans," he said, "it's feeding-time. What could be simpler?"

If his wife was to be trusted, he had given signs of his vocation at a very early age. Nothing, in fact, had ever interested him; his work, friendship, cafes, music, women,

outings, to all he was indifferent. He had never left his home town except once when he had been called to Algiers for family affairs, and even then he had alighted from the train at the first station after Oran, incapable of continuing the adventure. He took the first train back.

To Tarrou, who had shown surprise at the secluded life he led, he had given the following explanation, more or less. According to religion, the first half of a man's life is an upgrade; the second goes downhill. On the descending days he has no claim, they may be snatched from him at any moment; thus he can do nothing with them and the best thing, precisely, is to do nothing with them. He obviously had no compunction about contradicting himself, for a few minutes later he told Tarrou that God did not exist, since otherwise there would be no need for priests. But, from some observations which followed, Tarrou realized that the old fellow's philosophy was closely involved with the irritation caused by the house-to-house collections in aid of charities, which took place almost incessantly in that part of the town. What completed the picture of the old man was a desire he expressed several times, and which seemed deeply rooted: the desire to die at a very advanced age.

"Is he a saint?" Tarrou asked himself, and answered: "Yes, if saintliness is an aggregate of habits."

Meanwhile Tarrou was compiling a longish description of a day in the plague-stricken town; it was to give a full and accurate picture of the life of our fellow citizens during that summer. "Nobody laughs," Tarrou observes, "except the drunks, and they laugh too much." After which he embarks on his description.

"At daybreak light breaths of air fan the still empty streets. At this hour, between the night's victims and the death-agonies of the coming day, it is as if for a while plague stays its hand and takes breath. All shops are shut. But on some a notice: Closed owing to plague, shows that when the others open presently, these will not. Still half-asleep, the newsboys do not yet cry the news but, lounging at street corners, offer their wares to the lamp-posts, with the vague gestures of sleepwalkers. Soon, awakened by the early streetcars, they will fan out through the town, holding at arm's length sheets on which the word PLAGUE looms large. Will there be a plague autumn? Professor B. says: 'No.' Toll of the 94th day of plague: 124 deaths.

"In spite of the growing shortage of paper, which has compelled some dailies to reduce their pages, a new paper has been launched: the Plague Chronicle, which sets out 'to inform our townspeople, with scrupulous veracity, of the daily progress or recession of the disease; to supply them with the most authoritative opinions available as to its future course; to offer the hospitality of its columns to all, in whatever walk of life, who wish to join in combating the epidemic; to keep up the morale of the populace; to publish the latest orders issued by the authorities; and to centralize the efforts of all who desire to give active and wholehearted help in the present emergency.' Actually this newspaper very soon came to devote its columns to advertisements of new, 'infallible' antidotes against plague.

"Toward six in the morning all these papers are being sold to the lines that begin to form outside the shops over an hour before they open; then to the passengers alighting from the streetcars coming in, packed to capacity, from the suburbs. The cars are now the only means of transport, and they have much difficulty in progressing, what with people standing on the running-boards and hanging in clusters from the handrails. A queer thing is how the passengers all try to keep their backs turned to their neighbors, twisting themselves into grotesque attitudes in the attempt, the idea being, of course, to avoid contagion. At every stop a cataract of men and women is disgorged, each in haste to put a safe distance between himself or herself and the rest.

"When the first cars have gone by, the town gradually wakes up, early cafes open their doors, and you see an array of cards on the counter: No Coffee, Bring Your Own Sugar, and the like. Next the shops open and the streets grow livelier. And meanwhile the light is swelling and the sky, even at this early hour, beginning to grow leaden-hued with heat. This is the time when those who have nothing to do venture out on the boulevards. Most of them seem determined to counteract the plague by a lavish display of luxury. Daily, about eleven, you see a sort of dress parade of youths and girls, who make you realize the frantic desire for life that thrives in the heart of every great calamity. If the epidemic spreads, morals too will broaden, and we may see again the saturnalia of Milan, men and women dancing round the graves.

"At noon, in a flash, all the restaurants fill up. Very quickly small groups of people unable to find a seat form at the doors. Because of the intense heat the sky is losing its brightness. Under big awnings the aspirants to food wait their turn, aligned along the curbs of streets gaping and sizzling in the fires of noon. The reason for the restaurants' being so crowded is that they solve for many the feeding problem. But they do nothing to allay the fear of contagion.

Many of the customers spend several minutes methodically wiping their plates. Not long ago some restaurants put up notices: Our plates, knives, and forks guaranteed sterilized. But gradually they discontinued publicity of this order, since their customers came in any case. People, moreover, spend very freely. Choice wines, or wines alleged to be such, the costliest extras, a mood of reckless extravagance is setting in. It seems that there was something like a panic in a restaurant because a customer suddenly felt ill, went very white, and staggered precipitately to the door.

"Toward two o'clock the town slowly empties, it is the time when silence, sunlight, dust, and plague have the streets to themselves. Wave after wave of heat flows over the frontage of the tall gray houses during these long, languid hours. Thus the afternoon wears on, slowly merging into an evening that settles down like a red winding-sheet on the serried tumult of the town. At the start of the great heat, for some unascertained reason, the evenings found the streets almost empty. But now the least ripple of cooler air brings an easing of the strain, if not a flutter of hope. Then all stream out into the open, drug themselves with talking, start arguing or love-making, and in the last glow of sunset the town, freighted with lovers two by two and loud with voices, drifts like a helmless ship into the throbbing darkness. In vain a zealous evangelist with a felt hat and flowing tie threads his way through the crowd, crying without cease: 'God is great and good. Come unto Him.' On the contrary, they all make haste toward some trivial objective that seems of more immediate interest than God.

"In the early days, when they thought this epidemic was much like other epidemics, religion held its ground. But once these people realized their instant peril, they gave their thoughts to pleasure. And all the hideous fears that stamp their faces in the daytime are transformed in the fiery, dusty nightfall into a sort of hectic exaltation, an unkempt freedom fevering their blood.

"And I, too, I'm no different. But what matter? Death means nothing to men like me. It's the event that proves them right. It was Tarrou who had asked Rieux for the interview he refers to in his diary. On that evening, as it happened, just before Tarrou arrived, the doctor had gazed for some moments at his mother, who was sitting very still in a corner of the dining-room. Once her household tasks were over, she spent most of her time in that chair. Her hands folded in her lap, she sat there waiting. Rieux wasn't even sure it was for him she waited. However, something always changed in his mother's face when he came in. The silent resignation that a laborious life had given it seemed to light up with a sudden glow. Then she returned to her tranquillity. That evening she was gazing out of the window at the now empty street. The street lighting had been reduced by two thirds, and only at long intervals a lamp cast flickering gleams through the thick darkness of the town.

"Will they keep to the reduced lighting as long as the plague lasts?" Mme Rieux asked.

"I expect so."

"Let's hope it doesn't last till winter. It would be terribly depressing."

"Yes," Rieux said.

He saw his mother's gaze settle on his forehead. He knew that the worry and overwork of the last few days had scored their traces there.

"Didn't things go well today?" his mother asked.

"Oh, much as usual."

As usual! That was to say the new consignment of serum sent from Paris seemed less effective than the first, and the death-rate was rising. It was still impossible to administer prophylactic inoculations elsewhere than in families already attacked; if its use was to be generalized, very large quantities of the vaccine would have been needed. Most of the buboes refused to burst, it was as if they underwent a seasonal hardening, and the victims suffered horribly. During the last twenty-four hours there had been two cases of a new form of the epidemic; the plague was becoming pneumonic.

On this very day, in the course of a meeting, the much-harassed doctors had pressed the Prefect, the unfortunate man seemed quite at his wits' end, to issue new regulations to prevent contagion being carried from mouth to mouth, as happens in pneumonic plague. The Prefect had done as they wished, but as usual they were groping, more or less, in the dark.

Looking at his mother, he felt an uprush of a half-forgotten emotion, the love of his boyhood, at the sight of her soft brown gaze intent on him.

"Don't you ever feel alarmed, Mother?"

"Oh, at my age there isn't much left to fear."

"The days are very long, and just now I'm hardly ever at home."

"I don't mind waiting, if I know you're going to come back. And when you aren't here, I think of what you're doing. Have you any news?"

"Yes, if I'm to believe the last telegram, everything's going as well as could be expected. But I know she says that to prevent my worrying."

The doorbell rang. The doctor gave his mother a smile and went to open the door.

In the dim light on the landing Tarrou looked like a big gray bear. Rieux gave his visitor a seat facing his desk, while he himself remained standing behind the desk chair. Between them was the only light in the room, a desk lamp.

Tarrou came straight to the point. "I know," he said, "that I can talk to you quite frankly."

Rieux nodded.

"In a fortnight, or a month at most," Tarrou continued, "you'll serve no purpose here. Things will have got out of hand."

"I agree."

"The sanitary department is inefficient, understaffed, for one thing, and you're worked off your feet."

Rieux admitted this was so.

"Well," Tarrou said, "I've heard that the authorities are thinking of a sort of conscription of the population, and all men in good health will be required to help in fighting the plague."

"Your information was correct. But the authorities are in none too good odor as it is, and the Prefect can't make up his mind."

"If he daren't risk compulsion, why not call for voluntary help?"

"It's been done. The response was poor."

"It was done through official channels, and half-heartedly. What they're short on is imagination. Officialdom can never cope with something really catastrophic. And the remedial measures they think up are hardly adequate for a common cold. If we let them carry on like this they'll soon be dead, and so shall we."

"That's more than likely," Rieux said. "I should tell you, however, that they're thinking of using the prisoners in the jails for what we call the 'heavy work.'

"

"I'd rather free men were employed."

"So would I. But might I ask why you feel like that?"

"I loathe men's being condemned to death."

Rieux looked Tarrou in the eyes.

"So what?" he asked.

"It's this I have to say. I've drawn up a plan for voluntary groups of helpers.

Get me empowered to try out my plan, and then let's sidetrack officialdom. In any case the authorities have their hands more than full already. I have friends in many walks of life; they'll form a nucleus to start from. And, of course, I'll take part in it myself."

"I need hardly tell you," Rieux replied, "that I accept your suggestion most gladly. One can't have too many helpers, especially in a job like mine under present conditions. I undertake to get your plan approved by the authorities.

Anyhow, they've, no choice. But?" Rieux pondered. "But I take it you know that work of this kind may prove fatal to the worker. And I feel I should ask you this; have you weighed the dangers?"

Tarrou's gray eyes met the doctor's gaze serenely.

"What did you think of Paneloux's sermon, doctor?"

The question was asked in a quite ordinary tone, and Rieux answered in the same tone.

"I've seen too much of hospitals to relish any idea of collective punishment.

But, as you know, Christians sometimes say that sort of thing without really thinking it. They're better than they seem."

"However, you think, like Paneloux, that the plague has its good side; it opens men's eyes and forces them to take thought?"

The doctor tossed his head impatiently.

"So does every ill that flesh is heir to. What's true of all the evils in the world is true of plague as well. It helps men to rise above themselves. All the same, when you see the misery it brings, you'd need to be a madman, or a coward, or stone blind, to give in tamely to the plague."

Rieux had hardly raised his voice at all; but Tarrou made a slight gesture as if to calm him. He was smiling.

"Yes." Rieux shrugged his shoulders. "But you haven't answered my question yet.

Have you weighed the consequences?"

Tarrou squared his shoulders against the back of the chair, then moved his head forward into the light.

"Do you believe in God, doctor?"

Again the question was put in an ordinary tone. But this time Rieux took longer to find his answer.

"No, but what does that really mean? I'm fumbling in the dark, struggling to make something out. But I've long ceased finding that original."

"Isn't that it, the gulf between Paneloux and you?"

"I doubt it. Paneloux is a man of learning, a scholar. He hasn't come in contact with death; that's why he can speak with such assurance of the truth, with a capital T. But every country priest who visits his parishioners and has heard a man gasping for breath on his deathbed thinks as I do. He'd try to relieve human suffering before trying to point out its excellence." Rieux stood up; his face was now in shadow. "Let's drop the subject," he said, "as you won't answer."

Tarrou remained seated in his chair; he was smiling again.

"Suppose I answer with a question."

The doctor now smiled, too.

"You like being mysterious, don't you? Yes, fire away."

"My question's this," said Tarrou. "Why do you yourself show such devotion, considering you don't believe in God? I suspect your answer may help me to mine."

His face still in shadow, Rieux said that he'd already answered: that if he believed in an all-powerful God he would cease curing the sick and leave that to Him. But no one in the world believed in a God of that sort; no, not even Paneloux, who believed that he believed in such a God. And this was proved by the fact that no one ever threw himself on Providence completely. Anyhow, in this respect Rieux believed himself to be on the right road, in fighting against creation as he found it.

"Ah," Tarrou remarked. "So that's the idea you have of your profession?"

"More or less." The doctor came back into the light.

Tarrou made a faint whistling noise with his lips, and the doctor gazed at him.

"Yes, you're thinking it calls for pride to feel that way. But I assure you I've no more than the pride that's needed to keep me going. I have no idea what's awaiting me, or what will happen when all this ends. For the moment I know this; there are sick people and they need curing. Later on, perhaps, they'll think things over; and so shall I. But what's wanted now is to make them well. I defend them as best I can, that's all."

"Against whom?"

Rieux turned to the window. A shadow-line on the horizon told of the presence of the sea. He was conscious only of his exhaustion, and at the same time was struggling against a sudden, irrational impulse to unburden himself a little more to his companion; an eccentric, perhaps, but who, he guessed, was one of his own kind.

"I haven't a notion, Tarrou; I assure you I haven't a notion. When I entered this profession, I did it 'abstractedly,' so to speak; because I had a desire for it, because it meant a career like another, one that young men often aspire to. Perhaps, too, because it was particularly difficult for a workman's son, like myself. And then I had to see people die. Do you know that there are some who refuse to die? Have you ever heard a woman scream 'Never!' with her last gasp? Well, I have. And then I saw that I could never get hardened to it. I was young then, and I was outraged by the whole scheme of things, or so I thought.

Subsequently I grew more modest. Only, I've never managed to get used to seeing people die. That's all I know. Yet after all?"

Rieux fell silent and sat down. He felt his mouth dry.

"After all?" Tarrou prompted softly.

"After all," the doctor repeated, then hesitated again, fixing his eyes on Tarrou, "it's something that a man of your sort can understand most likely, but, since the order of the world is shaped by death, mightn't it be better for God if we refuse to believe in Him and struggle with all our might against death, without raising our eyes toward the heaven where He sits in silence."

Tarrou nodded.

"Yes. But your victories will never be lasting; that's all."

Rieux's face darkened.

"Yes, I know that. But it's no reason for giving up the struggle."

"No reason, I agree. Only, I now can picture what this plague must mean for you."

"Yes. A never ending defeat."

Tarrou stared at the doctor for a moment, then turned and tramped heavily toward the door. Rieux followed him and was almost at his side when Tarrou, who was staring at the floor, suddenly said:

"Who taught you all this, doctor?"

The reply came promptly:

"Suffering."

Rieux opened the door of his surgery and told Tarrou that he, too, was going out; he had a patient to visit in the suburbs. Tarrou suggested they should go together and he agreed. In the hall they encountered Mme Rieux, and the doctor introduced Tarrou to her.

"A friend of mine," he said.

"Indeed," said Mme Rieux, "I'm very pleased to make your acquaintance."

When she left them Tarrou turned to gaze after her. On the landing the doctor pressed a switch to turn on the lights along the stairs. But the stairs remained in darkness. Possibly some new light-saving order had come into force. Really, however, there was no knowing; for some time past, in the streets no less than in private houses, everything had been going out of order. It might be only that the concierge, like nearly everyone in the town, was ceasing to bother about his duties, The doctor had no time to follow up his thoughts; Tarrou's voice came from behind him.

"Just one word more, doctor, even if it sounds to you a bit nonsensical. You are perfectly right."

The doctor merely gave a little shrug, unseen in the darkness.

"To tell the truth, all that's outside my range. But you? what do you know about it?"

"Ah," Tarrou replied quite coolly, "I've little left to learn."

Rieux paused and, behind him, Tarrou's foot slipped on a step. He steadied himself by gripping the doctor's shoulder.

"Do you really imagine you know everything about life?"

The answer came through the darkness in the same cool, confident tone.

"Yes."

Once in the street, they realized it must be quite late, eleven perhaps. All was silence in the town, except for some vague rustlings. An ambulance bell clanged faintly in the distance. They stepped into the car and Rieux started the engine.

"You must come to the hospital tomorrow," he said, "for an injection. But, before embarking on this adventure, you'd better know your chances of coming out of it alive; they're one in three."

"That sort of reckoning doesn't hold water; you know it, doctor, as well as I. A hundred years ago plague wiped out the entire population of a town in Persia, with one exception. And the sole survivor was precisely the man whose job it was to wash the dead bodies, and who carried on throughout the epidemic."

"He pulled off his one-in-three chance, that's all." Rieux had lowered his voice. "But you're right; we know next to nothing on the subject."

They were entering the suburbs. The headlights lit up empty streets. The car stopped. Standing in front of it, Rieux asked Tarrou if he'd like to come in.

Tarrou said: "Yes." A glimmer of light from the sky lit up their faces.

Suddenly Rieux gave a short laugh, and there was much friendliness in it.

"Out with it, Tarrou! What on earth prompted you to take a hand in this?"

"I don't know. My code of morals, perhaps."

"Your code of morals? What code?"

"Comprehension."

Tarrou turned toward the house and Rieux did not see his face again until they were in the old asthma patient's room.

NEXT day Tarrou set to work and enrolled a first team of workers, soon to be followed by many others.

However, it is not the narrator's intention to ascribe to these sanitary groups more importance than their due. Doubtless today many of our fellow citizens are apt to yield to the temptation of exaggerating the services they rendered. But the narrator is inclined to think that by attributing overimportance to praiseworthy actions one may, by implication, be paying indirect but potent homage to the worse side of human nature. For this attitude implies that such actions shine out as rare exceptions, while callousness and apathy are the general rule. The narrator does not share that view. The evil that is in the world always comes of ignorance, and good intentions may do as much harm as malevolence, if they lack understanding. On the whole, men are more good than bad; that, however, isn't the real point. But they are more or less ignorant, and it is this that we call vice or virtue; the most incorrigible vice being that of an ignorance that fancies it knows everything and therefore claims for itself the right to kill. The soul of the murderer is blind; and there can be no true goodness nor true love without the utmost clear-sightedness.

Hence the sanitary groups, whose creation was entirely Tarrou's work, should be considered with objectivity as well as with approval. And this is why the narrator declines to vaunt in over-glowing terms a courage and a devotion to which he attributes only a relative and reasonable importance. But he will continue being the chronicler of the troubled, rebellious hearts of our townspeople under the impact of the plague.

Those who enrolled in the "sanitary squads," as they were called, had, indeed, no such great merit in doing as they did, since they knew it was the only thing to do, and the unthinkable thing would then have been not to have brought themselves to do it. These groups enabled our townsfolk to come to grips with the disease and convinced them that, now that plague was among us, it was up to them to do whatever could be done to fight it. Since plague became in this way some men's duty, it revealed itself as what it really was; that is, the concern of all.

So far, so good. But we do not congratulate a schoolmaster on teaching that two and two make four, though we may, perhaps, congratulate him on having chosen his laudable vocation. Let us then say it was praiseworthy that Tarrou and so many others should have elected to prove that two and two make four rather than the contrary; but let us add that this good will of theirs was one that is shared by the schoolmaster and by all who have the same feelings as the schoolmaster, and, be it said to the credit of mankind, they are more numerous than one would think, such, anyhow, is the narrator's conviction. Needless to say, he can see quite clearly a point that could be made against him, which is that these men were risking their lives. But again and again there comes a time in history when the man who dares to say that two and two make four is punished with death.

The schoolteacher is well aware of this. And the question is not one of knowing what punishment or reward attends the making of this calculation. The question is that of knowing whether two and two do make four. For those of our townsfolk who risked their lives in this predicament the issue was whether or not plague was in their midst and whether or not they must fight against it.

Many fledgling moralists in those days were going about our town proclaiming there was nothing to be done about it and we should bow to the inevitable. And Tarrou, Rieux, and their friends might give one answer or another, but its conclusion was always the same, their certitude that a fight must be put up, in this way or that, and there must be no bowing down. The essential thing was to save the greatest possible number of persons from dying and being doomed to unending separation. And to do this there was only one resource: to fight the plague. There was nothing admirable about this attitude; it was merely logical.

Thus it was only natural that old Dr. Castel should plod away with unshaken confidence, never sparing himself, at making anti-plague serum on the spot with the makeshift equipment at his disposal. Rieux shared his hope that a vaccine made with cultures of the bacilli obtained locally would take effect more actively than serum coming from outside, since the local bacillus differed slightly from the normal plague bacillus as defined in textbooks of tropical diseases. And Castel expected to have his first supply ready within a surprisingly short period.

That, too, is why it was natural that Grand, who had nothing of the hero about him, should now be acting as a sort of general secretary to the sanitary squads.

A certain number of the groups organized by Tarrou were working in the congested areas of the town, with a view to improving the sanitary conditions there. Their duties were to see that houses were kept in a proper hygienic state and to list attics and cellars that had not been disinfected by the official sanitary service. Other teams of volunteers accompanied the doctors on their house-to-house visits, saw to the evacuation of infected persons, and subsequently, owing to the shortage of drivers, even drove the vehicles conveying sick persons and dead bodies. All this involved the upkeep of registers and statistics, and Grand undertook the task.

From this angle, the narrator holds that, more than Rieux or Tarrou, Grand was the true embodiment of the quiet courage that inspired the sanitary groups. He had said yes without a moment's hesitation and with the large-hearted-ness that was a second nature with him. All he had asked was to be allotted light duties: he was too old for anything else. He could give his time from six to eight every evening. When Rieux thanked him with some warmth, he seemed surprised. "Why, that's not difficult! Plague is here and we've got to make a stand, that's obvious. Ah, I only wish everything were as simple!" And he went back to his phrase. Sometimes in the evening, when he had filed his reports and worked out his statistics, Grand and Rieux would have a chat. Soon they formed the habit of including Tarrou in their talks and Grand unburdened himself with increasingly apparent pleasure to his two companions. They began to take a genuine interest in the laborious literary task to which he was applying himself while plague raged around him. Indeed, they, too, found in it a relaxation of the strain.

"How's your young lady on horseback progressing?" Tarrou would ask. And invariably Grand would answer with a wry smile: "Trotting along, trotting along!" One evening Grand announced that he had definitely discarded the adjective "elegant" for his horsewoman.

From now on it was replaced by "slim."

"That's more concrete," he explained.

Soon after, he read out to his two friends the new version of the sentence:

" 'One fine morning in May a slim young horsewoman might have been seen riding a handsome sorrel mare along the flowery avenues of the Bois de Boulogne.'

"Don't you agree with me one sees her better that way? And I've put 'one fine morning in May' because 'in the month of May' tended rather to drag out the trot, if you see what I mean."

Next he showed some anxiety about the adjective "handsome." In his opinion it didn't convey enough, and he set to looking for an epithet that would promptly and clearly "photograph" the superb animal he saw with his mind's eye. "Plump" wouldn't do; though concrete enough, it sounded perhaps a little disparaging, also a shade vulgar. "Beautifully groomed" had tempted him for a moment, but it was cumbrous and made the rhythm limp somewhat. Then one evening he announced triumphantly that he had got it: "A black sorrel mare." To his thinking, he explained, "black" conveyed a hint of elegance and opulence.

"It won't do," Rieux said. "Why not?"

"Because 'sorrel' doesn't mean a breed of horse; it's a color."

"What color?"

"Well, er, a color that, anyhow, isn't black." Grand seemed greatly troubled.

"Thank you," he said warmly. "How fortunate you're here to help me! But you see how difficult it is."

"How about 'glossy'?" Tarrou suggested.

Grand gazed at him meditatively, then "Yes!" he exclaimed. "That's good." And slowly his lips parted in a smile.

Some days later he confessed that the word "flowery" was bothering him considerably. As the only towns he knew were Oran and Montelimar, he sometimes asked his friends to tell him about the avenues of the Bois de Boulogne, what sort of flowers grew in them and how they were disposed. Actually neither Rieux nor Tarrou had ever gathered the impression that those avenues were "flowery," but Grand's conviction on the subject shook their confidence in their memories.

He was amazed at their uncertainty. "It's only artists who know how to use their eyes," was his conclusion. But one evening the doctor found him in a state of much excitement. For "flowery" he had substituted "flower-strewn." He was rubbing his hands. "At last one can see them, smell them! Hats off, gentlemen!" Triumphantly he read out the sentence:

"One fine morning in May a slim young horsewoman might have been seen riding a glossy sorrel mare along the flower-strewn avenues of the Bois de Boulogne."

But, spoken aloud, the numerous "s" sounds had a disagreeable effect and Grand stumbled over them, lisping here and there. He sat down, crestfallen; then he asked the doctor if he might go. Some hard thinking lay ahead of him.

It was about this time, as was subsequently learned, that he began to display signs of absentmindedness in the office. A serious view was taken of these lapses of attention, as the municipality not only was working at high pressure with a reduced staff, but was constantly having new duties thrust upon it. His department suffered, and his chief took him severely to task, pointing out that he was paid to do certain work and was failing to do it as it should be done. "I am told that you are acting as a voluntary helper in the sanitary groups. You do this out of office hours, so it's no concern of mine. But the best way of making yourself useful in a terrible time like this is to do your work well. Otherwise all the rest is useless."

"He's right," Grand said to Rieux.

"Yes, he's right," the doctor agreed.

"But I can't steady my thoughts; it's the end of my phrase that's worrying me, I don't seem able to sort it out."

The plethora of sibilants in the sentence still offended his ear, but he saw no way of amending them without using what were, to his mind, inferior synonyms.

And that "flower-strewn" which had rejoiced him when he first lit on it now seemed unsatisfactory. How could one say the flowers were "strewn" when presumably they had been planted along the avenues, or else grew there naturally? On some evenings, indeed, he looked more tired than Rieux.

Yes, this unavailing quest which never left his mind had worn him out; none the less, he went on adding up the figures and compiling the statistics needed for the sanitary groups. Patiently every evening he brought his totals up to date, illustrated them with graphs, and racked his brains to present his data in the most exact, clearest form. Quite often he went to see Rieux at one of the hospitals and asked to be given a table in an

office or the dispensary. He would settle down at it with his papers, exactly as he settled down at his desk in the Municipal Office, and wave each completed sheet to dry the ink in the warm air, noisome with disinfectants and the disease itself. At these times he made honest efforts not to think about his "horsewoman," and concentrate on what he had to do.

Yes, if it is a fact that people like to have examples given them, men of the type they call heroic, and if it is absolutely necessary that this narrative should include a "hero," the narrator commends to his readers, with, to his thinking, perfect justice, this insignificant and obscure hero who had to his credit only a little goodness of heart and a seemingly absurd ideal. This will render to the truth its due, to the addition of two and two its sum of four, and to heroism the secondary place that rightly falls to it, just after, never before, the noble claim of happiness. It will also give this chronicle its character, which is intended to be that of a narrative made with good feelings, that is to say, feelings that are neither demonstrably bad nor overcharged with emotion in the ugly manner of a stage-play.

Such at least was Dr. Rieux's opinion when he read in newspapers or heard on the radio the messages and encouragement the outer world transmitted to the plague-ridden populace. Besides the comforts sent by air or overland, compassionate or admiring comments were lavished on the henceforth isolated town, by way of newspaper articles or broadcast talks. And invariably their epical or prize-speech verbiage jarred on the doctor. Needless to say, he knew the sympathy was genuine enough. But it could be expressed only in the conventional language with which men try to express what unites them with mankind in general; a vocabulary quite unsuited, for example, to Grand's small daily effort, and incapable of describing what Grand stood for under plague conditions.

Sometimes at midnight, in the great silence of the sleep-bound town, the doctor turned on his radio before going to bed for the few hours' sleep he allowed himself. And from the ends of the earth, across thousands of miles of land and sea, kindly, well-meaning speakers tried to voice their fellow-feeling, and indeed did so, but at the same time proved the utter incapacity of every man truly to share in suffering that he cannot see. "Oran! Oran!" In vain the call rang over oceans, in vain Rieux listened hopefully; always the tide of eloquence began to flow, bringing home still more the unbridgeable gulf that lay between Grand and the speaker. "Oran, we're with you!" they called emotionally. But not, the doctor told himself, to love or to die together? "and that's the only way.

They're too remote."

And, as it so happens, what has yet to be recorded before coming to the culmination, during the period when the plague was gathering all its forces to fling them at the town and lay it waste, is the long, heartrendingly monotonous struggle put up by some obstinate people like Rambert to recover their lost happiness and to balk the plague of that part of themselves which they were ready to defend in the last ditch. This was their way of resisting the bondage closing in upon them, and while their resistance lacked the active virtues of the other, it had (to the narrator's thinking) its point, and moreover it bore witness, even lit its futility and incoherences, to a salutary pride.

Rambert fought to prevent the plague from besting him. Once assured that there was no way of getting out of the town by lawful methods, he decided, as he told Rieux, to have recourse to others. He began by sounding cafe waiters. A waiter usually knows

much of what's going on behind the scenes. But the first he spoke to knew only of the very heavy penalties imposed on such attempts at evasion. In one of the cafes he visited he was actually taken for a stool-pigeon and curtly sent about his business. It was not until he happened to meet Cottard at Rieux's place that he made a little headway. On that day he and Rieux had been talking again about his unsuccessful efforts to interest the authorities in his case, and Cottard heard the tail end of the conversation.

Some days later Cottard met him in the street and greeted him with the hail-fellow-well-met manner that he now used on all occasions.

"Hello, Rambert! Still no luck?"

"None whatever."

"It's no good counting on the red-tape merchants. They couldn't understand if they tried."

"I know that, and I'm trying to find some other way. But it's damned difficult."

"Yes," Cottard replied. "It certainly is."

He, however, knew a way to go about it, and he explained to Rambert, who was much surprised to learn this, that for some time past he had been going the rounds of the cafes, had made a number of acquaintances, and had learned of the existence of an "organization" handling this sort of business. The truth was that Cottard, who had been beginning to live above his means, was now involved in smuggling ventures concerned with rationed goods. Selling contraband cigarettes and inferior liquor at steadily rising prices, he was on the way to building up a small fortune.

"Are you quite sure of this?" Rambert asked.

"Quite. I had a proposal of the sort made to me the other day."

"But you didn't accept it."

"Oh, come, there's no need to be suspicious." Cottard's tone was genial. "I didn't accept it because, personally, I've no wish to leave. I have my reasons."

After a short silence he added: "You don't ask me what my reasons are, I notice."

"I take it," Rambert replied, "that they're none of my business."

"That's so, in a way, of course. But from another angle? Well, let's put it like this: I've been feeling much more at ease here since plague settled in."

Rambert made no comment. Then he asked:

"And how does one approach this organization, as you call it?"

"Ah," Cottard replied, "that's none too easy. Come with me."

It was four in the afternoon. The town was warming up to boiling-point under a sultry sky. Nobody was about, all shops were shuttered. Cottard and Rambert walked some distance without speaking, under the arcades. This was an hour of the day when the plague lay low, so to speak; the silence, the extinction of all color and movement, might have been due as much to the fierce sunlight as to the epidemic, and there was no telling if the air was heavy with menace or merely with dust and heat. You had to look closely and take thought to realize that plague was here. For it betrayed its presence only by negative signs. Thus Cottard, who had affinities with it, drew Rambert's attention to the absence of the dogs that in normal times would have been seen sprawling in the shadow of the doorways, panting, trying to find a nonexistent patch of coolness.

They went along the boulevard des Palmiers, crossed the Place d'Armes, and then turned down toward the docks. On the left was a cafe painted green, with a wide awning of coarse yellow canvas projecting over the sidewalk. Cottard and Rambert wiped their brows on entering. There were some small iron tables, also painted green, and folding chairs. The room was empty, the air humming with flies; in a yellow cage on the bar a parrot squatted on its perch, all its feathers drooping. Some old pictures of military scenes, covered with grime and cobwebs, adorned the walls. On the tables, including that at which Rambert was sitting, bird-droppings were drying, and he was puzzled whence they came until, after some wing-flappings, a handsome cock came hopping out of his retreat in a dark corner.

Just then the heat seemed to rise several degrees more. Cottard took off his coat and banged on the table-top. A very small man wearing a long blue apron that came nearly to his neck emerged from a doorway at the back, shouted a greeting to Cottard, and, vigorously kicking the cock out of his way, came up to the table. Raising his voice to drown the cock's indignant cacklings, he asked what the gentlemen would like. Cottard ordered white wine and asked: "Where's Garcia?" The dwarf replied that he'd not shown up at the cafe for several days.

"Think he'll come this evening?"

"Well, I ain't in his secrets, but you know when he usually comes, don't you?"

"Yes. Really, it's nothing very urgent; I only want him to know this friend of mine."

The barkeeper rubbed his moist hands on the front of his apron.

"Ah, so this gentleman's in business too?"

"Yes," Cottard said.

The little man made a snuffling noise.

"All right. Come back this evening. I'll send the kid to warn him."

After they had left, Rambert asked what the business in question might be.

"Why, smuggling, of course. They get the stuff in past the sentries at the gates. There's plenty money in it."

"I see." Rambert paused for a moment, then asked: "And, I take it, they've friends in court?"

"You've said it!"

In the evening the awning was rolled up, the parrot squawking in its cage, and the small tables were surrounded by men in their shirt-sleeves. When Cottard entered, one man, with a white shirt gaping on a brick-red chest and a straw hat planted well back on his head, rose to his feet. He had a sun-tanned face, regular features, small black eyes, very white teeth, and two or three rings on his fingers. He looked about thirty.

"Hi!" he said to Cottard, ignoring Rambert. "Let's have one at the bar."

They drank three rounds in silence.

"How about a stroll?" Garcia suggested.

They walked toward the harbor. Garcia asked what he was wanted to do. Cottard explained that it wasn't really for a deal that he wanted to introduce his friend, M. Rambert, but only for what he called a "get-away." Puffing at his cigarette, Garcia walked straight ahead. He asked some questions, always referring to Rambert as "he" and appearing not to notice his presence.

"Why does he want to go?"

"His wife is in France."

"Ah!" After a short pause he added: "What's his job?"

"He's a journalist."

"Is he, now? Journalists have long tongues."

"I told you he's a friend of mine," Cottard replied.

They walked on in silence until they were near the wharves, which were now railed off. Then they turned in the direction of a small tavern from which came a smell of fried sardines.

"In any case," Garcia said finally, "it's not up my alley. Raoul's your man. And I'll have to get in touch with him. It's none too easy."

"That so?" Cottard sounded interested. "He's lying low, is he?"

Garcia made no answer. At the door of the tavern he halted and for the first time addressed Rambert directly.

"The day after tomorrow, at eleven, at the corner of the customs barracks in the upper town." He made as if to go, then seemed to have an afterthought. "It's going to cost something, you know." He made the observation in a quite casual tone.

Rambert nodded. "Naturally."

On the way back the journalist thanked Cottard.

"Don't mention it, old chap. I'm only too glad to help you. And then, you're a journalist, I dare say you'll put in a word for me one day or another."

Two days later Rambert and Cottard climbed the wide shadeless street leading to the upper part of the town. The barracks occupied by the customs officers had been partly transformed into a hospital, and a number of people were standing outside the main entrance, some of them hoping to be allowed to visit a patient, a futile hope, since such visits were strictly prohibited, and others to glean some news of an invalid, news that in the course of an hour would have ceased to count. For these reasons there were always a number of people and a certain amount of movement at this spot, a fact that probably accounted for its choice by Garcia for his meeting with Rambert.

"It puzzles me," Cottard remarked, "why you're so keen on going. Really, what's happening here is extremely interesting."

"Not to me," Rambert replied.

"Well, yes, one's running some risks, I grant you. All the same, when you come to think of it, one ran quite as much risk in the old days crossing a busy street."

Just then Rieux's car drew up level with them. Tarrou was at the wheel, and Rieux seemed half-asleep. He roused himself to make the introductions.

"We know each other," Tarrou said. "We're at the same hotel." He then offered to drive Rambert back to the center.

"No, thanks. We've an appointment here."

Rieux looked hard at Rambert.

"Yes," Rambert said.

"What's that?" Cottard sounded surprised. "The doctor knows about it?"

"There's the magistrate." Tarrou gave Cottard a warning glance.

Cottard's look changed. M. Othon was striding down the street toward them, briskly, yet with dignity. He took off his hat as he came up with them.

"Good morning, Monsieur Othon," said Tarrou.

The magistrate returned the greeting of the men in the car and, turning to Rambert and Cottard, who were in the background, gave them a quiet nod. Tarrou introduced Cottard and the journalist. The magistrate gazed at the sky for a moment, sighed, and remarked that these were indeed sad times.

"I've been told, Monsieur Tarrou," he continued, "that you are helping to enforce the prophylactic measures. I need hardly say how commendable that is, a fine example. Do you think, Dr. Rieux, that the epidemic will get worse?"

Rieux replied that one could only hope it wouldn't, and the magistrate replied that one must never lose hope, the ways of Providence were inscrutable.

Tarrou asked if his work had increased as the result of present conditions.

"Quite the contrary. Criminal cases of what we call the first instance are growing rarer. In fact, almost my only work just now is holding inquiries into more serious breaches of the new regulations. Our ordinary laws have never been so well respected."

"That's because, by contrast, they necessarily appear good ones," Tarrou observed.

The magistrate, who seemed unable to take his gaze off the sky, abruptly dropped his mildly meditative air and stared at Tarrou.

"What does that matter? It's not the law that counts, it's the sentence. And that is something we must all accept."

"That fellow," said Tarrou when the magistrate was out of hearing, "is Enemy Number One."

He pressed the starter.

Some minutes later Rambert and Cottard saw Garcia approaching. Without making any sign of recognition he came straight up to them and, by way of greeting, said: "You'll have to wait a bit."

There was complete silence in the crowd around them, most of whom were women.

Nearly all were carrying parcels; they had the vain hope of somehow smuggling these in to their sick relatives, and the even crazier idea that the latter could eat the food they'd brought. The gate was guarded by armed sentries, and now and then an eerie cry resounded in the courtyard between the barrack rooms and the entrance. Whenever this happened, anxious eyes turned toward the sick-wards.

The three men were watching the scene when a brisk "Good morning" from behind them made them swing round. In spite of the heat Raoul was wearing a well-cut dark suit and a felt hat with rolled-up brim. He was tall and strongly built, his face rather pale. Hardly moving his lips, he said quickly and clearly:

"Let's walk down to the center. You, Garcia, needn't come."

Garcia lit a cigarette and remained there while they walked away. Placing himself between Rambert and Cottard, Raoul set the pace, a fast one.

"Garcia's explained the situation," he said. "We can fix it. But I must warn you it'll cost you a cool ten thousand."

Rambert said he agreed to these terms.

"Lunch with me tomorrow at the Spanish restaurant near the docks."

Rambert said: "Right," and Raoul shook his hand, smiling for the first time.

After he had gone, Cottard said he wouldn't be able to come to lunch next day, as he had an engagement, but anyhow Rambert didn't need him any more.

When next day Rambert entered the Spanish restaurant, everyone turned and stared at him. The dark, cellarlike room, below the level of the small yellow street, was patronized only by men, mostly Spaniards, judging by their looks. Raoul was sitting at a table at the back of the room. Once he had beckoned to the journalist and Rambert started

to go toward him, the curiosity left the faces of others and they bent over their plates again. Raoul had beside him a tall, thin, ill-shaven man, with enormously wide shoulders, an equine face, and thinning hair. His shirtsleeves were rolled up, displaying long, skinny arms covered with black hair. When Rambert was introduced he gave three slow nods. His own name, however, was not announced and Raoul, when referring to him, always said "our friend."

"Our friend here thinks he may be able to help you. He is going?" Raoul broke off, as the waitress had just come to take Rambert's order. "He is going to put you in touch with two of our friends who will introduce you to some sentries whom we've squared. But that doesn't mean you can start right away. You'll have to leave it to the sentries to decide on the best moment. The simplest thing will be for you to stay some nights with one of them; his home is quite near the gate. The first thing is for our friend here to give you the contacts needed; then when everything's set, you'll settle with him for the expenses."

Again the "friend" slowly moved his equine head up and down, without ceasing to munch the tomato and pimento salad he was shoveling into his mouth. After which he began to speak, with a slight Spanish accent. He asked Rambert to meet him, the next day but one, at eight in the morning, in the Cathedral porch.

"Another two days' wait," Rambert observed.

"It ain't so easy as all that, you see," Raoul said. "Them boys take some finding."

Horse-face nodded slow approval once more. Some time was spent looking for a subject of conversation. The problem was solved easily enough when Rambert discovered that horse-face was an ardent football-player. He, too, had been very keen on soccer. They discussed the French championship, the merits of professional English teams, and the technique of passing. By the end of the meal horse-face was in high good humor, was calling Rambert "old boy," and trying to convince him that the most sporting position by far on the football field was that of center half. "You see, old boy, it's the center half that does the placing. And that's the whole art of the game, isn't it?" Rambert was inclined to agree, though he, personally, had always played center forward. The discussion proceeded peacefully until a radio was turned on and, after at first emitting a series of sentimental songs, broke into the announcement that there had been a hundred and thirty-seven plague deaths on the previous day. No one present betrayed the least emotion. Horse-face merely shrugged and stood up.

Raoul and Rambert followed his example.

As they were going out, the center half shook Rambert's hand vigorously. "My name's Gonzales," he said.

To Rambert the next two days seemed endless. He looked up Rieux and described to him the latest developments, then accompanied the doctor on one of his calls. He took leave of him on the doorstep of a house where a patient, suspected to have plague, was awaiting him. There was a sound of footsteps and voices in the hall; the family were being warned of the doctor's visit.

"I hope Tarrou will be on time," Rieux murmured. He looked worn out.

"Is the epidemic getting out of hand?" Rambert asked.

Rieux said it wasn't that; indeed, the death-graph was rising less steeply. Only they lacked adequate means of coping with the disease.

"We're short of equipment. In all the armies of the world a shortage of equipment is usually compensated for by manpower. But we're short of man-power, too."

"Haven't doctors and trained assistants been sent from other towns?"

"Yes," Rieux said. "Ten doctors and a hundred helpers. That sounds a lot, no doubt. But it's barely enough to cope with the present state of affairs. And it will be quite inadequate if things get worse."

Rambert, who had been listening to the sounds within the house, turned to Rieux with a friendly smile.

"Yes," he said, "you'd better make haste to win your battle." Then a shadow crossed his face. "You know," he added in a low tone: "it's not because of that I'm leaving."

Rieux replied that he knew it very well, but Rambert went on to say: "I don't think I'm a coward, not as a rule, anyhow. And I've had opportunities of putting it to the test. Only there are some thoughts I simply cannot endure."

The doctor looked him in the eyes.

"You'll see her again," he said.

"Maybe. But I just can't stomach the thought that it may last on and on, and all the time she'll be growing older. At thirty one's beginning to age, and one's got to squeeze all one can out of life. But I doubt if you can understand."

Rieux was replying that he thought he could, when Tarrou came up, obviously much excited.

"I've just asked Paneloux to join us."

"Well?" asked the doctor.

"He thought it over, then said yes."

"That's good," the doctor said. "I'm glad to know he's better than his sermon."

"Most people are like that," Tarrou replied. "It's only a matter of giving them the chance." He smiled and winked at Rieux. "That's my job in life, giving people chances."

"Excuse me," Rambert said, "I've got to be off."

On Thursday, the day of the appointment, Rambert entered the Cathedral porch at five minutes to eight. The air was still relatively cool. Small fleecy clouds, which presently the sun would swallow at a gulp, were drifting across the sky. A faint smell of moisture rose from the lawns, parched though they were. Still masked by the eastward houses, the sun was warming up Joan of Arc's helmet only, and it made a solitary patch of brightness in the Cathedral square. A clock struck eight. Rambert took some steps in the empty porch. From inside came a low sound of intoning voices, together with stale wafts of incense and dank air.

Then the voices ceased. Ten small black forms came out of the building and hastened away toward the center of the town. Rambert grew impatient. Other black forms climbed the steps and entered the porch. He was about to light a cigarette when it struck him that smoking might be frowned on here.

At eight fifteen the organ began to play, very softly. Rambert entered. At first he could see nothing in the dim light of the aisle; after a moment he made out in the nave the small black forms that had preceded him. They were all grouped in a corner, in front of a makeshift altar on which stood a statue of St. Roch, carved in haste by one of our local sculptors. Kneeling, they looked even smaller than before, blobs of clotted darkness

hardly more opaque than the gray, smoky haze in which they seemed to float. Above them the organ was playing endless variations.

When Rambert stepped out of the Cathedral, he saw Gonzales already going down the steps on his way back to the town.

"I thought you'd cleared off, old boy," he said to the journalist. "Considering how late it is."

He proceeded to explain that he'd gone to meet his friends at the place agreed on, which was quite near by, at ten to eight, the time they'd fixed, and waited twenty minutes without seeing them.

"Something must have held them up. There's lots of snags, you know, in our line of business."

He suggested another meeting at the same time on the following day, beside the war memorial. Rambert sighed and pushed his hat back on his head.

"Don't take it so hard," Gonzales laughed. "Why, think of all the swerves and runs and passes you got to make to score a goal."

"Quite so," Rambert agreed. "But the game lasts only an hour and a half."

The war memorial at Oran stands at the one place where one has a glimpse of the sea, a sort of esplanade following for a short distance the brow of the cliff overlooking the harbor. Next day, being again the first to arrive at the meeting-place, Rambert whiled away the time reading the list of names of those who had died for their country. Some minutes later two men strolled up, gave him a casual glance, then, resting their elbows on the parapet of the esplanade, gazed down intently at the empty, lifeless harbor. Both wore short-sleeved jerseys and blue trousers, and were of much the same height. The journalist moved away and, seated on a stone bench, studied their appearance at leisure. They were obviously youngsters, not more than twenty. Just then he saw Gonzales coming up.

"Those are our friends," he said, after apologizing for being late. Then he led Rambert to the two youths, whom he introduced as Marcel and Louis. They looked so much alike that Rambert had no doubt they were brothers.

"Right," said Gonzales. "Now you know each other, you can get down to business."

Marcel, or Louis, said that their turn of guard duty began in two days and lasted a week; they'd have to watch out for the night when there was the best chance of bringing it off. The trouble was that there were two other sentries, regular soldiers, besides themselves, at the west gate. These two men had better be kept out of the business; one couldn't depend on them, and anyhow it would pile up expenses unnecessarily. Some evenings, however, these two sentries spent several hours in the back room of a near-by bar. Marcel, or Louis, said that the best thing Rambert could do would be to stay at their place, which was only a few minutes' walk from the gate, and wait till one of them came to tell him the coast was clear. It should then be quite easy for him to "make his get-away."

But there was no time to lose; there had been talk about setting up duplicate sentry posts a little farther out.

Rambert agreed and handed some of his few remaining cigarettes to the young men.

The one who had not yet spoken asked Gonzales if the question of expenses had been settled and whether an advance would be given.

"No," Gonzales said, "and you needn't bother about that; he's a pal of mine.

He'll pay when he leaves."

Another meeting was arranged. Gonzales suggested their dining together on the next day but one, at the Spanish restaurant. It was at easy walking-distance from where the young men lived. "For the first night," he added, "I'll keep you company, old boy."

Next day on his way to his bedroom Rambert met Tarrou coming down the stairs at the hotel.

"Like to come with me?" he asked. "I'm just off to see Rieux."

Rambert hesitated.

"Well, I never feel sure I'm not disturbing him."

"I don't think you need worry about that; he's talked about you quite a lot."

The journalist pondered. Then, "Look here," he said. "If you've any time to spare after dinner, never mind how late, why not come to the hotel, both of you, and have a drink with me?"

"That will depend on Rieux." Tarrou sounded doubtful. "And on the plague," said Tarrou.

At eleven o'clock that night, however, Rieux and Tarrou entered the small, narrow bar of the hotel. Some thirty people were crowded into it, all talking at the top of their voices. Coming from the silence of the plague-bound town, the two newcomers were startled by the sudden burst of noise, and halted in the doorway. They understood the reason for it when they saw that liquor was still to be had here. Rambert, who was perched on a stool at a corner of the bar, beckoned to them. With complete coolness he elbowed away a noisy customer beside him to make room for his friends.

"You've no objection to a spot of something strong?"

"No," Tarrou replied. "Quite the contrary."

Rieux sniffed the pungency of bitter herbs in the drink that Rambert handed him.

It was hard to make oneself heard in the din of voices, but Rambert seemed chiefly concerned with drinking. The doctor couldn't make up his mind whether he was drunk yet. At one of the two tables that occupied all the remaining space beyond the half-circle round the bar, a naval officer, with a girl on each side of him, was describing to a fat, red-faced man a typhus epidemic at Cairo. "They had camps, you know," he was saying, "for the natives, with tents for the sick ones and a ring of sentries all round. If a member of the family came along and tried to smuggle in one of those damn-fool native remedies, they fired at sight.

A bit tough, I grant you, but it was the only thing to do." At the other table, round which sat a bevy of bright young people, the talk was incomprehensible, half drowned by the stridence of St. James Infirmary coming from a loud-speaker just above their heads.

"Any luck?" Rieux had to raise his voice.

"I'm getting on," Rambert replied. "In the course of the week, perhaps."

"A pity!" Tarrou shouted.

"Why?"

"Oh," Rieux put in, "Tarrou said that because he thinks you might be useful to us here. But, personally, I understand your wish to get away only too well."

Tarrou stood the next round of drinks.

Rambert got off his stool and looked him in the eyes for the first time.

"How could I be useful?"

"Why, of course," Tarrou replied, slowly reaching toward his glass, "in one of our sanitary squads."

The look of brooding obstinacy that Rambert so often had came back to his face, and he climbed again on to his stool.

"Don't you think these squads of ours do any good?" asked Tarrou, who had just taken a sip of his glass and was gazing hard at Rambert.

"I'm sure they do," the journalist replied, and drank off his glass.

Rieux noticed that his hand was shaking, and he decided, definitely, that the man was far gone in drink.

Next day, when for the second time Rambert entered the Spanish restaurant, he had to make his way through a group of men who had taken chairs out on the sidewalk and were sitting in the green-gold evening light, enjoying the first breaths of cooler air. They were smoking an acrid-smelling tobacco. The restaurant itself was almost empty. Rambert went to the table at the back at which Gonzales had sat when they met for the first time. He told the waitress he would wait a bit. It was seven thirty.

In twos and threes the men from outside began to dribble in and seat themselves at the tables. The waitresses started serving them, and a tinkle of knives and forks, a hum of conversation, began to fill the cellarlike room. At eight Rambert was still waiting. The lights were turned on. A new set of people took the other chairs at his table. He ordered dinner. At half past eight he had finished without having seen either Gonzales or the two young men.

He smoked several cigarettes. The restaurant was gradually emptying. Outside, night was falling rapidly. The curtains hung across the doorway were billowing in a warm breeze from the sea. At nine Rambert realized that the restaurant was quite empty and the waitress was eying him curiously. He paid, went out, and, noticing that a cafe across the street was open, settled down there at a place from which he could keep an eye on the entrance of the restaurant. At half past nine he walked slowly back to his hotel, racking his brains for some method of tracking down Gonzales, whose address he did not know, and bitterly discouraged by the not unlikely prospect of having to start the tiresome business all over again.

It was at this moment, as he walked in the dark streets along which ambulances were speeding, that it suddenly struck him, as he informed Dr. Rieux subsequently, that all this time he'd practically forgotten the woman he loved, so absorbed had he been in trying to find a rift in the walls that cut him off from her. But at this same moment, now that once more all ways of escape were sealed against him, he felt his longing for her blaze up again, with a violence so sudden, so intense, that he started running to his hotel, as if to escape the burning pain that none the less pervaded him, racing like wildfire in his blood.

Very early next day, however, he called on Rieux, to ask him where he could find Cottard.

"The only thing to do is to pick up the thread again where I dropped it."

"Come tomorrow night," Rieux said. "Tarrou asked me to invite Cottard here, I don't know why. He's due to come at ten. Come at half past ten."

When Cottard visited the doctor next day, Tarrou and Rieux were discussing the case of one of Rieux's patients who against all expectation had recovered.

"It was ten to one against," Tarrou commented. "He was in luck."

"Oh, come now," Cottard said. "It can't have been plague, that's all."

They assured him there was no doubt it was a case of plague.

"That's impossible, since he recovered. You know as well as I do, once you have plague your number's up."

"True enough, as a general rule," Rieux replied. "But if you refuse to be beaten, you have some pleasant surprises."

Cottard laughed.

"Precious few, anyhow. You saw the number of deaths this evening?"

Tarrou, who was gazing amiably at Cottard, said he knew the latest figures, and that the position was extremely serious. But what did that prove? Only that still more stringent measures should be applied.

"How? You can't make more stringent ones than those we have now."

"No. But every person in the town must apply them to himself."

Cottard stared at him in a puzzled manner, and Tarrou went on to say that there were far too many slackers, that this plague was everybody's business, and everyone should do his duty. For instance, any able-bodied man was welcome in the sanitary squads.

"That's an idea," said Cottard, "but it won't get you anywhere. The plague has the whip hand of you and there's nothing to be done about it."

"We shall know whether that is so", Tarrou's voice was carefully controlled, "only when we've tried everything."

Meanwhile Rieux had been sitting at his desk, copying out reports. Tarrou was still gazing at the little business man, who was stirring uneasily in his chair.

"Look here, Monsieur Cottard, why don't you join us?"

Picking up his derby hat, Cottard rose from his chair with an offended expression.

"It's not my job," he said. Then, with an air of bravado, he added: "What's more, the plague suits me quite well and I see no reason why I should bother about trying to stop it."

As if a new idea had just waylaid him, Tarrou struck his forehead.

"Why, of course, I was forgetting. If it wasn't for that, you'd be arrested."

Cottard gave a start and gripped the back of the chair, as if he were about to fall. Rieux had stopped writing and was observing him with grave interest.

"Who told you that?" Cottard almost screamed.

"Why, you yourself!" Tarrou looked surprised. "At least, that's what the doctor and I have gathered from the way you speak."

Losing all control of himself, Cottard let out a volley of oaths.

"Don't get excited," Tarrou said quietly. "Neither I nor the doctor would dream of reporting you to the police. What you may have done is no business of ours.

And, anyway, we've never had much use for the police. Come, now! Sit down again."

Cottard looked at the chair, then hesitantly lowered himself into it. He heaved a deep sigh.

"It's something that happened ages ago," he began. "Somehow they've dug it up. I thought it had all been forgotten. But somebody started talking, damn him! They sent for me and told me not to budge till the inquiry was finished. And I felt pretty sure they'd end up by arresting me."

"Was it anything serious?" Tarrou asked.

"That depends on what you mean by 'serious.' It wasn't murder, anyhow."

"Prison or transportation with hard labor?"

Cottard was looking almost abject.

"Well, prison, if I'm lucky." But after a moment he grew excited again. "It was all a mistake. Everybody makes mistakes. And I can't bear the idea of being pulled in for that, of being torn from my home and habits and everyone I know."

"And is that the reason," Tarrou asked, "why you had the bright idea of hanging yourself?"

"Yes. It was a damn-fool thing to do, I admit."

For the first time Rieux spoke. He told Cottard that he quite understood his anxiety, but perhaps everything would come right in the end.

"Oh, for the moment I've nothing to fear."

"I can see," Tarrou said, "that you're not going to join in our effort."

Twiddling his hat uneasily, Cottard gazed at Tarrou with shifty eyes.

"I hope you won't bear me a grudge."

"Certainly not. But", Tarrou smiled, "do try at least not to propagate the microbe deliberately."

Cottard protested that he'd never wanted the plague, it was pure chance that it had broken out, and he wasn't to blame if it happened to make things easier for him just now. Then he seemed to pluck up courage again and when Rambert entered was shouting almost aggressively:

"What's more, I'm pretty sure you won't get anywhere."

Rambert learned to his chagrin that Cottard didn't know where Gonzales lived; he suggested that they'd better pay another visit to the small cafe. They made an appointment for the following day. When Rieux gave him to understand that he'd like to be kept posted, Rambert proposed that he and Tarrou should look him up one night at the end of the week. They could come as late as they liked and would be sure to find him in his room.

Next morning Cottard and Rambert went to the cafe and left a message for Garcia, asking him to come that evening, or if this could not be managed, next day. They waited for him in vain that evening. Next day Garcia turned up. He listened in silence to what Rambert had to say; then informed him he had no idea what had happened, but knew that several districts of the town had been isolated for twenty-four hours for a house-to-house inspection. Quite possibly Gonzales and the two youngsters hadn't been able to get through the cordon. All he could do was to put them in touch once more with Raoul. Naturally this couldn't be done before the next day but one.

"I see," Rambert said. "I'll have to start it all over again, from scratch."

On the next day but one, Raoul, whom Rambert met at a street corner, confirmed Garcia's surmise; the low-lying districts had, in fact, been isolated and a cordon put round them. The next thing was to get in contact with Gonzales. Two days later Rambert was lunching with the footballer.

"It's too damn silly," Gonzales said. "Of course you should have arranged some way of seeing each other."

Rambert heartily agreed.

"Tomorrow morning," Gonzales continued, "we'll look up the kids and try to get a real move on."

When they called next day, however, the youngsters were out. A note was left fixing a meeting for the following day at noon, outside the high school. When Rambert came back to his hotel, Tarrou was struck by the look on his face.

"Not feeling well?" he asked.

"It's having to start it all over again that's got me down." Then he added:

"You'll come tonight, won't you?"

When the two friends entered Rambert's room that night, they found him lying on the bed. He got up at once and filled the glasses he had ready. Before lifting his to his lips, Rieux asked him if he was making progress. The journalist replied that he'd started the same round again and got to the same point as before; in a day or two he was to have his last appointment. Then he took a sip of his drink and added gloomily: "Needless to say, they won't turn up."

"Oh come! That doesn't follow because they let you down last time."

"So you haven't understood yet?" Rambert shrugged his shoulders almost scornfully.

"Understood what?"

"The plague."

"Ah!" Rieux exclaimed.

"No, you haven't understood that it means exactly that, the same thing over and over and over again."

He went to a corner of the room and started a small phonograph.

"What's that record?" Tarrou asked. "I've heard it before."

"It's St. James Infirmary."

While the phonograph was playing, two shots rang out in the distance.

"A dog or a get-away," Tarrou remarked.

When, a moment later, the record ended, an ambulance bell could be heard clanging past under the window and receding into silence.

"Rather a boring record," Rambert remarked. "And this must be the tenth time I've put it on today."

"Are you really so fond of it?"

"No, but it's the only one I have." And after a moment he added: "That's what I said 'it' was, the same thing over and over again."

He asked Rieux how the sanitary groups were functioning. Five teams were now at work, and it was hoped to form others. Sitting on the bed, the journalist seemed to be studying his fingernails. Rieux was gazing at his squat, powerfully built form, hunched up on the edge of the bed.

Suddenly he realized that Rambert was returning his gaze.

"You know, doctor, I've given a lot of thought to your campaign. And if I'm not with you, I have my reasons. No, I don't think it's that I'm afraid to risk my skin again. I took part in the Spanish Civil War."

"On which side?" Tarrou asked.

"The losing side. But since then I've done a bit of thinking."

"About what?"

"Courage. I know now that man is capable of great deeds. But if he isn't capable of a great emotion, well, he leaves me cold."

"One has the idea that he is capable of everything," Tarrou remarked.

"I can't agree; he's incapable of suffering for a long time, or being happy for a long time. Which means that he's incapable of anything really worth while." He looked at the two men in turn, then asked: "Tell me, Tarrou, are you capable of dying for love?"

"I couldn't say, but I hardly think so, as I am now."

"You see. But you're capable of dying for an idea; one can see that right away.

Well, personally, I've seen enough of people who die for an idea. I don't believe in heroism; I know it's easy and I've learned it can be murderous. What interests me is living and dying for what one loves."

Rieux had been watching the journalist attentively. With his eyes still on him he said quietly:

"Man isn't an idea, Rambert."

Rambert sprang off the bed, his face ablaze with passion.

"Man is an idea, and a precious small idea, once he turns his back on love. And that's my point; we, mankind, have lost the capacity for love. We must face that fact, doctor. Let's wait to acquire that capacity or, if really it's beyond us, wait for the deliverance that will come to each of us anyway, without his playing the hero. Personally, I look no farther."

Rieux rose. He suddenly appeared very tired.

"You're right, Rambert, quite right, and for nothing in the world would I try to dissuade you from what you're going to do; it seems to me absolutely right and proper. However, there's one thing I must tell you: there's no question of heroism in all this. It's a matter of common decency. That's an idea which may make some people smile, but the only means of righting a plague is, common decency."

"What do you mean by 'common decency'?" Rambert's tone was grave.

"I don't know what it means for other people. But in my case I know that it consists in doing my job."

"Your job! I only wish I were sure what my job is!" There was a mordant edge to Rambert's voice. "Maybe I'm all wrong in putting love first."

Rieux looked him in the eyes.

"No," he said vehemently, "you are not wrong."

Rambert gazed thoughtfully at them.

"You two," he said, "I suppose you've nothing to lose in all this. It's easier, that way, to be on the side of the angels."

Rieux drained his glass.

"Come along," he said to Tarrou. "We've work to do."

He went out.

Tarrou followed, but seemed to change his mind when he reached the door. He stopped and looked at the journalist.

"I suppose you don't know that Rieux's wife is in a sanatorium, a hundred miles or so away."

Rambert showed surprise and began to say something; but Tarrou had already left the room.

At a very early hour next day Rambert rang up the doctor.

"Would you agree to my working with you until I find some way of getting out of the town?"

There was a moment's silence before the reply came.

"Certainly, Rambert. Thanks."

PART III

Thus week by week the prisoners of plague put up what fight they could. Some, like Rambert, even contrived to fancy they were still behaving as free men and had the power of choice. But actually it would have been truer to say that by this time, mid-August, the plague had swallowed up everything and everyone. No longer were there individual destinies; only a collective destiny, made of plague and the emotions shared by all. Strongest of these emotions was the sense of exile and of deprivation, with all the crosscurrents of revolt and fear set up by these. That is why the narrator thinks this moment, registering the climax of the summer heat and the disease, the best for describing, on general lines and by way of illustration, the excesses of the living, burials of the dead, and the plight of parted lovers.

It was at this time that a high wind rose and blew for several days through the plague-stricken city. Wind is particularly dreaded by the inhabitants of Oran, since the plateau on which the town is built presents no natural obstacle, and it can sweep our streets with unimpeded violence. During the months when not a drop of rain had refreshed the town, a gray crust had formed on everything, and this flaked off under the wind, disintegrating into dust-clouds. What with the dust and scraps of paper whirled against peoples' legs, the streets grew emptier. Those few who went out could be seen hurrying along, bent forward, with handkerchiefs or their hands pressed to their mouths. At nightfall, instead of the usual throng of people, each trying to prolong a day that might well be his last, you met only small groups hastening home or to a favorite cafe. With the result that for several days when twilight came, it fell much quicker at this time of the year, the streets were almost empty, and silent but for the long-drawn stridence of the wind. A smell of brine and seaweed came from the unseen, storm-tossed sea. And in the growing darkness the almost empty town, palled in dust, swept by bitter sea-spray, and loud with the shrilling of the wind, seemed a lost island of the damned.

Hitherto the plague had found far more victims in the more thickly populated and less well-appointed outer districts than in the heart of the town. Quite suddenly, however, it launched a new attack and established itself in the business center. Residents accused the wind of carrying infection, "broadcasting germs," as the hotel manager put it. Whatever the reason might be, people living in the central districts realized that their turn had come when each night they heard oftener and oftener the ambulances clanging past, sounding the plague's dismal, passionless tocsin under their windows.

The authorities had the idea of segregating certain particularly affected central areas and permitting only those whose services were indispensable to cross the cordon. Dwellers in these districts could not help regarding these regulations as a sort of taboo specially directed at themselves, and thus they came, by contrast, to envy residents in other areas their freedom. And the latter, to cheer themselves up in despondent moments,

fell to picturing the lot of those others less free than themselves. "Anyhow, there are some worse off than I," was a remark that voiced the only solace to be had in those days.

About the same time we had a recrudescence of outbreaks of fire, especially in the residential area near the west gate. It was found, after inquiry, that people who had returned from quarantine were responsible for these fires. Thrown off their balance by bereavement and anxiety, they were burning their houses under the odd delusion that they were killing off the plague in the holocaust.

Great difficulty was experienced in fighting these fires, whose numbers and frequency exposed whole districts to constant danger, owing to the high wind. When the attempts made by the authorities to convince these well-meaning incendiaries that the official fumigation of their houses effectively removed any risk of infection had proved unavailing, it became necessary to decree very heavy penalties for this type of arson. And most likely it was not the prospect of mere imprisonment that deterred these unhappy people, but the common belief that a sentence of imprisonment was tantamount to a death sentence, owing to the very high mortality prevailing in the town jail. It must be admitted that there was some foundation for this belief. It seemed that, for obvious reasons, the plague launched its most virulent attacks on those who lived, by choice or by necessity, in groups: soldiers, prisoners, monks, and nuns. For though some prisoners are kept solitary, a prison forms a sort of community, as is proved by the fact that in our town jail the guards died of plague in the same proportion as the prisoners. The plague was no respecter of persons and under its despotic rule everyone, from the warden down to the humblest delinquent, was under sentence and, perhaps for the first time, impartial justice reigned in the prison.

Attempts made by the authorities to redress this leveling-out by some sort of hierarchy?the idea was to confer a decoration on guards who died in the exercise of their duties, came to nothing. Since martial law had been declared and the guards might, from a certain angle, be regarded as on active service, they were awarded posthumously the military medal. But though the prisoners raised no protest, strong exception was taken in military circles, and it was pointed out, logically enough, that a most regrettable confusion in the public mind would certainly ensue. The civil authority conceded the point and decided that the simplest solution was to bestow on guards who died at their post a "plague medal." Even so, since as regards the first recipients of the military medal the harm had been done and there was no question of withdrawing the decoration from them, the military were still dissatisfied. Moreover, the plague medal had the disadvantage of having far less moral effect than that attaching to a military award, since in time of pestilence a decoration of this sort is too easily acquired. Thus nobody was satisfied.

Another difficulty was that the jail administration could not follow the procedure adopted by the religious and, in a less degree, the military authorities. The monks in the two monasteries of the town had been evacuated and lodged for the time being with religious-minded families. In the same way, whenever possible, small bodies of men had been moved out of barracks and billeted in schools or public buildings. Thus the disease, which apparently had forced on us the solidarity of a beleaguered town, disrupted at the same time longestablished communities and sent men out to live, as individuals, in relative isolation. This, too, added to the general feeling of unrest.

Indeed, it can easily be imagined that these changes, combined with the high wind, also had an incendiary effect on certain minds. There were frequent attacks on the gates of the town, and the men who made them now were armed.

Shots were exchanged, there were casualties, and some few got away. Then the sentry posts were reinforced, and such attempts quickly ceased. None the less, they sufficed to start a wave of revolutionary violence, though only on a small scale. Houses that had been burnt or closed by the sanitary control were looted. However, it seemed unlikely that these excesses were premeditated. Usually it was some chance incentive that led normally well-behaved people to acts which promptly had their imitators. Thus you sometimes saw a man, acting on some crazy impulse, dash into a blazing house under the eyes of its owner, who was standing by, dazed with grief, watching the flames. Seeing his indifference, many of the onlookers would follow the lead given by the first man, and presently the dark street was full of running men, changed to hunched, misshapen gnomes by the flickering glow from the dying flames and the ornaments or furniture they carried on their shoulders.

It was incidents of this sort that compelled the authorities to declare martial law and enforce the regulations deriving from it. Two looters were shot, but we may doubt if this made much impression on the others; with so many deaths taking place every day, these two executions went unheeded, a mere drop in the ocean.

Actually scenes of this kind continued to take place fairly often, without the authorities' making even a show of intervening. The only regulation that seemed to have some effect on the populace was the establishment of a curfew hour. From eleven onwards, plunged in complete darkness, Oran seemed a huge necropolis.

On moonlight nights the long, straight streets and dirty white walls, nowhere darkened by the shadow of a tree, their peace untroubled by footsteps or a dog's bark, glimmered in pale recession. The silent city was no more than an assemblage of huge, inert cubes, between which only the mute effigies of great men, carapaced in bronze, with their blank stone or metal faces, conjured up a sorry semblance of what the man had been. In lifeless squares and avenues these tawdry idols lorded it under the lowering sky; stolid monsters that might have personified the rule of immobility imposed on us, or, anyhow, its final aspect, that of a defunct city in which plague, stone, and darkness had effectively silenced every voice.

But there was darkness also in men's hearts, and the true facts were as little calculated to reassure our townsfolk as the wild stories going round about the burials. The narrator cannot help talking about these burials, and a word of excuse is here in place. For he is well aware of the reproach that might be made him in this respect; his justification is that funerals were taking place throughout this period and, in a way, he was compelled, as indeed everybody was compelled, to give heed to them. In any case it should not be assumed that he has a morbid taste for such ceremonies; quite the contrary, he much prefers the society of the living and, to give a concrete illustration, sea-bathing. But the bathing-beaches were out of bounds and the company of the living ran a risk, increasing as the days went by, of being perforce converted into the company of the dead. That was, indeed, self-evident.

True, one could always refuse to face this disagreeable fact, shut one's eyes to it, or thrust it out of mind, but there is a terrible cogency in the self-evident; ultimately it breaks down all defenses. How, for instance, continue to ignore the funerals on the day when somebody you loved needed one?

Actually the most striking feature of our funerals was their speed. Formalities had been whittled down, and, generally speaking, all elaborate ceremonial suppressed. The plague victim died away from his family and the customary vigil beside the dead body was forbidden, with the result that a person dying in the evening spent the night alone, and those who died in the daytime were promptly buried. Needless to say, the family was notified, but in most cases, since the deceased had lived with them, its members were in quarantine and thus immobilized. When, however, the deceased had not lived with his family, they were asked to attend at a fixed time; after, that is to say, the body had been washed and put in the coffin and when the journey to the cemetery was about to begin.

Let us suppose that these formalities were taking place at the auxiliary hospital of which Dr. Rieux was in charge. This converted school had an exit at the back of the main building. A large storeroom giving on the corridor contained the coffins. On arrival, the family found a coffin already nailed up in the corridor. Then came the most important part of the business: the signing of official forms by the head of the family. Next the coffin was loaded on a motor-vehicle, a real hearse or a large converted ambulance. The mourners stepped into one of the few taxis still allowed to ply and the vehicles drove hell-for-leather to the cemetery by a route avoiding the center of the town. There was a halt at the gate, where police officers applied a rubber stamp to the official exit permit, without which it was impossible for our citizens to have what they called a last resting-place. The policeman stood back and the cars drew up near a plot of ground where a number of graves stood open, waiting for inmates. A priest came to meet the mourners, since church services at funerals were now prohibited. To an accompaniment of prayers the coffin was dragged from the hearse, roped up, and carried to the graveside; the ropes were slipped and it came heavily to rest at the bottom of the grave. No sooner had the priest begun to sprinkle holy water than the first sod rebounded from the lid. The ambulance had already left and was being sprayed with disinfectant, and while spadefuls of clay thudded more and more dully on the rising layer of earth, the family were bundling into the taxi. A quarter of an hour later they were back at home.

The whole process was put through with the maximum of speed and the minimum of risk. It cannot be denied that, anyhow in the early days, the natural feelings of the family were somewhat outraged by these lightning funerals. But obviously in time of plague such sentiments can't be taken into account, and all was sacrificed to efficiency. And though, to start with, the morale of the population was shaken by this summary procedure, for the desire to have a "proper funeral" is more widespread than is generally believed, as time went on, fortunately enough, the food problem became more urgent and the thoughts of our townsfolk were diverted to more instant needs. So much energy was expended on filling up forms, hunting round for supplies, and lining up that people had no time to think of the manner in which others were dying around them and they themselves would die one day. Thus the growing complications of our everyday life, which might have been an affliction, proved to be a blessing in disguise. Indeed, had not the epidemic, as already mentioned, spread its ravages, all would have been for the best.

For then coffins became scarcer; also there was a shortage of winding-sheets, and of space in the cemetery. Something had to be done about this, and one obvious step, justified by its practical convenience, was to combine funerals and, when necessary, multiply the trips between the hospital and the burial-place.

At one moment the stock of coffins in Rieux's hospital was reduced to five. Once filled, all five were loaded together in the ambulance. At the cemetery they were emptied out and the iron-gray corpses put on stretchers and deposited in a shed reserved for that purpose, to wait their turn. Meanwhile the empty coffins, after being sprayed with antiseptic fluid, were rushed back to the hospital, and the process was repeated as often as necessary. This system worked excellently and won the approval of the Prefect. He even told Rieux that it was really a great improvement on the death-carts driven by Negroes of which one reads in accounts of former visitations of this sort.

"Yes," Rieux said. "And though the burials are much the same, we keep careful records of them. That, you will agree, is progress."

Successful, however, as the system proved itself in practice, there was something so distasteful in the last rites as now performed that the Prefect felt constrained to forbid relations of the deceased being present at the actual interment. They were allowed to come only as far as the cemetery gates, and even that was not authorized officially. For things had somewhat changed as regards the last stage of the ceremony. In a patch of open ground dotted with lentiscus trees at the far end of the cemetery, two big pits had been dug. One was reserved for the men, the other for the women. Thus, in this respect, the authorities still gave thought to propriety and it was only later that, by the force of things, this last remnant of decorum went by the board, and men and women were flung into the death-pits indiscriminately. Happily, this ultimate indignity synchronized with the plague's last ravages.

In the period we are now concerned with, the separation of the sexes was still in force and the authorities set great store by it. At the bottom of each pit a deep layer of quicklime steamed and seethed. On the lips of the pit a low ridge of quicklime threw up bubbles that burst in the air above it. When the ambulance had finished its trips, the stretchers were carried to the pits in Indian file.

The naked, somewhat contorted bodies were slid off into the pit almost side by side, then covered with a layer of quicklime and another of earth, the latter only a few inches deep, so as to leave space for subsequent consignments. On the following day the next of kin were asked to sign the register of burials, which showed the distinction that can be made between men and, for example, dogs; men's deaths are checked and entered up.

Obviously all these activities called for a considerable staff, and Rieux was often on the brink of a shortage. Many of the gravediggers, stretcher-bearers, and the like, public servants to begin with, and later volunteers, died of plague. However stringent the precautions, sooner or later contagion did its work. Still, when all is said and done, the really amazing thing is that, so long as the epidemic lasted, there was never any lack of men for these duties. The critical moment came just before the outbreak touched high-water mark, and the doctor had good reason for feeling anxious. There was then a real shortage of man-power both for the higher posts and for the rough work, as Rieux called it. But, paradoxically enough, once the whole town was in the grip of the disease, its very prevalence tended to make things easier, since the disorganization of the town's economic life threw a great number of persons out of work. Few of the workers thus made available were qualified for administrative posts, but the recruiting of men for the "rough work" became much easier. From now on, indeed, poverty showed itself a stronger stimulus than fear, especially as, owing to its risks, such work was highly paid. The sanitary authorities always had a waiting-list of applicants for work; whenever there was a vacancy the men at the top of the list were notified, and unless they too had laid off work for good, they never failed to appear when summoned. Thus the Prefect, who had always been reluctant to employ the prisoners in the jail, whether short-term men or lifers, was able to avoid recourse to this distasteful measure. As long, he said, as there were unemployed, we could afford to wait.

Thus until the end of August our fellow citizens could be conveyed to their last resting-place, if not under very decorous conditions, at least in a manner orderly enough for the authorities to feel that they were doing their duty by the dead and the bereaved. However, we may here anticipate a little and describe the pass to which we came in the final phase. From August onwards the plague mortality was and continued such as far to exceed the capacity of our small cemetery. Such expedients as knocking down walls and letting the dead encroach on neighboring land proved inadequate; some new method had to be evolved without delay. The first step taken was to bury the dead by night, which obviously permitted a more summary procedure. The bodies were piled into ambulances in larger and larger numbers. And the few belated wayfarers who, in defiance of the regulations, were abroad in the outlying districts after curfew hour, or whose duties took them there, often saw the long white ambulances hurtling past, making the nightbound streets reverberate with the dull clangor of their bells.

The corpses were tipped pell-mell into the pits and had hardly settled into place when spadefuls of quicklime began to sear their faces and the earth covered them indisdinctively, in holes dug steadily deeper as time went on.

Shortly afterwards, however, it became necessary to find new space and to strike out in a new direction. By a special urgency measure the denizens of grants in perpetuity were evicted from their graves and the exhumed remains dispatched to the crematorium. And soon the plague victims likewise had to go to a fiery end.

This meant that the old crematorium east of the town, outside the gates, had to be utilized. Accordingly the east-gate sentry post was moved farther out. Then a municipal employee had an idea that greatly helped the harassed authorities; he advised them to employ the streetcar line running along the coastal road, which was now unused. So the interiors of streetcars and trailers were adapted to this new purpose, and a branch line was laid down to the crematorium, which thus became a terminus.

During all the late summer and throughout the autumn there could daily be seen moving along the road skirting the cliffs above the sea a strange procession of passengerless streetcars swaying against the skyline. The residents in this area soon learned what was going on. And though the cliffs were patrolled day and night, little groups of people contrived to thread their way unseen between the rocks and would toss flowers into the open trailers as the cars went by. And in the warm darkness of the summer nights the cars could be heard clanking on their way, laden with flowers and corpses.

During the first few days an oily, foul-smelling cloud of smoke hung low upon the eastern districts of the town. These effluvia, all the doctors agreed, though unpleasant, were not in the least harmful. However, the residents of this part of the town threatened to migrate in a body, convinced that germs were raining down on them from the sky, with the result that an elaborate apparatus for diverting the smoke had to be installed to appease them. Thereafter only when a strong wind was blowing did a faint, sickly odor coming from the east remind them that they were living under a new order and that the plague fires were taking their nightly toll.

Such were the consequences of the epidemic at its culminating point. Happily it grew no worse, for otherwise, it may well be believed, the resourcefulness of our administration, the competence of our officials, not to mention the burning-capacity of our crematorium, would have proved unequal to their tasks. Rieux knew that desperate solutions had been mooted, such as throwing the corpses into the sea, and a picture had risen before him of hideous jetsam lolling in the shallows under the cliffs. He knew, too, that if there was another rise in the death-rate, no organization, however efficient, could stand up to it; that men would die in heaps, and corpses rot in the street, whatever the authorities might do, and the town would see in public squares the dying embrace the living in the frenzies of an all too comprehensible hatred or some crazy hope.

Such were the sights and apprehensions that kept alive in our townspeople their feeling of exile and separation. In this connection the narrator is well aware how regrettable is his inability to record at this point something of a really spectacular order, some heroic feat or memorable deed like those that thrill us in the chronicles of the past. The truth is that nothing is less sensational than pestilence, and by reason of their very duration great misfortunes are monotonous. In the memories of those who lived through them, the grim days of plague do not stand out like vivid flames, ravenous and inextinguishable, beaconing a troubled sky, but rather like the slow, deliberate progress of some monstrous thing crushing out all upon its path.

No, the real plague had nothing in common with the grandiose imaginings that had haunted Rieux's mind at its outbreak. It was, about all, a shrewd, unflagging adversary; a skilled organizer, doing his work thoroughly and well. That, it may be said in passing, is why, so as not to play false to the facts, and, still more, so as not to play false to himself, the narrator has aimed at objectivity.

He has made hardly any changes for the sake of artistic effect, except those elementary adjustments needed to present his narrative in a more or less coherent form. And in deference to this scruple he is constrained to admit that, though the chief source of distress, the deepest as well as the most widespread, was separation, and it is his duty to say more about it as it existed in the later stages of the plague, it cannot be denied that even this distress was coming to lose something of its poignancy.

Was it that our fellow citizens, even those who had felt the parting from their loved ones most keenly, were getting used to doing without them? To assume this would fall somewhat short of the truth. It would be more correct to say that they were wasting away emotionally as well as physically. At the beginning of the plague they had a vivid recollection of the absent ones and bitterly felt their loss. But though they could clearly recall the face, the smile and voice of the beloved, and this or that occasion when (as they now saw in retrospect) they had been supremely happy, they had trouble in picturing what he or she might be doing at the moment when they conjured up these memories, in a setting so hopelessly remote. In short, at these moments memory played its part, but their imagination failed them. During the second phase of the plague their memory failed them, too. Not that they had forgotten the face itself, but, what came to the same thing, it had lost fleshly substance and they no longer saw it in memory's mirror.

Thus, while during the first weeks they were apt to complain that only shadows remained to them of what their love had been and meant, they now came to learn that

even shadows can waste away, losing the faint hues of life that memory may give. And by the end of their long sundering they had also lost the power of imagining the intimacy that once was theirs or understanding what it can be to live with someone whose life is wrapped up in yours.

In this respect they had adapted themselves to the very condition of the plague, all the more potent for its mediocrity. None of us was capable any longer of an exalted emotion; all had trite, monotonous feelings. "It's high time it stopped," people would say, because in time of calamity the obvious thing is to desire its end, and in fact they wanted it to end. But when making such remarks, we felt none of the passionate yearning or fierce resentment of the early phase; we merely voiced one of the few clear ideas that lingered in the twilight of our minds. The furious revolt of the first weeks had given place to a vast despondency, not to be taken for resignation, though it was none the less a sort of passive and provisional acquiescence.

Our fellow citizens had fallen into line, adapted themselves, as people say, to the situation, because there was no way of doing otherwise. Naturally they retained the attitudes of sadness and suffering, but they had ceased to feel their sting. Indeed, to some, Dr. Rieux among them, this precisely was the most disheartening thing: that the habit of despair is worse than despair itself.

Hitherto those who were parted had not been utterly unhappy; there was always a gleam of hope in the night of their distress; but that gleam had now died out.

You could see them at street corners, in cafes or friends' houses, listless, indifferent, and looking so bored that, because of them, the whole town seemed like a railway waiting-room. Those who had jobs went about them at the exact tempo of the plague, with dreary perseverance. Everyone was modest. For the first time exiles from those they loved had no reluctance to talk freely about them, using the same words as everybody else, and regarding their deprivation from the same angle as that from which they viewed the latest statistics of the epidemic. This change was striking since until now they had jealously withheld their personal grief from the common stock of suffering; now they accepted its inclusion.

Without memories, without hope, they lived for the moment only. Indeed, the here and now had come to mean everything to them. For there is no denying that the plague had gradually killed off in all of us the faculty not of love only but even of friendship. Naturally enough, since love asks something of the future, and nothing was left us but a series of present moments.

However, this account of our predicament gives only the broad lines. Thus, while it is true that all who were parted came ultimately to this state, we must add that all did not attain it simultaneously; moreover, once this utter apathy had fallen on them, there were still flashes of lucidity, broken lights of memory that rekindled in the exiles a younger, keener sensibility. This happened when, for instance, they fell to making plans implying that the plague had ended. Or when, quite unexpectedly, by some kindly chance, they felt a twinge of jealousy, none the less acute for its objectlessness. Others, again, had sudden accesses of energy and shook off their languor on certain days of the week, for obvious reasons, on Sundays and Saturday afternoons, because these had been devoted to certain ritual pleasures in the days when the loved ones were still accessible.

Sometimes the mood of melancholy that descended on them with the nightfall acted as a sort of warning, not always fulfilled, however, that old memories were floating up to the surface. That evening hour which for believers is the time to look into their consciences is hardest of all hours on the prisoner or exile who has nothing to look into but the void. For a moment it held them in suspense; then they sank back into their lethargy, the prison door had closed on them once again.

Obviously all this meant giving up what was most personal in their lives.

Whereas in the early days of the plague they had been struck by the host of small details that, while meaning absolutely nothing to others, meant so much to them personally, and thus had realized, perhaps for the first time, the uniqueness of each man's life; now, on the other hand, they took an interest only in what interested everyone else, they had only general ideas, and even their tenderest affections now seemed abstract, items of the common stock. So completely were they dominated by the plague that sometimes the one thing they aspired to was the long sleep it brought, and they caught themselves thinking:

"A good thing if I get plague and have done with it!" But really they were asleep already; this whole period was for them no more than a long night's slumber. The town was peopled with sleepwalkers, whose trance was broken only on the rare occasions when at night their wounds, to all appearance closed, suddenly reopened. Then, waking with a start, they would run their fingers over the wounds with a sort of absentminded curiosity, twisting their lips, and in a flash their grief blazed up again, and abruptly there rose before them the mournful visage of their love. In the morning they harked back to normal conditions, in other words, the plague.

What impression, it may be asked, did these exiles of the plague make on the observer? The answer is simple; they made none. Or, to put it differently, they looked like everybody else, nondescript. They shared in the torpor of the town and in its puerile agitations. They lost every trace of a critical spirit, while gaining an air of sang-froid. You could see, for instance, even the most intelligent among them making a show like all the rest of studying the newspapers or listening to the radio, in the hope apparently of finding some reason to believe the plague would shortly end. They seemed to derive fantastic hopes or equally exaggerated fears from reading the linens that some journalist had scribbled at random, yawning with boredom at his desk. Meanwhile they drank their beer, nursed their sick, idled, or doped themselves with work, filed documents in offices, or played the phonograph at home, without betraying any difference from the rest of us. In other words, they had ceased to choose for themselves; plague had leveled out discrimination. This could be seen by the way nobody troubled about the quality of the clothes or food he bought. Everything was taken as it came.

And, finally, it is worth noting that those who were parted ceased to enjoy the curious privilege that had been theirs at the outset. They had lost love's egoism and the benefit they derived from it. Now, at least, the position was clear; this calamity was everybody's business. What with the gunshots echoing at the gates, the punctual thuds of rubber stamps marking the rhythm of lives and deaths, the files and fires, the panics and formalities, all alike were pledged to an ugly but recorded death, and, amidst noxious fumes and the muted clang of ambulances, all of us ate the same sour bread of exile, unconsciously waiting for the same reunion, the same miracle of peace regained. No doubt our love persisted, but in practice it served nothing; it was an inert mass within us, sterile as crime or a life sentence. It had declined on a patience that led nowhere, a dogged expectation. Viewed from this angle, the attitude of some of our fellow citizens

resembled that of the long queues one saw outside the food-shops. There was the same resignation, the same long-sufferance, inexhaustible and without illusions. The only difference was that the mental state of the food-seekers would need to be raised to a vastly higher power to make it comparable with the gnawing pain of separation, since this latter came from a hunger fierce to the point of insatiability. In any case, if the reader would have a correct idea of the mood of these exiles, we must conjure up once more those dreary evenings sifting down through a haze of dust and golden light upon the treeless streets filled with teeming crowds of men and women. For, characteristically, the sound that rose toward the terraces still bathed in the last glow of daylight, now that the noises of vehicles and motors, the sole voice of cities in ordinary times, had ceased, was but one vast rumor of low voices and incessant footfalls, the drumming of innumerable soles timed to the eerie whistling of the plague in the sultry air above, the sound of a huge concourse of people marking time, a never ending, stifling drone that, gradually swelling, filled the town from end to end, and evening after evening gave its truest, mournfulest expression to the blind endurance that had ousted love from all our hearts.

PART IV

Throughout September and October the town lay prostrate, at the mercy of the plague. There was nothing to do but to "mark time," and some hundreds of thousands of men and women went on doing this, through weeks that seemed interminable.

Mist, heat, and rain rang their changes in our streets. From the south came silent coveys of starlings and thrushes, flying very high, but always giving the town a wide berth, as though the strange implement of the plague described by Paneloux, the giant flail whirling and shrilling over the housetops, warned them off us. At the beginning of October torrents of rain swept the streets clean.

And all the time nothing more important befell us than that multitudinous marking time.

It was now that Rieux and his friends came to realize how exhausted they were.

Indeed, the workers in the sanitary squads had given up trying to cope with their fatigue. Rieux noticed the change coming over his associates, and himself as well, and it took the form of a strange indifference to everything. Men, for instance, who hitherto had shown a keen interest in every scrap of news concerning the plague now displayed none at all. Rambert, who had been temporarily put in charge of a quarantine station, his hotel had been taken over for this purpose, could state at any moment the exact number of persons under his observation, and every detail of the procedure he had laid down for the prompt evacuation of those who suddenly developed symptoms of the disease was firmly fixed in his mind. The same was true of the statistics of the effects of anti-plague inoculations on the persons in his quarantine station. Nevertheless, he could not have told you the week's total of plague deaths, and he could not even have said if the figure was rising or falling. And meanwhile, in spite of everything, he had not lost hope of being able to "make his get-away" from one day to another.

As for the others, working themselves almost to a standstill throughout the day and far into the night, they never bothered to read a newspaper or listen to the radio. When told of some unlooked-for recovery, they made a show of interest, but actually

received the news with the stolid indifference that we may imagine the fighting man in a great war to feel who, worn out by the incessant strain and mindful only of the duties daily assigned to him, has ceased even to hope for the decisive battle or the bugle-call of armistice.

Though he still worked out methodically the figures relating to the plague, Grand would certainly have been quite unable to say to what they pointed. Unlike Rieux, Rambert, and Tarrou, who obviously had great powers of endurance, he had never had good health. And now, in addition to his duties in the Municipal Office, he had his night work and his secretarial post under Rieux. One could see that the strain was telling on him, and if he managed to keep going, it was thanks to two or three fixed ideas, one of which was to take, the moment the plague ended, a complete vacation, of a week at least, which he would devote, "hats off," to his work in progress. He was also becoming subject to accesses of sentimentality and at such times would unburden himself to Rieux about Jeanne.

Where was she now, he wondered; did her thoughts sometimes turn to him when she read the papers? It was Grand to whom one day Rieux caught himself talking, much to his own surprise, about his wife, and in the most commonplace terms, something he had never done as yet to anyone.

Doubtful how far he could trust his wife's telegrams, their tone was always reassuring, he had decided to wire the house physician of the sanatorium. The reply informed him that her condition had worsened, but everything was being done to arrest further progress of the disease. He had kept the news to himself so far and could only put it down to his nervous exhaustion that he passed it on to Grand. After talking to the doctor about Jeanne, Grand had asked some questions about Mme Rieux and, on hearing Rieux's reply, said: "You know, it's wonderful, the cures they bring off nowadays." Rieux agreed, merely adding that the long separation was beginning to tell on him, and, what was more, he might have helped his wife to make a good recovery; whereas, as things were, she must be feeling terribly lonely. After which he fell silent and gave only evasive answers to Grand's further questions.

The others were in much the same state. Tarrou held his own better, but the entries in his diary show that while his curiosity had kept its depth, it had lost its diversity. Indeed, throughout this period the only person, apparently, who really interested him was Cottard. In the evening, at Rieux's apartment, where he had come to live now that the hotel was requisitioned as a quarantine center, he paid little or no attention to Grand and the doctor when they read over the day's statistics. At the earliest opportunity he switched the conversation over to his pet subject, small details of the daily life at Oran.

More perhaps than any of them, Dr. Castel showed signs of wear and tear. On the day when he came to tell Rieux that the anti-plague serum was ready, and they decided to try it for the first time on M. Othon's small son, whose case seemed all but hopeless, Rieux suddenly noticed, while he was announcing the latest statistics, that Castel was slumped in his chair, sound asleep. The difference in his old friend's face shocked him.

The smile of benevolent irony that always played on it had seemed to endow it with perpetual youth; now, abruptly left out of control, with a trickle of saliva between the slightly parted lips, it betrayed its age and the wastage of the years. And, seeing this, Rieux felt a lump come to his throat.

It was by such lapses that Rieux could gauge his exhaustion. His sensibility was getting out of hand. Kept under all the time, it had grown hard and brittle and seemed to snap completely now and then, leaving him the prey of his emotions.

No resource was left him but to tighten the stranglehold on his feelings and harden his heart protectively. For he knew this was the only way of carrying on.

In any case, he had few illusions left, and fatigue was robbing him of even these remaining few. He knew that, over a period whose end he could not glimpse, his task was no longer to cure but to diagnose. To detect, to see, to describe, to register, and then condemn, that was his present function. Sometimes a woman would clutch his sleeve, crying shrilly: "Doctor, you'll save him, won't you?"

But he wasn't there for saving life; he was there to order a sick man's evacuation. How futile was the hatred he saw on faces then! "You haven't a heart!" a woman told him on one occasion. She was wrong; he had one. It saw him through his twenty-hour day, when he hourly watched men dying who were meant to live. It enabled him to start anew each morning. He had just enough heart for that, as things were now. How could that heart have sufficed for saving life?

No, it wasn't medical aid that he dispensed in those crowded days, only information. Obviously that could hardly be reckoned a man's job. Yet, when all was said and done, who, in that terror-stricken, decimated populace, had scope for any activity worthy of his manhood? Indeed, for Rieux his exhaustion was a blessing in disguise. Had he been less tired, his senses more alert, that all-pervading odor of death might have made him sentimental. But when a man has had only four hours' sleep, he isn't sentimental. He sees things as they are; that is to say, he sees them in the garish light of justice, hideous, witless justice. And those others, the men and women under sentence to death, shared his bleak enlightenment. Before the plague he was welcomed as a savior. He was going to make them right with a couple of pills or an injection, and people took him by the arm on his way to the sickroom. Flattering, but dangerous. Now, on the contrary, he came accompanied by soldiers, and they had to hammer on the door with rifle-butts before the family would open it. They would have liked to drag him, drag the whole human race, with them to the grave. Yes, it was quite true that men can't do without their fellow men; that he was as helpless as these unhappy people and he, too, deserved the same faint thrill of pity that he allowed himself once he had left them.

Such, anyhow, were the thoughts that in those endless-seeming weeks ran in the doctor's mind, along with thoughts about his severance from his wife. And such, too, were his friends' thoughts, judging by the look he saw on their faces. But the most dangerous effect of the exhaustion steadily gaining on all engaged in the fight against the epidemic did not consist in their relative indifference to outside events and the feelings of others, but in the slackness and supine-ness that they allowed to invade their personal lives.

They developed a tendency to shirk every movement that didn't seem absolutely necessary or called for efforts that seemed too great to be worth while. Thus these men were led to break, oftener and oftener, the rules of hygiene they themselves had instituted, to omit some of the numerous disinfections they should have practiced, and sometimes to visit the homes of people suffering from pneumonic plague without taking steps to safeguard themselves against infection, because they had been notified only at the last moment and could not be bothered with returning to a sanitary service station, sometimes a considerable distance away, to have the necessary instillations. There lay the real danger; for the energy they devoted to righting the disease made them all the more liable to it. In short, they were gambling on their luck, and luck is not to be coerced.

There was, however, one man in the town who seemed neither exhausted nor discouraged; indeed, the living image of contentment. It was Cottard. Though maintaining contact with Rieux and Rambert, he still kept rather aloof, whereas he deliberately cultivated Tarrou, seeing him as often as Tarrou's scanty leisure permitted. He had two reasons for this: one, that Tarrou knew all about his case, and the other, that he always gave him a cordial welcome and made him feel at ease.

That was one of the remarkable things about Tarrou; no matter how much work he had put in, he was always a ready listener and an agreeable companion. Even when, some evenings, he seemed completely worn out, the next day brought him a new lease of energy. "Tarrou's a fellow one can talk to," Cottard once told Rambert, "because he's really human. He always understands."

This may explain why the entries in Tarrou's diary of this period tend to converge on Cottard's personality. It is obvious that Tarrou was attempting to give a full-length picture of the man and noted all his reactions and reflections, whether as conveyed to him by Cottard or interpreted by himself. Under the heading "Cottard and his Relations with the Plague," we find a series, of notes covering several pages and, in the narrator's opinion, these are well worth summarizing here.

One of the entries gives Tarrou's general impression of Cottard at this time:

"He is blossoming out. Expanding in geniality and good humor." For Cottard was anything but upset by the turn events were taking. Sometimes in Tarrou's company he voiced his true feelings in remarks of this order: "Getting worse every day, isn't it? Well, anyhow, everyone's in the same boat."

"Obviously," Tarrou comments, "he's in the same peril of death as everyone else, but that's just the point; he's in it with the others. And then I'm pretty sure he doesn't seriously think he runs much personal risk. He has got the idea into his head, apparently, and perhaps it's not so farfetched as it seems, that a man suffering from a dangerous ailment or grave anxiety is allergic to other ailments and anxieties. 'Have you noticed,' he asked me, 'that no one ever runs two diseases at once? Let's suppose you have an incurable disease like cancer or a galloping consumption, well, you'll never get plague or typhus; it's a physical impossibility. In fact, one might go farther; have you ever heard of a man with cancer being killed in an auto smash?' This theory, for what it's worth, keeps Cottard cheerful. The thing he'd most detest is being cut off from others; he'd rather be one of a beleaguered crowd than a prisoner alone. The plague has put an effective stop to police inquiries, sleuthings, warrants of arrest, and so forth. Come to that, we have no police nowadays; no crimes past or present, no more criminals, only condemned men hoping for the most capricious of pardons; and among these are the police themselves."

Thus Cottard (if we may trust Tarrou's diagnosis) had good grounds for viewing the symptoms of mental confusion and distress in those around him with an understanding and an indulgent satisfaction that might have found expression in the remark: "Prate away, my friends, but I had it first!"

"When I suggested to him," Tarrou continues, "that the surest way of not being cut off from others was having a clean conscience, he frowned. 'If that is so, everyone's always cut off from everyone else.' And a moment later he added: 'Say what you like, Tarrou, but let me tell you this: the one way of making people hang together is to give 'em a spell of plague. You've only got to look around you.' Of course I see his point, and I understand how congenial our present mode of life must be to him. How could he fail to recognize at every turn reactions that were his; the efforts everyone makes to keep on the right side of other people; the obligingness sometimes shown in helping someone who has lost his way, and the ill humor shown at other times; the way people flock to the luxury restaurants, their pleasure at being there and their reluctance to leave; the crowds lining up daily at the picture-houses, filling theaters and music halls and even dance halls, and flooding boisterously out into the squares and avenues; the shrinking from every contact and, notwithstanding, the craving for human warmth that urges people to one another, body to body, sex to sex?

Cottard has been through all that obviously, with one exception; we may rule out women in his case. With that mug of his! And I should say that when tempted to visit a brothel he refrains; it might give him a bad name and be held up against him one day.

"In short, this epidemic has done him proud. Of a lonely man who hated loneliness it has made an accomplice. Yes, 'accomplice' is the word that fits, and doesn't he relish his complicity! He is happily at one with all around him, with their superstitions, their groundless panics, the susceptibilities of people whose nerves are always on the stretch; with their fixed idea of talking the least possible about plague and nevertheless talking of it all the time; with their abject terror at the slightest headache, now they know headache to be an early symptom of the disease; and, lastly, with their frayed, irritable sensibility that takes offense at trifling oversights and brings tears to their eyes over the loss of a trouser-button."

Tarrou often went out with Cottard in the evening, and he describes how they would plunge together into the dark crowds filling the streets at nightfall; how they mingled, shoulder to shoulder, in the black-and-white moving mass lit here and there by the fitful gleam of a street-lamp; and how they let themselves be swept along with the human herd toward resorts of pleasure whose companionable warmth seemed a safeguard from the plague's cold breath. What Cottard had some months previously been looking for in public places, luxury and the lavish life, the frenzied orgies he had dreamed of without being able to procure them, these were now the quest of a whole populace. Though prices soared inevitably, never had so much money been squandered, and while bare necessities were often lacking, never had so much been spent on superfluities. All the recreations of leisure, due though it now was to unemployment, multiplied a hundredfold. Sometimes Tarrou and Cottard would follow for some minutes one of those amorous couples who in the past would have tried to hide the passion drawing them to each other, but now, pressed closely to each other's side, paraded the streets among the crowd, with the trancelike self-absorption of great lovers, oblivious of the people around them.

Cottard watched them gloatingly. "Good work, my dears!" he'd exclaim. "Go to it!" Even his voice had changed, grown louder; as Tarrou wrote, he was "blossoming out" in the congenial atmosphere of mass excitement, fantastically large tips clinking on cafe tables, love-affairs shaping under his eyes.

However, Tarrou seemed to detect little if any spiteful-ness in Cottard's attitude. His "I've been through the mill myself" had more pity than triumph in it. "I suspect," Tarrou wrote, "that he's getting quite fond of these people shut up under their little patch of sky within their city walls. For instance, he'd like to explain to them, if he had a

chance, that it isn't so terrible as all that. 'You hear them saying,' he told me, ' "After the plague I'll do this or that."... They're eating their hearts out instead of staying put. And they don't even realize their privileges. Take my case: could I say "After my arrest I'll do this or that"? Arrest's a beginning, not an end. Whereas plague....

Do you know what I think? They're fretting simply because they won't let themselves go. And I know what I'm talking about.' "

"Yes, he knows what he's talking about," Tarrou added. "He has an insight into the anomalies in the lives of the people here who, though they have an instinctive craving for human contacts, can't bring themselves to yield to it, because of the mistrust that keeps them apart. For it's common knowledge that you can't trust your neighbor; he may pass the disease to you without your knowing it, and take advantage of a moment of inadvertence on your part to infect you. When one has spent one's days, as Cottard has, seeing a possible police spy in everyone, even in persons he feels drawn to, it's easy to understand this reaction. One can have fellow-feelings toward people who are haunted by the idea that when they least expect it plague may lay its cold hand on their shoulders, and is, perhaps, about to do so at the very moment when one is congratulating oneself on being safe and sound. So far as this is possible, he is at ease under a reign of terror. But I suspect that, just because he has been through it before them, he can't wholly share with them the agony of this feeling of uncertainty that never leaves them. It comes to this: like all of us who have not yet died of plague he fully realizes that his freedom and his life may be snatched from him at any moment. But since he, personally, has learned what it is to live in a state of constant fear, he finds it normal that others should come to know this state. Or perhaps it should be put like this: fear seems to him more bearable under these conditions than it was when he had to bear its burden alone. In this respect he's wrong, and this makes him harder to understand than other people. Still, after all, that's why he is worth a greater effort to understand."

Tarrou's notes end with a story illustrating the curious state of mind arrived at no less by Cottard than by other dwellers in the plague-stricken town. The story re-creates as nearly as may be the curiously feverish atmosphere of this period, and that is why the narrator attaches importance to it.

One evening Cottard and Tarrou went to the Municipal Opera House, where Gluck's Orpheus was being given. Cottard had invited Tarrou. A touring operatic company had come to Oran in the spring for a series of performances. Marooned there by the outbreak of plague and finding themselves in difficulties, the company and the management of the opera house had come to an agreement under which they were to give one performance a week until further notice. Thus for several months our theater had been resounding every Friday evening with the melodious laments of Orpheus and Eurydice's vain appeals. None the less, the opera continued in high favor and played regularly to full houses. From their seats, the most expensive, Cottard and Tarrou could look down at the orchestra seats filled to capacity with the cream of Oran society. It was interesting to see how careful they were, as they went to their places, to make an elegant entrance. While the musicians were discreetly tuning up, men in evening dress could be seen moving from one row to another, bowing gracefully to friends under the flood of light bathing the proscenium. In the soft hum of well-mannered conversation they regained the confidence denied them when they walked the dark streets of the town; evening dress was a sure charm against plague.

Throughout the first act Orpheus lamented suavely his lost Eurydice, with women in Grecian tunics singing melodious comments on his plight, and love was hymned in alternating strophes. The audience showed their appreciation in discreet applause. Only a few people noticed that in his song of the second act Orpheus introduced some tremolos not in the score and voiced an almost exaggerated emotion when begging the lord of the Underworld to be moved by his tears. Some rather jerky movements he indulged in gave our connoisseurs of stagecraft an impression of clever, if slightly overdone, effects, intended to bring out the emotion of the words he sang.

Not until the big duet between Orpheus and Eurydice in the third act, at the precise moment when Eurydice was slipping from her lover, did a flutter of surprise run through the house. And as though the singer had been waiting for this cue or, more likely, because the faint sounds that came to him from the orchestra seats confirmed what he was feeling, he chose this moment to stagger grotesquely to the footlights, his arms and legs splayed out under his antique robe, and fall down in the middle of the property sheepfold, always out of place, but now, in the eyes of the spectators, significantly, appallingly so.

For at the same moment the orchestra stopped playing, the audience rose and began to leave the auditorium, slowly and silently at first, like worshippers leaving church when the service ends, or a death-chamber after a farewell visit to the dead, women lifting their skirts and moving with bowed heads, men steering the ladies by the elbow to prevent their brushing against the tip-up seats at the ends of the rows. But gradually their movements quickened, whispers rose to exclamations, and finally the crowd stampeded toward the exits, wedged together in the bottlenecks, and pouring out into the street in a confused mass, with shrill cries of dismay.

Cottard and Tarrou, who had merely risen from their seats, gazed down at what was a dramatic picture of their life in those days: plague on the stage in the guise of a disarticulated mummer, and in the auditorium the toys of luxury, so futile now, forgotten fans and lace shawls derelict on the red plush seats.

DURING the first part of September Rambert had worked conscientiously at Rieux's side. He had merely asked for a few hours' leave on the day he was due to meet Gonzales and the two youngsters again outside the boys' school. Gonzales kept the appointment, at noon, and while he and the journalist were talking, they saw the two boys coming toward them, laughing. They said they'd had no luck last time, but that was only to be expected. Anyhow, it wasn't their turn for guard duty this week. Rambert must have patience till next week; then they'd have another shot at it. Rambert observed that "patience" certainly was needed in this business. Gonzales suggested they should all meet again on the following Monday, and this time Rambert had better move in to stay with Marcel and Louis.

"We'll make a date, you and I. If I don't turn up, go straight to their place.

I'll give you the address." But Marcel, or Louis, told him that the safest thing was to take his pal there right away, then he'd be sure of finding it. If he wasn't too particular, there was enough grub for the four of them. That way he'd get the hang of things. Gonzales agreed it was a good idea, and the four of them set off toward the harbor.

Marcel and Louis lived on the outskirts of the dockyard, near the gate leading to the cliff road. It was a small Spanish house with gaily painted shutters and bare, dark rooms. The boys' mother, a wrinkled old Spanish woman with a smiling face, produced a dish of which the chief ingredient was rice. Gonzales showed surprise, as rice had been unprocurable for some time in the town. "We fix it up at the gate," Marcel explained. Rambert ate and drank heartily, and Gonzales informed him he was "a damned good sort." Actually the journalist was thinking solely of the coming week.

It turned out that he had a fortnight to wait, as the periods of guard duty were extended to two weeks, to reduce the number of shifts. During that fortnight Rambert worked indefatigably, giving every ounce of himself, with his eyes shut, as it were, from dawn till night. He went to bed very late and always slept like a log. This abrupt transition from a life of idleness to one of constant work had left him almost void of thoughts or energy. He talked little about his impending escape. Only one incident is worth noting: after a week he confessed to the doctor that for the first time he'd got really drunk. It was the evening before; on leaving the bar he had an impression that his groin was swollen and he had pains in his armpits when he moved his arms. "I'm in for it!" he thought.

And his only reaction, an absurd one, as he frankly admitted to Rieux, had been to start running to the upper town and when he reached a small square, from which if not the sea, a fairly big patch of open sky could be seen, to call to his wife with a great cry, over the walls of the town. On returning home and failing to discover any symptoms of plague on his body, he had felt far from proud of having given way like that. Rieux, however, said he could well understand one's being moved to act thus. "Or, anyhow, one may easily feel inclined that way."

"Monsieur Othon was talking to me about you this morning," Rieux suddenly remarked, when Rambert was bidding him good night. "He asked me if I knew you, and I told him I did. Then he said: 'If he's a friend of yours advise him not to associate with smugglers. It's bound to attract attention.' "

"Meaning what?"

"It means you'd better hurry up."

"Thanks." Rambert shook the doctor's hand.

In the doorway he suddenly swung round. Rieux noticed that, for the first time since the outbreak of plague, he was smiling.

"Then why don't you stop my going? You could easily manage it."

Rieux shook his head with his usual deliberateness. It was none of his business, he said. Rambert had elected for happiness, and he, Rieux, had no argument to put up against him. Personally he felt incapable of deciding which was the right course and which the wrong in such a case as Rambert's.

"If that's so, why tell me to hurry up?"

It was Rieux who now smiled.

"Perhaps because I, too, would like to do my bit for happiness."

Next day, though they were working together most of the time, neither referred to the subject. On the following Sunday Rambert moved into the little Spanish house. He was given a bed in the living-room. As the brothers did not come home for meals and he'd been told to go out as little as possible, he was always alone but for occasional meetings with the boys' mother. She was a dried-up little wisp of a woman, always

dressed in black, busy as a bee, and she had a nut-brown, wrinkled face and immaculately white hair. No great-talker, she merely smiled genially when her eyes fell on Rambert.

On one of the few occasions when she spoke, it was to ask him if he wasn't afraid of infecting his wife with plague. He replied that there might be some risk of that, but only a very slight one; while if he stayed in the town, there was a fair chance of their never seeing each other again.

The old woman smiled. "Is she nice?"

"Very nice."

"Pretty?"

"I think so."

"Ah," she nodded, "that explains it."

Rambert reflected. No doubt that explained it, but it was impossible that that alone explained it.

The old woman went to Mass every morning. "Don't you believe in God?" she asked him.

On Rambert's admitting he did not, she said again that "that explained it."

"Yes," she added, "you're right. You must go back to her. Or else what would be left you?"

Rambert spent most of the day prowling round the room, gazing vaguely at the distempered walls, idly fingering the fans that were their only decoration, or counting the woollen balls on the tablecloth fringe. In the evening the youngsters came home; they hadn't much to say, except that the time hadn't come yet. After dinner Marcel played the guitar, and they drank an anise-flavored liqueur. Rambert seemed lost in thought.

On Wednesday Marcel announced: "It's for tomorrow night, at midnight. Be ready on time." Of the two men sharing the sentry post with them, he explained, one had got plague and the other, who had slept in the same room, was now under observation. Thus for two or three days Marcel and Louis would be alone at the post.

They'd fix up the final details in the course of the night, and he could count on them to see it through. Rambert thanked them.

"Pleased?" the old woman asked.

He said yes, but his thoughts were elsewhere.

The next day was very hot and muggy and a heat-mist veiled the sun. The total of deaths had jumped up. But the old Spanish woman lost nothing of her serenity.

"There's so much wickedness in the world," she said. "So what can you expect?"

Like Marcel and Louis, Rambert was stripped to the waist. But, even so, sweat was trickling down his chest and between his shoulder-blades. In the dim light of the shuttered room their torsos glowed like highly polished mahogany. Rambert kept prowling round like a caged animal, without speaking. Abruptly at four in the afternoon he announced that he was going out.

"Don't forget," Marcel said. "At midnight sharp. Everything's set."

Rambert went to the doctor's apartment. Rieux's mother told him he would find the doctor at the hospital in the upper town. As before, a crowd was circling in front of the entrance gates. "Move on, there!" a police sergeant with bulging eyes bawled every few minutes. And the crowd kept moving, but always in a circle. "No use hanging round here." The sergeant's coat was soaked in sweat. They knew it was "no use," but they stayed on, despite the devastating heat.

Rambert showed his pass to the sergeant, who told him to go to Tarrou's office.

Its door opened on the courtyard. He passed Father Paneloux, who was coming out of the office.

Tarrou was sitting at a black wood desk, with his sleeves rolled up, mopping up with his handkerchief a trickle of sweat in the bend of his arm. The office, a small, white-painted room, smelt of drugs and damp cloth.

"Still here?" asked Tarrou.

"Yes. I'd like to have a word with Rieux."

"He's in the ward. Look here! Don't you think you could fix up whatever you've come for without seeing him?"

"Why?"

"He's overdoing it. I spare him as much as I can."

Rambert gazed thoughtfully at Tarrou. He'd grown thinner, his eyes and features were blurred with fatigue, his broad shoulders sagged. There was a knock at the door. A male attendant, wearing a white mask, entered. He laid a little sheaf of cards on Tarrou's desk and, his voice coming thickly through the cloth, said:

"Six," then went out. Tarrou looked at the journalist and showed him the cards, spreading them fanwise.

"Neat little gadgets, aren't they? Well, they're deaths.

Last night's deaths." Frowning, he slipped the cards together. "The only thing that's left us is accountancy!"

Taking his purchase on the table, Tarrou rose to his feet.

"You're off quite soon, I take it?"

"Tonight, at midnight."

Tarrou said he was glad to hear it, and Rambert had better look after himself for a bit.

"Did you say that, sincerely?"

Tarrou shrugged his shoulders.

"At my age one's got to be sincere. Lying's too much effort."

"Excuse me, Tarrou," the journalist said, "but I'd greatly like to see the doctor."

"I know. He's more human than I. All right, come along."

"It's not that." Rambert stumbled over his words and broke off.

Tarrou stared at him; then, unexpectedly, his face broke into a smile.

They walked down a narrow passage; the walls were painted pale green, and the light was glaucous, like that in an aquarium. Before they reached the glazed double door at the end of the passage, behind which shadowy forms could be seen moving, Tarrou took Rambert into a small room, all the wall space of which was occupied by cupboards. Opening one of these, he took from a sterilizer two masks of cotton-wool enclosed in muslin, handed one to Rambert, and told him to put it on.

The journalist asked if it was really any use. Tarrou said no, but it inspired confidence in others.

They opened the glazed door. It led into a very large room, all the windows of which were shut, in spite of the great heat. Electric fans buzzed near the ceiling, churning up the stagnant, overheated air above two long rows of gray beds. Groans shrill or stifled rose on all sides, blending in a monotonous dirgelike refrain. Men in white moved slowly from bed to bed under the garish light flooding in from high, barred windows. The

appalling heat in the ward made Rambert ill at ease, and he had difficulty in recognizing Rieux, who was bending over a groaning form. The doctor was lancing the patient's groin, while two nurses, one on each side, held his legs apart. Presently Rieux straightened up, dropped his instruments into a tray that an attendant held out to him, and remained without moving for some moments, gazing down at the man, whose wound was now being dressed.

"Any news?" he asked Tarrou, who had come beside him.

"Paneloux is prepared to replace Rambert at the quarantine station. He has put in a lot of useful work already. All that remains is to reorganize group number three, now that Rambert's going."

Rieux nodded.

"Castel has his first lot of serum ready now," Tarrou continued. "He's in favor of its being tried at once."

"Good," Rieux said. "That's good news."

"And Rambert's come."

Rieux looked round. His eyes narrowed above the mask when he saw the journalist.

"Why have you come?" he asked. "Surely you should be elsewhere?"

Tarrou explained that it was fixed for midnight, to which Rambert added: "That's the idea, anyhow."

Whenever any of them spoke through the mask, the muslin bulged and grew moist over the lips. This gave a sort of unreality to the conversation; it was like a colloquy of statues.

"I'd like to have a word with you," Rambert said.

"Right. I'm just going. Wait for me in Tarrou's office."

A minute or so later Rambert and Rieux were sitting at the back of the doctor's car. Tarrou, who was at the wheel, looked round as he let in the gear.

"Gas is running out," he said. "We'll have to foot-slog it tomorrow."

"Doctor," Rambert said, "I'm not going. I want to stay with you."

Tarrou made no movement; he went on driving. Rieux seemed unable to shake off his fatigue.

"And what about her?" His voice was hardly audible.

Rambert said he'd thought it over very carefully, and his views hadn't changed, but if he went away, he would feel ashamed of himself, and that would embarrass his relations with the woman he loved.

Showing more animation, Rieux told him that was sheer nonsense; there was nothing shameful in preferring happiness.

"Certainly," Rambert replied. "But it may be shameful to be happy by oneself."

Tarrou, who had not spoken so far, now remarked, without turning his head, that if Rambert wished to take a share in other people's unhappiness, he'd have no time left for happiness. So the choice had to be made.

"That's not it," Rambert rejoined. "Until now I always felt a stranger in this town, and that I'd no concern with you people. But now that

I've seen what I have seen, I know that I belong here whether I want it or not. This business is everybody's business." When there was no reply from either of the others, Rambert seemed to grow annoyed. "But you know that as well as I do, damn it! Or else what are you up to in that hospital of yours? Have you made a definite choice and turned down happiness?"

Rieux and Tarrou still said nothing, and the silence lasted until they were at the doctor's home. Then Rambert repeated his last question in a yet more emphatic tone.

Only then Rieux turned toward him, raising himself with an effort from the cushion.

"Forgive me, Rambert, only, well, I simply don't know. But stay with us if you want to." A swerve of the car made him break off. Then, looking straight in front of him, he said: "For nothing in the world is it worth turning one's back on what one loves. Yet that is what I'm doing, though why I do not know."

He sank back on the cushion. "That's how it is," he added wearily, "and there's nothing to be done about it. So let's recognize the fact and draw the conclusions."

"What conclusions?"

"Ah," Rieux said, "a man can't cure and know at the same time. So let's cure as quickly as we can. That's the more urgent job."

At midnight Tarrou and Rieux were giving Rambert the map of the district he was to keep under surveillance. Tarrou glanced at his watch. Looking up, he met Rambert's gaze.

"Have you let them know?" he asked.

The journalist looked away.

"I'd sent them a note", he spoke with an effort, "before coming to see you."

Toward the close of October Castel's anti-plague serum was tried for the first time. Practically speaking, it was Rieux's last card. If it failed, the doctor was convinced the whole town would be at the mercy of the epidemic, which would either continue its ravages for an unpredictable period or perhaps die out abruptly of its own accord.

The day before Castel called on Rieux, M. Othon's son had fallen ill and all the family had to go into quarantine. Thus the mother, who had only recently come out of it, found herself isolated once again. In deference to the official regulations the magistrate had promptly sent for Dr. Rieux the moment he saw symptoms of the disease in his little boy. Mother and father were standing at the bedside when Rieux entered the room. The boy was in the phase of extreme prostration and submitted without a whimper to the doctor's examination. When Rieux raised his eyes he saw the magistrate's gaze intent on him, and, behind, the mother's pale face. She was holding a handkerchief to her mouth, and her big, dilated eyes followed each of the doctor's movements.

"He has it, I suppose?" the magistrate asked in a toneless voice.

"Yes." Rieux gazed down at the child again.

The mother's eyes widened yet more, but she still said nothing. M. Othon, too, kept silent for a while before saying in an even lower tone:

"Well, doctor, we must do as we are told to do."

Rieux avoided looking at Mme Othon, who was still holding her handkerchief to her mouth.

"It needn't take long," he said rather awkwardly, "if you'll let me use your phone."

The magistrate said he would take him to the telephone. But before going, the doctor turned toward Mme Othon.

"I regret very much indeed, but I'm afraid you'll have to get your things ready.

You know how it is."

Mme Othon seemed disconcerted. She was staring at the floor.

Then, "I understand," she murmured, slowly nodding her head. "I'll set about it at once."

Before leaving, Rieux on a sudden impulse asked the Othons if there wasn't anything they'd like him to do for them. The mother gazed at him in silence. And now the magistrate averted his eyes.

"No," he said, then swallowed hard. "But, save my son."

In the early days a mere formality, quarantine had now been reorganized by Rieux and Rambert on very strict lines.

In particular they insisted on having members of the family of a patient kept apart. If, unawares, one of them had been infected, the risks of an extension of the infection must not be multiplied. Rieux explained this to the magistrate, who signified his approval of the procedure. Nevertheless, he and his wife exchanged a glance that made it clear to Rieux how keenly they both felt the separation thus imposed on them. Mme Othon and her little girl could be given rooms in the quarantine hospital under Rambert's charge. For the magistrate, however, no accommodation was available except in an isolation camp the authorities were now installing in the municipal stadium, using tents supplied by the highway department. When Rieux apologized for the poor accommodation, M.

Othon replied that there was one rule for all alike, and it was only proper to abide by it.

The boy was taken to the auxiliary hospital and put in a ward of ten beds which had formerly been a classroom. After some twenty hours Rieux became convinced that the case was hopeless. The infection was steadily spreading, and the boy's body putting up no resistance. Tiny, half-formed, but acutely painful buboes were clogging the joints of the child's puny limbs. Obviously it was a losing fight.

Under the circumstances Rieux had no qualms about testing Castel's serum on the boy. That night, after dinner, they performed the inoculation, a lengthy process, without getting the slightest reaction. At daybreak on the following day they gathered round the bed to observe the effects of this test inoculation on which so much hung.

The child had come out of his extreme prostration and was tossing about convulsively on the bed. From four in the morning Dr. Castel and Tarrou had been keeping watch and noting, stage by stage, the progress and remissions of the malady. Tarrou's bulky form was slightly drooping at the head of the bed, while at its foot, with Rieux standing beside him, Castel was seated, reading, with every appearance of calm, an old leather-bound book. One by one, as the light increased in the former classroom, the others arrived. Paneloux, the first to come, leaned against the wall on the opposite side of the bed to Tarrou. His face was drawn with grief, and the accumulated weariness of many weeks, during which he had never spared himself, had deeply seamed his somewhat prominent forehead. Grand came next. It was seven o'clock, and he apologized for being out of breath; he could only stay a moment, but wanted to know if any definite results had been observed. Without speaking, Rieux pointed to the child. His eyes shut, his teeth clenched, his features frozen in an agonized grimace, he was rolling his head from side to side on the bolster. When there was just light enough to make out the half-obliterated figures of an equation chalked on a blackboard that still hung on the wall at the far end of the room, Rambert entered. Posting himself at the foot of the next bed, he took a package of cigarettes from his pocket. But after his first glance at the child's face he put it back.

From his chair Castel looked at Rieux over his spectacles.

"Any news of his father?"

"No," said Rieux. "He's in the isolation camp."

The doctor's hands were gripping the rail of the bed, his eyes fixed on the small tortured body. Suddenly it stiffened, and seemed to give a little at the waist, as slowly the arms and legs spread out X-wise. From the body, naked under an army blanket, rose a smell of damp wool and stale sweat. The boy had gritted his teeth again. Then very gradually he relaxed, bringing his arms and legs back toward the center of the bed, still without speaking or opening his eyes, and his breathing seemed to quicken. Rieux looked at Tarrou, who hastily lowered his eyes.

They had already seen children die, for many months now death had shown no favoritism, but they had never yet watched a child's agony minute by minute, as they had now been doing since daybreak. Needless to say, the pain inflicted on these innocent victims had always seemed to them to be what in fact it was: an abominable thing. But hitherto they had felt its abomination in, so to speak, an abstract way; they had never had to witness over so long a period the death-throes of an innocent child.

And just then the boy had a sudden spasm, as if something had bitten him in the stomach, and uttered a long, shrill wail. For moments that seemed endless he stayed in a queer, contorted position, his body racked by convulsive tremors; it was as if his frail frame were bending before the fierce breath of the plague, breaking under the reiterated gusts of fever. Then the storm-wind passed, there came a lull, and he relaxed a little; the fever seemed to recede, leaving him gasping for breath on a dank, pestilential shore, lost in a languor that already looked like death. When for the third time the fiery wave broke on him, lifting him a little, the child curled himself up and shrank away to the edge of the bed, as if in terror of the flames advancing on him, licking his limbs. A moment later, after tossing his head wildly to and fro, he flung off the blanket. From between the inflamed eyelids big tears welled up and trickled down the sunken, leaden-hued cheeks. When the spasm had passed, utterly exhausted, tensing his thin legs and arms, on which, within forty-eight hours, the flesh had wasted to the bone, the child lay flat, racked on the tumbled bed, in a grotesque parody of crucifixion.

Bending, Tarrou gently stroked with his big paw the small face stained with tears and sweat. Castel had closed his book a few moments before, and his eyes were now fixed on the child. He began to speak, but had to give a cough before continuing, because his voice rang out so harshly.

"There wasn't any remission this morning, was there, Rieux?"

Rieux shook his head, adding, however, that the child was putting up more resistance than one would have expected. Paneloux, who was slumped against the wall, said in a low voice:

"So if he is to die, he will have suffered longer." Light was increasing in the ward. The occupants of the other nine beds were tossing about and groaning, but in tones that seemed deliberately subdued. Only one, at the far end of the ward, was screaming, or rather uttering little exclamations at regular intervals, which seemed to convey surprise more than pain. Indeed, one had the impression that even for the sufferers the frantic terror of the early phase had passed, and there was a sort of mournful resignation in their present attitude toward the disease. Only the child went on fighting with all his little might. Now and then Rieux took his pulse, less because this served any purpose than as an escape from his utter helplessness, and when he closed his eyes, he seemed to feel its tumult mingling with the fever of his own blood. And then, at one with the tortured child, he struggled to sustain him with all the remaining strength of his own body. But, linked for a few moments, the rhythms of their heartbeats soon fell apart, the child escaped him, and again he knew his impotence. Then he released the small, thin wrist and moved back to his place. The light on the whitewashed walls was changing from pink to yellow. The first waves of another day of heat were beating on the windows. They hardly heard Grand saying he would come back as he turned to go. All were waiting. The child, his eyes still closed, seemed to grow a little calmer. His clawlike fingers were feebly plucking at the sides of the bed. Then they rose, scratched at the blanket over his knees, and suddenly he doubled up his limbs, bringing his thighs above his stomach, and remained quite still. For the first time he opened his eyes and gazed at Rieux, who was standing immediately in front of him. In the small face, rigid as a mask of grayish clay, slowly the lips parted and from them rose a long, incessant scream, hardly varying with his respiration, and filling the ward with a fierce, indignant protest, so little childish that it seemed like a collective voice issuing from all the sufferers there. Rieux clenched his jaws, Tarrou looked away. Rambert went and stood beside Castel, who closed the book lying on his knees. Paneloux gazed down at the small mouth, fouled with the sores of the plague and pouring out the angry death-cry that has sounded through the ages of mankind. He sank on his knees, and all present found it natural to hear him say in a voice hoarse but clearly audible across that nameless, never ending wail:

"My God, spare this child!"

But the wail continued without cease and the other sufferers began to grow restless. The patient at the far end of the ward, whose little broken cries had gone on without a break, now quickened their tempo so that they flowed together in one unbroken cry, while the others' groans grew louder. A gust of sobs swept through the room, drowning Paneloux's prayer, and Rieux, who was still tightly gripping the rail of the bed, shut his eyes, dazed with exhaustion and disgust.

When he opened them again, Tarrou was at his side.

"I must go," Rieux said. "I can't bear to hear them any longer."

But then, suddenly, the other sufferers fell silent. And now the doctor grew aware that the child's wail, after weakening more and more, had fluttered out into silence. Around him the groans began again, but more faintly, like a far echo of the fight that now was over. For it was over. Castel had moved round to the other side of the bed and said the end had come. His mouth still gaping, but silent now, the child was lying among the tumbled blankets, a small, shrunken form, with the tears still wet on his cheeks.

Paneloux went up to the bed and made the sign of benediction. Then gathering up his cassock, he walked out by the passage between the beds.

"Will you have to start it all over again?" Tarrou asked Castel.

The old doctor nodded slowly, with a twisted smile.

"Perhaps. After all, he put up a surprisingly long resistance."

Rieux was already on his way out, walking so quickly and with such a strange look on his face that Paneloux put out an arm to check him when he was about to pass him in the doorway.

"Come, doctor," he began.

Rieux swung round on him fiercely.

"Ah! That child, anyhow, was innocent, and you know it as well as I do!"

He strode on, brushing past Paneloux, and walked across the school playground.

Sitting on a wooden bench under the dingy, stunted trees, he wiped off the sweat that was beginning to run into his eyes. He felt like shouting imprecations, anything to loosen the stranglehold lashing his heart with steel. Heat was flooding down between the branches of the fig trees. A white haze, spreading rapidly over the blue of the morning sky, made the air yet more stifling. Rieux lay back wearily on the bench. Gazing up at the ragged branches, the shimmering sky, he slowly got back his breath and fought down his fatigue.

He heard a voice behind him. "Why was there that anger in your voice just now?

What we'd been seeing was as unbearable to me as it was to you."

Rieux turned toward Paneloux.

"I know. I'm sorry. But weariness is a kind of madness. And there are times when the only feeling I have is one of mad revolt."

"I understand," Paneloux said in a low voice. "That sort of thing is revolting because it passes our human understanding. But perhaps we should love what we cannot understand."

Rieux straightened up slowly. He gazed at Paneloux, summoning to his gaze all the strength and fervor he could muster against his weariness. Then he shook his head.

"No, Father. I've a very different idea of love. And until my dying day I shall refuse to love a scheme of things in which children are put to torture."

A shade of disquietude crossed the priest's face. "Ah, doctor," he said sadly, "I've just realized what is meant by 'grace.'"

Rieux had sunk back again on the bench. His lassitude had returned and from its depths he spoke, more gently:

"It's something I haven't got; that I know. But I'd rather not discuss that with you. We're working side by side for something that unites us, beyond blasphemy and prayers. And it's the only thing that matters."

Paneloux sat down beside Rieux. It was obvious that he was deeply moved.

"Yes, yes," he said, "you, too, are working for man's salvation."

Rieux tried to smile.

"Salvation's much too big a word for me. I don't aim so high. I'm concerned with man's health; and for me his health comes first."

Paneloux seemed to hesitate. "Doctor?" he began, then fell silent. Down his face, too, sweat was trickling. Murmuring: "Good-by for the present," he rose.

His eyes were moist. When he turned to go, Rieux, who had seemed lost in thought, suddenly rose and took a step toward him.

"Again, please forgive me. I can promise there won't be another outburst of that kind."

Paneloux held out his hand, saying regretfully:

"And yet, I haven't convinced you!"

"What does it matter? What I hate is death and disease, as you well know. And whether you wish it or not, we're allies, facing them and fighting them together." Rieux was still holding Paneloux's hand. "So you see", but he refrained from meeting the priest's eyes, "God Himself can't part us now."

Since joining Rieux's band of workers Paneloux had spent his entire time in hospitals and places where he came in contact with plague. He had elected for the place among his fellow workers that he judged incumbent on him, in the forefront of the fight. And constantly since then he had rubbed shoulders with death. Though theoretically immunized by periodical inoculations, he was well aware that at any moment death might claim him too, and he had given thought to this. Outwardly he had lost nothing of his serenity. But from the day on which he saw a child die, something seemed to change in him. And his face bore traces of the rising tension of his thoughts. When one day he told Rieux with a smile that he was working on a short essay entitled "Is a Priest Justified in Consulting a Doctor?" Rieux had gathered that something graver lay behind the question than the priest's tone seemed to imply. On the doctor's saying he would greatly like to have a look at the essay, Paneloux informed him that he would shortly be preaching at a Mass for men, and his sermon would convey some at least of his considered opinions on the question.

"I hope you'll come, doctor. The subject will interest you.".

A high wind was blowing on the day Father Paneloux preached his second sermon.

The congregation, it must be admitted, was sparser than on the first occasion, partly because this kind of performance had lost its novelty for our townsfolk.

Indeed, considering the abnormal conditions they were up against, the very word "novelty" had lost all meaning. Moreover, most people, assuming they had not altogether abandoned religious observances, or did not combine them naively with a thoroughly immoral way of living, had replaced normal religious practice by more or less extravagant superstitions. Thus they were readier to wear prophylactic medals of St. Roch than to go to Mass.

An illustration may be found in the remarkable interest shown in prophecies of all descriptions. True, in the spring, when the epidemic was expected to end abruptly at any moment, no one troubled to take another's opinion as to its probable duration, since everyone had persuaded himself that it would have none.

But as the days went by, a fear grew up that the calamity might last indefinitely, and then the ending of the plague became the target of all hopes.

As a result copies of predictions attributed to soothsayers or saints of the Catholic Church circulated freely from hand to hand. The local printing firms were quick to realize the profit to be made by pandering to this new craze and printed large numbers of the prophecies that had been going round in manuscript.

Finding that the public appetite for this type of literature was still unsated, they had researches made in the municipal libraries for all the mental pabulum of the kind available in old chronicles, memoirs, and the like. And when this source ran dry, they commissioned journalists to write up forecasts, and, in this respect at least, the journalists proved themselves equal to their prototypes of earlier ages.

Some of these prophetic writings were actually serialized in our newspapers and read with as much avidity as the love-stories that had occupied these columns in the piping times of health. Some predictions were based on far-fetched arithmetical calculations, involving the figures of the year, the total of deaths, and the number of months the plague had so far lasted. Others made comparisons with the great pestilences of former times, drew parallels (which the forecasters called "constants"), and claimed to deduce conclusions bearing on the present calamity. But our most popular prophets were undoubtedly those who in an apocalyptic jargon had announced sequences of events, any one of which might be construed as applicable to the present state of affairs and was abstruse enough to admit of almost any interpretation. Thus Nostradamus and St. Odilia were consulted daily, and always with happy results.

Indeed, the one thing these prophecies had in common was that, ultimately, all were reassuring. Unfortunately, though, the plague was not.

Thus superstition had usurped the place of religion in the life of our town, and that is why the church in which Paneloux preached his sermon was only three-quarters full. That evening, when Rieux arrived, the wind was pouring in great gusts through the swing-doors and filling the aisles with sudden drafts. And it was in a cold, silent church, surrounded by a congregation of men exclusively, that Rieux watched the Father climb into the pulpit. He spoke in a gender, more thoughtful tone than on the previous occasion, and several times was noticed to be stumbling over his words. A yet more noteworthy change was that instead of saying "you" he now said "we."

However, his voice grew gradually firmer as he proceeded. He started by recalling that for many a long month plague had been in our midst, and we now knew it better, after having seen it often seated at our tables or at the bedsides of those we loved. We had seen it walking at our side, or waiting for our coming at the places where we worked. Thus we were now, perhaps, better able to comprehend what it was telling us unceasingly; a message to which, in the first shock of the visitation, we might not have listened with due heed. What he, Father Paneloux, had said in his first sermon still held good, such, anyhow, was his belief. And yet, perhaps, as may befall any one of us (here he struck his breast), his words and thoughts had lacked in charity. However this might be, one thing was not to be gainsaid; a fact that always, under all circumstances, we should bear in mind.

Appearances notwithstanding, all trials, however cruel, worked together for good to the Christian. And, indeed, what a Christian should always seek in his hour of trial was to discern that good, in what it consisted and how best he could turn it to account.

At this stage the people near Rieux seemed to settle in against the arm-rests of their pews and make themselves as comfortable as they could. One of the big padded entrance doors was softly thudding in the wind, and someone got up to secure it. As a result, Rieux's attention wandered and he did not follow well what Paneloux now went on to say. Apparently it came to this: we might try to explain the phenomenon of the plague, but, above all, should learn what it had to teach us. Rieux gathered that, to the Father's thinking, there was really nothing to explain.

His interest quickened when, in a more emphatic tone, the preacher said that there were some things we could grasp as touching God, and others we could not.

There was no doubt as to the existence of good and evil and, as a rule, it was easy to see the difference between them. The difficulty began when we looked into the nature of evil, and among things evil he included human suffering. Thus we had apparently needful pain, and apparently needless pain; we had Don Juan cast into hell, and a child's death. For while it is right that a libertine should be struck down, we see no reason for a child's suffering. And, truth to tell, nothing was more important on earth than a child's suffering, the horror it inspires in us, and the reasons we must find to account for it. In other manifestations of life God made things easy for us and, thus far, our religion had no

merit. But in this respect He put us, so to speak, with our backs to the wall. Indeed, we all were up against the wall that plague had built around us, and in its lethal shadow we must work out our salvation. He, Father Paneloux, refused to have recourse to simple devices enabling him to scale that wall. Thus he might easily have assured them that the child's sufferings would be compensated for by an eternity of bliss awaiting him. But how could he give that assurance when, to tell the truth, he knew nothing about it? For who would dare to assert that eternal happiness can compensate for a single moment's human suffering? He who asserted that would not be a true Christian, a follower of the Master who knew all the pangs of suffering in his body and his soul. No, he, Father Paneloux, would keep faith with that great symbol of all suffering, the tortured body on the Cross; he would stand fast, his back to the wall, and face honestly the terrible problem of a child's agony. And he would boldly say to those who listened to his words today: "My brothers, a time of testing has come for us all. We must believe everything or deny everything. And who among you, I ask, would dare to deny everything?"

It crossed Rieux's mind that Father Paneloux was dallying with heresy in speaking thus, but he had no time to follow up the thought. The preacher was declaring vehemently that this uncompromising duty laid on the Christian was at once his ruling virtue and his privilege. He was well aware that certain minds, schooled to a more indulgent and conventional morality, might well be dismayed, not to say outraged, by the seemingly excessive standard of Christian virtue about which he was going to speak. But religion in a time of plague could not be the religion of every day. While God might accept and even desire that the soul should take its ease and rejoice in happier times, in periods of extreme calamity He laid extreme demands on it. Thus today God had vouchsafed to His creatures an ordeal such that they must acquire and practice the greatest of all virtues: that of the All or Nothing.

Many centuries previously a profane writer had claimed to reveal a secret of the Church by declaring that purgatory did not exist. He wished to convey that there could be no half measures, there was only the alternative between heaven and hell; you were either saved or damned. That, according to Paneloux, was a heresy that could spring only from a blind, disordered soul. Nevertheless, there may well have been periods of history when purgatory could not be hoped for; periods when it was impossible to speak of venial sin. Every sin was deadly, and any indifference criminal. It was all or it was nothing.

The preacher paused, and Rieux heard more clearly the whistling of the wind outside; judging by the sounds that came in below the closed doors, it had risen to storm pitch. Then he heard Father Paneloux's voice again. He was saying that the total acceptance of which he had been speaking was not to be taken in the limited sense usually given to the words; he was not thinking of mere resignation or even of that harder virtue, humility. It involved humiliation, but a humiliation to which the person humiliated gave full assent. True, the agony of a child was humiliating to the heart and to the mind. But that was why we had to come to terms with it. And that, too, was why, and here Paneloux assured those present that it was not easy to say what he was about to say, since it was God's will, we, too, should will it. Thus and thus only the Christian could face the problem squarely and, scorning subterfuge, pierce to the heart of the supreme issue, the essential choice. And his choice would be to believe everything, so as not to be forced into denying everything. Like those worthy women who, after learning that buboes were the natural issues through which the body cast out infection, went to their church and

prayed: "Please, God, give him buboes," thus the Christian should yield himself wholly to the divine will, even though it passed his understanding. It was wrong to say: "This I understand, but that I cannot accept"; we must go straight to the heart of that which is unacceptable, precisely because it is thus that we are constrained to make our choice. The sufferings of children were our bread of affliction, but without this bread our souls would die of spiritual hunger.

The shuffling sounds which usually followed the moment when the preacher paused were beginning to make themselves heard when, unexpectedly, he raised his voice, making as if to put himself in his hearers' place and ask what then was the proper course to follow. He made no doubt that the ugly word "fatalism" would be applied to what he said. Well, he would not boggle at the word, provided he were allowed to qualify it with the adjective "active." Needless to say, there was no question of imitating the Abyssinian Christians of whom he had spoken previously. Nor should one even think of acting like those Persians who in time of plague threw their infected garments on the Christian sanitary workers and loudly called on Heaven to give the plague to these infidels who were trying to avert a pestilence sent by God. But, on the other hand, it would be no less wrong to imitate the monks at Cairo who, when plague was raging in the town, distributed the Host with pincers at the Mass, so as to avoid contact with wet, warm mouths in which infection might be latent. The plague-stricken Persians and the monks were equally at fault. For the former a child's agony did not count; with the latter, on the contrary, the natural dread of suffering ranked highest in their conduct. In both cases the real problem had been shirked; they had closed their ears to God's voice.

But, Paneloux continued, there were other precedents of which he would now remind them. If the chronicles of the Black Death at Marseille were to be trusted, only four of the eighty-one monks in the Mercy Monastery survived the epidemic. And of these four three took to flight. Thus far the chronicler, and it was not his task to tell us more than the bare facts. But when he read that chronicle, Father Paneloux had found his thoughts fixed on that monk who stayed on by himself, despite the death of his seventy-seven companions, and, above all, despite the example of his three brothers who had fled. And, bringing down his fist on the edge of the pulpit, Father Paneloux cried in a ringing voice:

"My brothers, each one of us must be the one who stays!" There was no question of not taking precautions or failing to comply with the orders wisely promulgated for the public weal in the disorders of a pestilence. Nor should we listen to certain moralists who told us to sink on our knees and give up the struggle. No, we should go forward, groping our way through the darkness, stumbling perhaps at times, and try to do what good lay in our power. As for the rest, we must hold fast, trusting in the divine goodness, even as to the deaths of little children, and not seeking personal respite.

At this point Father Paneloux evoked the august figure of Bishop Belzunce during the Marseille plague. He reminded his hearers how, toward the close of the epidemic, the Bishop, having done all that it behooved him, shut himself up in his palace, behind high walls, after laying in a stock of food and drink. With a sudden revulsion of feeling, such as often comes in times of extreme tribulation, the inhabitants of Marseille, who had idolized him hitherto, now turned against him, piled up corpses round his house in order to infect it, and even flung bodies over the walls to make sure of his death. Thus in a moment of weakness the Bishop had proposed to isolate himself from the outside world,

and, lo and behold, corpses rained down on his head! This had a lesson for us all; we must convince ourselves that there is no island of escape in time of plague. No, there was no middle course. We must accept the dilemma and choose either to hate God or to love God. And who would dare to choose to hate Him?

"My brothers", the preacher's tone showed he was nearing the conclusion of his sermon, "the love of God is a hard love. It demands total self-surrender, disdain of our human personality. And yet it alone can reconcile us to suffering and the deaths of children, it alone can justify them, since we cannot understand them, and we can only make God's will ours. That is the hard lesson I would share with you today. That is the faith, cruel in men's eyes, and crucial in God's, which we must ever strive to compass. We must aspire beyond ourselves toward that high and fearful vision. And on that lofty plane all will fall into place, all discords be resolved, and truth flash forth from the dark cloud of seeming injustice. Thus in some churches of the south of France plague victims have lain sleeping many a century under the flagstones of the chancel, and priests now speak above their tombs, and the divine message they bring to men rises from that charnel, to which, nevertheless, children have contributed their share."

When Rieux was preparing to leave the church a violent gust swept up the nave through the half-open doors and buffeted the faces of the departing congregation. It brought with it a smell of rain, a tang of drenched sidewalks, warning them of the weather they would encounter outside. An old priest and a young deacon who were walking immediately in front of Rieux had much difficulty in keeping their headdress from blowing away. But this did not prevent the elder of the two from discussing the sermon they had heard. He paid tribute to the preacher's eloquence, but the boldness of thought Paneloux had shown gave him pause. In his opinion the sermon had displayed more uneasiness than real power, and at Paneloux's age a priest had no business to feel uneasy. The young deacon, his head bowed to protect his face from the wind, replied that he saw much of the Father, had followed the evolution of his views, and believed his forthcoming pamphlet would be bolder still; indeed it might well be refused the imprimatur.

"You don't mean to say so! What's the main idea?" asked the old priest.

They were now in the Cathedral square and for some moments the roar of the wind made it impossible for the younger man to speak. When there was a slight lull, he said briefly to his companion:

"That it's illogical for a priest to call in a doctor."

Tarrou, when told by Rieux what Paneloux had said, remarked that he'd known a priest who had lost his faith during the war, as the result of seeing a young man's face with both eyes destroyed.

"Paneloux is right," Tarrou continued. "When an innocent youth can have his eyes destroyed, a Christian should either lose his faith or consent to having his eyes destroyed. Paneloux declines to lose his faith, and he will go through with it to the end. That's what he meant to say."

It may be that this remark of Tarrou's throws some light on the regrettable events which followed, in the course of which the priest's conduct seemed inexplicable to his friends. The reader will judge for himself.

A few days after the sermon Paneloux had to move out of his rooms. It was a time when many people were obliged to change their residence owing to the new conditions created by the plague. Thus Tarrou, when his hotel was requisitioned, had gone to live with Rieux, and now the Father had to vacate the lodgings provided for him by his Order and stay in the house of a pious old lady who had so far escaped the epidemic. During the process of moving, Paneloux had been feeling more run down than ever, mentally as well as physically. And it was this that put him in the bad books of his hostess. One evening when she was enthusiastically vaunting the merits of St. Odilia's prophecies, the priest betrayed a slight impatience, due probably to fatigue. All his subsequent efforts to bring the good lady round to, anyhow, a state of benevolent neutrality came to nothing. He had made a bad impression and it went on rankling. So each night on his way to his bedroom, where almost all the furniture was dotted with crochet covers, he had to contemplate the back of his hostess seated in her drawing-room and carry away with him a memory of the sour "Good night, Father," she flung at him over her shoulder. It was on one such evening that he felt, like a flood bursting the dikes, the turbulent onrush in his wrists and temples of the fever latent in his blood for several days past.

The only available account of what followed comes from the lips of the old lady.

Next morning she rose early, as was her wont. After an hour or so, puzzled at not seeing the Father leave his room, she brought herself, not without some hesitation, to knock at his door. She found him still in bed after a sleepless night. He had difficulty in breathing and looked more flushed than usual. She had suggested most politely (as she put it) that a doctor should be called in, but her suggestion had been brushed aside with a curtness that she described as "quite unmannerly." So she had no alternative but to. leave the room. Later in the morning the Father rang and asked if he could see her. He apologized for his lack of courtesy and assured her that what he was suffering from could not be plague, as he had none of the symptoms; it was no more than a passing indisposition. The lady replied with dignity that her suggestion had not been prompted by any apprehension of that sort, she took no thought for her personal security, which was in God's hands, but that she felt a certain measure of responsibility for the Father's welfare while he was under her roof. When he said nothing, his hostess, wishing (according to her account) to do her duty by him, offered to send for her doctor. Father Paneloux told her not to trouble, adding some explanations that seemed to the old lady incoherent, not to say nonsensical.

The only thing she gathered, and it was precisely this that appeared to her so incomprehensible, was that the Father refused to hear of a doctor's visit because it was against his principles. Her impression was that her guest's mind had been unhinged by fever, and she confined herself to bringing him a cup of tea.

Resolutely mindful of the obligations imposed on her by the situation, she visited the invalid regularly every two hours. What struck her most about him was his restlessness, which continued throughout the day. He would throw off the blankets, then pull them back, and he kept running his hand over his forehead, which was glistening with sweat. Every now and then he sat up in bed and tried to clear his throat with a thick, grating cough, which sounded almost like retching. At these moments he seemed to be vainly struggling to force up from his lungs a clot of some semi-solid substance that was choking him. After each unavailing effort, he sank back, utterly exhausted, on the pillow. Then he would raise himself again a little and stare straight in front of him with a fixity even more dismaying than the paroxysms which had preceded it. Even now the old lady

was reluctant to annoy her guest by calling in the doctor. After all, it might be no more than an attack of fever, spectacular as were its manifestations.

However, in the afternoon she made another attempt to talk to the priest, but she could get out of him no more than a few rambling phrases. She renewed her proposal to call in the doctor. Whereat Paneloux sat up and in a stifled voice emphatically declined to see a doctor. Under these circumstances it seemed best to the old lady to wait till the following morning; if the Father's condition showed no more improvement she would ring up the number announced ten times daily on the radio by the Ransdoc Information Bureau. Still conscious of her obligations, she resolved to visit the invalid from time to time in the course of the night and give him any attention he might need. But after bringing him a decoction of herbal tea she decided to lie down for a while. Only at daybreak did she wake up, and then she hurried to the priest's room.

Father Paneloux was lying quite still; his face had lost its deep flush of the previous day and had now a deathly pallor, all the more impressive because the cheeks had kept their fullness. He was gazing up at the bead fringe of a lamp hanging above the bed. When the old lady came in he turned his head to her. As she quaintly put it, he looked as if he'd been severely thrashed all the night long, and more dead than alive. She was greatly struck by the apathy of his voice when, on her asking how he was feeling, he replied that he was in a bad way, he did not need a doctor, and all he wished was to be taken to the hospital, so as to comply with the regulations. Panic-stricken, she hurried to the telephone.

Rieux came at noon. After hearing what the old lady had to say he replied briefly that Paneloux was right, but it was probably too late. The Father welcomed him with the same air of complete indifference. Rieux examined him and was surprised to find none of the characteristic symptoms of bubonic or pneumonic plague, except congestion and obstruction of the lungs. But his pulse was so weak and his general state so alarming that there was little hope of saving him.

"You have none of the specific symptoms of the disease," Rieux told him. "But I admit one can't be sure, and I must isolate you."

The Father smiled queerly, as if for politeness' sake, but said nothing. Rieux left the room to telephone, then came back and looked at the priest.

"I'll stay with you," he said gently.

Paneloux showed a little more animation and a sort of warmth came back to his eyes when he looked up at the doctor. Then, speaking with such difficulty that it was impossible to tell if there was sadness in his voice, he said:

"Thanks. But priests can have no friends. They have given their all to God."

He asked for the crucifix that hung above the head of the bed; when given it, he turned away to gaze at it.

At the hospital Paneloux did not utter a word. He submitted passively to the treatment given him, but never let go of the crucifix. However, his case continued doubtful, and Rieux could not feel sure how to diagnose it. For several weeks, indeed, the disease had seemed to make a point of confounding diagnoses. In the case of Paneloux, what followed was to show that this uncertainty had no consequence.

His temperature rose. Throughout the day the cough grew louder, racking the enfeebled body. At last, at nightfall, Father Paneloux brought up the clot of matter that was choking him; it was red. Even at the height of his fever Paneloux's eyes kept their

blank serenity, and when, next morning, he was found dead, his body drooping over the bedside, they betrayed nothing. Against his name the index card recorded: "Doubtful case."

All Souls' Day that year was very different from what it had been in former years. True, the weather was seasonable; there had been sudden change, and the great heat had given place to mild autumnal air. As in other years a cool wind blew all day, and big clouds raced from one horizon to the other, trailing shadows over the houses upon which fell again, when they had passed, the pale gold light of a November sky.

The first waterproofs made their appearance. Indeed, one was struck by the number of glossy, rubberized garments to be seen. The reason was that our newspapers had informed us that two hundred years previously, during the great pestilences of southern Europe, the doctors wore oiled clothing as a safeguard against infection. The shops had seized this opportunity of unloading their stock of out-of-fashion waterproofs, which their purchasers fondly hoped would guarantee immunity from germs.

But these familiar aspects of All Souls' Day could not make us forget that the cemeteries were left unvisited. In previous years the rather sickly smell of chrysanthemums had filled the streetcars, while long lines of women could be seen making pilgrimage to the places where members of the family were buried, to lay flowers on the graves. This was the day when they made amends for the oblivion and dereliction in which their dead had slept for many a long month.

But in the plague year people no longer wished to be reminded of their dead.

Because, indeed, they were thinking all too much about them as it was. There was no more question of revisiting them with a shade of regret and much melancholy.

They were no longer the forsaken to whom, one day in the year, you came to justify yourself. They were intruders whom you would rather forget. This is why the Day of the Dead this year was tacitly but willfully ignored. As Cottard dryly remarked, Tarrou noted that the habit of irony was growing on him more and more, each day was for us a Day of the Dead.

And, in fact, the balefires of the pestilence were blazing ever more merrily in the crematorium. It is true that the actual number of deaths showed no increase.

But it seemed that plague had settled in for good at its most virulent, and it took its daily toll of deaths with the punctual zeal of a good civil servant.

Theoretically, and in the view of the authorities, this was a hopeful sign. The fact that the graph after its long rising curve had flattened out seemed to many, Dr. Richard for example, reassuring. "The graph's good today," he would remark, rubbing his hands. To his mind the disease had reached what he called high-water mark. Thereafter it could but ebb. He gave the credit of this to Dr.

Castel's new serum, which, indeed, had brought off some quite unlooked-for recoveries. While not dissenting, the old doctor reminded him that the future remained uncertain; history proved that epidemics have a way of recrudescing when least expected. The authorities, who had long been desirous of giving a fillip to the morale of the populace, but had so far been prevented by the plague from doing so, now proposed to convene a meeting of the medical corps and ask for an announcement on the subject. Unfortunately, just before the meeting was due to take place, Dr. Richard, too, was carried off by the plague, then precisely at "high-water mark."

The effect of this regrettable event, which, sensational as it was, actually proved nothing, was to make our authorities swing back to pessimism as inconsequently as they had previously indulged in optimism. As for Castel, he confined himself to preparing his serums with the maximum of care. By this time no public place or building had escaped conversion into a hospital or quarantine camp with the exception of the Prefect's offices, which were needed for administrative purposes and committee meetings. In a general way, however, owing to the relative stability of the epidemic at this time, Rieux's organizations were still able to cope with the situation. Though working constantly at high pressure, the doctors and their helpers were not forced to contemplate still greater efforts. All they had to do was to carry on automatically, so to speak, their all but superhuman task. The pneumonic type of infection, cases of which had already been detected, was now spreading all over the town; one could almost believe that the high winds were kindling and fanning its flames in people's chests. The victims of pneumonic plague succumbed much more quickly, after coughing up blood-stained sputum. This new form of the epidemic looked like being more contagious as well as even more fatal. However, the opinions of experts had always been divided on this matter. For greater safety all sanitary workers wore masks of sterilized muslin. On the face of it, the disease should have extended its ravages. But, the cases of bubonic plague showing a decrease, the death-rate remained constant.

Meanwhile the authorities had another cause for anxiety in the difficulty of maintaining the food-supply. Profiteers were taking a hand and purveying at enormous prices essential foodstuffs not available in the shops. The result was that poor families were in great straits, while the rich went short of practically nothing. Thus, whereas plague by its impartial ministrations should have promoted equality among our townsfolk, it now had the opposite effect and, thanks to the habitual conflict of cupidities, exacerbated the sense of injustice rankling in men's hearts. They were assured, of course, of the inerrable equality of death, but nobody wanted that kind of equality.

Poor people who were feeling the pinch thought still more nostalgically of towns and villages in the near-by countryside, where bread was cheap and life without restrictions. Indeed, they had a natural if illogical feeling that they should have been permitted to move out to these happier places. The feeling was embodied in a slogan shouted in the streets and chalked up on walls: "Bread or fresh air!" This half-ironical battle-cry was the signal for some demonstrations that, though easily repressed, made everyone aware that an ugly mood was developing among us.

The newspapers, needless to say, complied with the instructions given them: optimism at all costs. If one was to believe what one read in them, our populace was giving "a fine example of courage and composure." But in a town thrown back upon itself, in which nothing could be kept secret, no one had illusions about the "example" given by the public. To form a correct idea about the courage and composure talked about by our journalists you had only to visit one of the quarantine depots or isolation camps established by our authorities. As it so happens, the narrator, being fully occupied elsewhere, had no occasion to visit any of them, and must fall back on Tarrou's diary for a description of the conditions in these places.

Tarrou gives an account of a visit he made, accompanied by Rambert, to the camp located in the municipal stadium.

The stadium lies on the outskirts of the town, between a street along which runs a car line and a stretch of waste land extending to the extreme edge of the plateau on which Oran is built. It was already surrounded by high concrete walls and all that was needed to make escape practically impossible was to post sentries at the four entrance gates. The walls served another purpose: they screened the unfortunates in quarantine from the view of people on the road.

Against this advantage may be set the fact that the inmates could hear all day, though they could not see them, the passing streetcars, and recognize by the increased volume of sound coming from the road the hours when people had knocked off work or were going to it. And this brought home to them that the life from which they were debarred was going on as before, within a few yards of them, and that those high walls parted two worlds as alien to each other as two different planets.

Tarrou and Rambert chose a Sunday afternoon for their visit to the stadium. They were accompanied by Gonzales, the football-player, with whom Rambert had kept in contact and who had let himself be persuaded into undertaking, in rotation with others, the surveillance of the camp. This visit was to enable Rambert to introduce Gonzales to the camp commandant. When they met that afternoon, Gonzales's first remark was that this was exactly the time when, before the plague, he used to start getting into his football togs. Now that the sports fields had been requisitioned, all that was of the past, and Gonzales was feeling, and showed it, at a loose end. This was one of the reasons why he had accepted the post proposed by Rambert, but he made it a condition that he was to be on duty during week-ends only.

The sky was overcast and, glancing up at it, Gonzales observed regretfully that a day like this, neither too hot nor rainy, would have been perfect for a game.

And then he fell to conjuring up, as best he could, the once familiar smell of embrocation in the dressing-rooms, the stands crowded with people, the colored shirts of the players, showing up brightly against the tawny soil, the lemons at intermission or bottled lemonade that titillated parched throats with a thousand refreshing pin-pricks. Tarrou also records how on the way, as they walked the shabby outer streets, the footballer gave kicks to all the small loose stones. His object was to shoot them into the sewer-holes of the gutters, and whenever he did this, he would shout: "Goal!" When he had finished his cigarette he spat the stub in front of him and tried to catch it on his toe before it touched the ground. Some children were playing near the stadium, and when one of them sent a ball toward the three men, Gonzales went out of his way to return it neatly.

On entering the stadium they found the stands full of people. The field was dotted with several hundred red tents, inside which one had glimpses of bedding and bundles of clothes or rugs. The stands had been kept open for the use of the internees in hot or rainy weather. But it was a rule of the camp that everyone must be in his tent at sunset. Shower-baths had been installed under the stands, and what used to be the players' dressing-rooms converted into offices and infirmaries. The majority of the inmates of the camp were sitting about on the stands. Some, however, were strolling on the touchlines, and a few, squatting at the entrances of their tents, were listlessly contemplating the scene around them. In the stands many of those slumped on the wooden tiers had a look of vague expectancy.

"What do they do with themselves all day?" Tarrou asked Rambert.

"Nothing."

Almost all, indeed, had empty hands and idly dangling arms. Another curious thing about this multitude of derelicts was its silence.

"When they first came there was such a din you couldn't hear yourself speak,"

Rambert said. "But as the days went by they grew quieter and quieter."

In his notes Tarrou gives what to his mind would explain this change. He pictures them in the early days bundled together in the tents, listening to the buzz of flies, scratching themselves, and, whenever they found an obliging listener, shrilly voicing their fear or indignation. But when the camp grew overcrowded, fewer and fewer people were inclined to play the part of sympathetic listener. So they had no choice but to hold their peace and nurse their mistrust of everything and everyone. One had, indeed, a feeling that suspicion was falling, dewlike, from the grayly shining sky over the brick-red camp.

Yes, there was suspicion in the eyes of all. Obviously, they were thinking, there must be some good reason for the isolation inflicted on them, and they had the air of people who are puzzling over their problem and are afraid. Everyone Tarrou set eyes on had that vacant gaze and was visibly suffering from the complete break with all that life had meant to him. And since they could not be thinking of their death all the time, they thought of nothing. They were on vacation.

"But worst of all," Tarrou writes, "is that they're forgotten, and they know it.

Their friends have forgotten them because they have other things to think about, naturally enough. And those they love have forgotten them because all their energies are devoted to making schemes and taking steps to get them out of the camp. And by dint of always thinking about these schemes and steps they have ceased thinking about those whose release they're trying to secure. And that, too, is natural enough. In fact, it comes to this: nobody is capable of really thinking about anyone, even in the worst calamity. For really to think about someone means thinking about that person every minute of the day, without letting one's thoughts be diverted by anything, by meals, by a fly that settles on one's cheek, by household duties, or by a sudden itch somewhere. But there are always flies and itches. That's why life is difficult to live. And these people know it only too well."

The camp manager came up; a gentleman named Othon, he said, would like to see them. Leaving Gonzales in the office, he led the others to a corner of the grandstand, where they saw M. Othon sitting by himself. He rose as they approached.

The magistrate was dressed exactly as in the past and still wore a stiff collar.

The only changes Tarrou noted were that the tufts of hair over his temples were not brushed back and that one of his shoelaces was undone. M. Othon appeared very tired and not once did he look his visitors in the face. He said he was glad to see them and requested them to thank Dr. Rieux for all he had done.

Some moments of silence ensued, then with an effort the magistrate spoke again:

"I hope Jacques did not suffer too much."

This was the first time Tarrou heard him utter his son's name, and he realized that something had changed. The sun was setting and, flooding through a rift in the clouds, the level rays raked the stands, tingeing their faces with a yellow glow.

"No," Tarrou said. "No, I couldn't really say he suffered."

When they took their leave, the magistrate was still gazing toward the light.

They called in at the office to say good-by to Gonzales, whom they found studying the duty roster. The footballer was laughing when he shook hands with them.

"Anyhow, I'm back in the good old dressing-room," he chuckled. "That's something to go on with."

Soon after, when the camp manager was seeing Tarrou and Rambert out, they heard a crackling noise coming from the stands. A moment later the loud-speakers, which in happier times served to announce the results of games or to introduce the teams, informed the inmates of the camp that they were to go back to their tents for the evening meal. Slowly everyone filed off the stands and shuffled toward the tents. After all were under canvas two small electric trucks, of the kind used for transporting baggage on railroad platforms, began to wend their way between the tents. While the occupants held forth their arms, two ladles plunged into the two big caldrons on each truck and neatly tipped their contents into the waiting mess-kits. Then the truck moved on to the next tent.

"Very efficient," Tarrou remarked.

The camp manager beamed as he shook hands.

"Yes, isn't it? We're great believers in efficiency in this camp."

Dusk was falling. The sky had cleared and the camp was bathed in cool, soft light. Through the hush of evening came a faint tinkle of spoons and plates.

Above the tents bats were circling, vanishing abruptly into the darkness. A streetcar squealed on a switch outside the walls.

"Poor Monsieur Othon!" Tarrou murmured as the gate closed behind them. "One would like to do something to help him. But how can you help a judge?"

There were other camps of much the same kind in the town, but the narrator, for lack of firsthand information and in deference to veracity, has nothing to add about them. This much, however, he can say; the mere existence of these camps, the smell of crowded humanity coming from them, the baying of their loud-speakers in the dusk, the air of mystery that clung about them, and the dread these forbidden places inspired told seriously on our fellow citizens' morale and added to the general nervousness and apprehension. Breaches of the peace and minor riots became more frequent.

As November drew to a close, the mornings turned much colder. Heavy downpours had scoured the streets and washed the sky clean of clouds. In the mornings a weak sunlight bathed the town in a cold, sparkling sheen. The air warmed up, however, as night approached. It was such a night that Tarrou chose for telling something of himself to Dr. Rieux.

After a particularly tiring day, about ten o'clock Tarrou proposed to the doctor that they should go together for the evening visit to Rieux's old asthma patient. There was a soft glow above the housetops in the Old Town and a light breeze fanned their faces at the street crossings. Coming from the silent streets, they found the old man's loquacity rather irksome at first. He launched into a long harangue to the effect that some folks were getting fed up, that it was always the same people had all the jam, and things couldn't go on like that indefinitely, one day there'd be, he rubbed his hands, "a fine old row." He continued expatiating on this theme all the time the doctor was attending to him.

They heard footsteps overhead. Noticing Tarrou's upward glance, the old woman explained that it was the girls from next door walking on the terrace. She added that one had a lovely view up there, and that as the terraces in this part of the town often joined up

with the next one on one side, the women could visit their neighbors without having to go into the street.

"Why not go up and have a look?" the old man suggested. "You'll get a breath of nice fresh air."

They found nobody on the terrace, only three empty chairs. On one side, as far as eye could reach, was a row of terraces, the most remote of which abutted on a dark, rugged mass that they recognized as the hill nearest the town. On the other side, spanning some streets and the unseen harbor, their gaze came to rest on the horizon, where sea and sky merged in a dim, vibrant grayness. Beyond a black patch that they knew to be the cliffs a sudden glow, whose source they could not see, sprang up at regular intervals; the lighthouse at the entrance of the fairway was still functioning for the benefit of ships that, passing Oran's unused harbor, went on to other ports along the coast. In a sky swept crystal-clear by the night wind, the stars showed like silver flakes, tarnished now and then by the yellow gleam of the revolving light. Perfumes of spice and warm stone were wafted on the breeze.

Everything was very still.

"A pleasant spot," said Rieux as he lowered himself into a chair. "You'd think that plague had never found its way up here."

Tarrou was gazing seawards, his back to the doctor.

"Yes," he replied after a moment's silence, "it's good to be here."

Then, settling into the chair beside Rieux, he fixed his eyes on his face. Three times the glow spread up the sky and died away. A faint clatter of crockery rose from a room opening on the street below. A door banged somewhere in the house.

"Rieux," Tarrou said in a quite ordinary tone, "do you realize that you've never tried to find out anything about me, the man I am? Can I regard you as a friend?"

"Yes, of course, we're friends; only so far we haven't had much time to show it."

"Good. That gives me confidence. Suppose we now take an hour off, for friendship?"

Rieux smiled by way of answer.

"Well, here goes!"

There was a long faint hiss some streets off, the sound of a car speeding on the wet pavement. It died away; then some vague shouts a long way off broke the stillness again. Then, like a dense veil slowly falling from the starry sky on the two men, silence returned. Tarrou had moved and now was sitting on the parapet, facing Rieux, who was slumped back in his chair. All that could be seen of him was a dark, bulky form outlined against the glimmering sky. He had much to tell; what follows gives it more or less in his own words.

"To make things simpler, Rieux, let me begin by saying I had plague already, long before I came to this town and encountered it here. Which is tantamount to saying I'm like everybody else. Only there are some people who don't know it, or feel at ease in that condition; others know and want to get out of it.

Personally, I've always wanted to get out of it.

"When I was young I lived with the idea of my innocence; that is to say, with no idea at all. I'm not the self-tormenting kind of person, and I made a suitable start in life. I brought off everything I set my hand to, I moved at ease in the field of the intellect, I got on excellently with women, and if I had occasional qualms, they passed as lightly as they came. Then one day I started thinking.

And now?

"I should tell you I wasn't poor in my young days, as you were. My father had an important post, he was prosecuting attorney; but to look at him, you'd never have guessed it; he appeared, and was, a kindly, good-natured man. My mother was a simple, rather shy woman, and I've always loved her greatly; but I'd rather not talk about her. My father was always very kind to me, and I even think he tried to understand me. He wasn't a model husband. I know that now, but I can't say it shocks me particularly. Even in his infidelities he behaved as one could count on his behaving and never gave rise to scandal. In short, he wasn't at all original and, now he's dead, I realize that, while no plaster saint, he was a very decent man as men go. He kept the middle way, that's all; he was the type of man for whom one has an affection of the mild but steady order, which is the kind that wears best.

"My father had one peculiarity; the big railway directory was his bedside book. Not that he often took a train; almost his only journeys were to Brittany, where he had a small country house to which we went every summer. But he was a walking timetable; he could tell you the exact times of departure and arrival of the Paris-Berlin expresses; how to get from Lyon to Warsaw, which trains to take and at what hours; the precise distance between any two capital cities you might mention. Could you tell me offhand how to get from Briancon to Chamonix? Even a station-master would scratch his head, I should say. Well, my father had the answer pat. Almost every evening he enlarged his knowledge of the subject, and he prided himself on it. This hobby of his much amused me; I would put complicated travel problems to him and check his answers afterwards by the railway directory. They were invariably correct. My father and I got on together excellently, thanks largely to these railway games we played in the evenings; I was exactly the audience he needed, attentive and appreciative. Personally I regarded this accomplishment of his as quite as admirable in its ways as most accomplishments.

"But I'm letting my tongue run away with me and attributing too much importance to that worthy man. Actually he played only an indirect role in the great change of heart about which I want to tell you. The most he did to me was to touch off a train of thoughts. When I was seventeen my father asked me to come to hear him speak in court. There was a big case on at the assizes, and probably he thought I'd see him to his best advantage. Also I suspect he hoped I'd be duly impressed by the pomp and ceremony of the law and encouraged to take up his profession. I could tell he was keen on my going, and the prospect of seeing a side of my father's character so different from that we saw at home appealed to me. Those were absolutely the only reasons I had for going to the trial. What happened in a court had always seemed to me as natural, as much in the order of things, as a military parade on the Fourteenth of July or a school speech day. My notions on the subject were purely abstract, and I'd never given it serious thought.

"The only picture I carried away with me of that day's proceedings was a picture of the criminal. I have little doubt he was guilty, of what crime is no great matter. That little man of about thirty, with sparse, sandy hair, seemed so eager to confess everything, so genuinely horrified at what he'd done and what was going to be done with him, that after a few minutes I had eyes for nothing and nobody else. He looked like a yellow owl scared blind by too much light. His tie was slightly awry, he kept biting his nails, those of one hand only, his right.... I needn't go on, need I? You've understood, he was a living human being.

"As for me, it came on me suddenly, in a flash of understanding; until then I'd thought of him only under his commonplace official designation, as 'the defendant.' And though I can't say I quite forgot my father, something seemed to grip my vitals at that moment and riveted all my attention on the little man in the dock. I hardly heard what was being said; I only knew that they were set on killing that living man, and an uprush of some elemental instinct, like a wave, had swept me to his side. And I did not really wake up until my father rose to address the court.

"In his red gown he was another man, no longer genial or good-natured; his mouth spewed out long, turgid phrases like an endless stream of snakes. I realized he was clamoring for the prisoner's death, telling the jury that they owed it to society to find him guilty; he went so far as to demand that the man should have his head cut off. Not exactly in those words, I admit. 'He must pay the supreme penalty,' was the formula. But the difference, really, was slight, and the result the same. He had the head he asked for. Only of course it wasn't he who did the actual job. I, who saw the whole business through to its conclusion, felt a far closer, far more terrifying intimacy with that wretched man than my father can ever have felt. Nevertheless, it fell to him, in the course of his duties, to be present at what's politely termed the prisoner's last moments, but what would be better called murder in its most despicable form.

"From that day on I couldn't even see the railway directory without a shudder of disgust. I took a horrified interest in legal proceedings, death sentences, executions, and I realized with dismay that my father must have often witnessed those brutal murders, on the days when, as I'd noticed without guessing what it meant, he rose very early in the morning. I remembered he used to wind his alarm-clock on those occasions, to make sure. I didn't dare to broach the subject with my mother, but I watched her now more closely and saw that their life in common had ceased to mean anything, she had abandoned hope. That helped me to 'forgive her,' as I put it to myself at the time. Later on, I learned that there'd been nothing to forgive; she'd been quite poor until her marriage, and poverty had taught her resignation.

"Probably you're expecting me to tell you that I left home at once. No, I stayed on many months, nearly a year, in fact. Then one evening my father asked for the alarm-clock as he had to get up early. I couldn't sleep that night. Next day, when he came home, I'd gone.

"To cut a long story short, I had a letter from my father, who had set inquiries on foot to find me, I went to see him, and, without explaining my reasons, told him quite calmly that I'd kill myself if he forced me to return. He wound up by letting me have my way, he was, as I've said, a kindly man at bottom, gave me a lecture on the silliness of wanting to 'live my life' (that was how he accounted for my conduct and I didn't undeceive him), and plenty of good advice. I could see he really felt it deeply and it was an effort for him to keep back his tears. Subsequently, but quite a long time after that, I formed a habit of visiting my mother periodically, and I always saw him on these occasions. 1 imagine these infrequent meetings satisfied my father. Personally, I hadn't the least antipathy to him, only a little sadness of heart. When he died I had my mother come to live with me, and she'd still be with me if she were alive.

"I've had to dwell on my start in life, since for me it really was the start of everything. I'll get on more quickly now. I came to grips with poverty when I was eighteen, after an easy life till then. I tried all sorts of jobs, and I didn't do too badly. But my real interest in life was the death penalty; I wanted to square accounts with that poor blind owl in the dock. So I became an agitator, as they say. I didn't want to be pestiferous, that's all. To my mind the social order around me was based on the death sentence, and by righting the established order I'd be fighting against murder. That was my view, others had told me so, and I still think that this belief of mine was substantially true. I joined forces with a group of people I then liked, and indeed have never ceased to like. I spent many years in close co-operation with them, and there's not a country in Europe in whose struggles I haven't played a part. But that's another story.

"Needless to say, I knew that we, too, on occasion, passed sentences of death.

But I was told that these few deaths were inevitable for the building up of a new world in which murder would cease to be. That also was true up to a point, and maybe I'm not capable of standing fast where that order of truths is concerned.

Whatever the explanation, I hesitated. But then I remembered that miserable owl in the dock and it enabled me to keep on. Until the day when I was present at an execution, it was in Hungary, and exactly the same dazed horror that I'd experienced as a youngster made everything reel before my eyes.

"Have you ever seen a man shot by a firing-squad? No, of course not; the spectators are hand-picked and it's like a private party, you need an invitation. The result is that you've gleaned your ideas about it from books and pictures. A post, a blindfolded man, some soldiers in the offing. But the real thing isn't a bit like that. Do you know that the firing-squad stands only a yard and a half from the condemned man? Do you know that if the victim took two steps forward his chest would touch the rifles? Do you know that, at this short range, the soldiers concentrate their fire on the region of the heart and their big bullets make a hole into which you could thrust your fist? No, you didn't know all that; those are things that are never spoken of. For the plague-stricken their peace of mind is more important than a human life. Decent folks must be allowed to sleep easy o' nights, mustn't they? Really it would be shockingly bad taste to linger on such details, that's common knowledge. But personally I've never been able to sleep well since then. The bad taste remained in my mouth and I've kept lingering on the details, brooding over them.

"And thus I came to understand that I, anyhow, had had plague through all those long years in which, paradoxically enough, I'd believed with all my soul that I was fighting it. I learned that I had had an indirect hand in the deaths of thousands of people; that I'd even brought about their deaths by approving of acts and principles which could only end that way. Others did not seem embarrassed by such thoughts, or anyhow never voiced them of their own accord.

But I was different; what I'd come to know stuck in my gorge. I was with them and yet I was alone. When I spoke of these matters they told me not to be so squeamish; I should remember what great issues were at stake. And they advanced arguments, often quite impressive ones, to make me swallow what none the less I couldn't bring myself to stomach. I replied that the most eminent of the plague-stricken, the men who wear red robes, also have excellent arguments to justify what they do, and once I admitted the arguments of necessity and force majeure put forward by the less eminent, I couldn't reject those of the eminent. To which they retorted that the surest way of playing the game of the red robes was to leave to them the monopoly of the death penalty. My reply to this was that if you gave in once, there was no reason for not continuing to give in. It seems to me that history has borne me out; today there's a sort of competition who will kill the most. They're all mad over murder and they couldn't stop killing men even if they wanted to.

"In any case, my concern was not with arguments. It was with the poor owl; with that foul procedure whereby dirty mouths stinking of plague told a fettered man that he was going to die, and scientifically arranged things so that he should die, after nights and nights of mental torture while he waited to be murdered in cold blood. My concern was with that hole in a man's chest. And I told myself that meanwhile, so far anyhow as I was concerned, nothing in the world would induce me to accept any argument that justified such butcheries. Yes, I chose to be blindly obstinate, pending the day when I could see my way more clearly.

"I'm still of the same mind. For many years I've been ashamed, mortally ashamed, of having been, even with the best intentions, even at many removes, a murderer in my turn. As time went on I merely learned that even those who were better than the rest could not keep themselves nowadays from killing or letting others kill, because such is the logic by which they live; and that we can't stir a finger in this world without the risk of bringing death to somebody. Yes, I've been ashamed ever since; I have realized that we all have plague, and I have lost my peace. And today I am still trying to find it; still trying to understand all those others and not to be the mortal enemy of anyone. I only know that one must do what one can to cease being plague-stricken, and that's the only way in which we can hope for some peace or, failing that, a decent death. This, and only this, can bring relief to men and, if not save them, at least do them the least harm possible and even, sometimes, a little good. So that is why I resolved to have no truck with anything which, directly or indirectly, for good reasons or for bad, brings death to anyone or justifies others' putting him to death.

"That, too, is why this epidemic has taught me nothing new, except that I must fight it at your side. I know positively, yes, Rieux, I can say I know the world inside out, as you may see, that each of us has the plague within him; no one, no one on earth is free from it. And I know, too, that we must keep endless watch on ourselves lest in a careless moment we breathe in somebody's face and fasten the infection on him. What's natural is the microbe. All the rest, health, integrity, purity (if you like), is a product of the human will, of a vigilance that must never falter. The good man, the man who infects hardly anyone, is the man who has the fewest lapses of attention. And it needs tremendous will-power, a never ending tension of the mind, to avoid such lapses. Yes, Rieux, it's a wearying business, being plague-stricken. But it's still more wearying to refuse to be it. That's why everybody in the world today looks so tired; everyone is more or less sick of plague. But that is also why some of us, those who want to get the plague out of their systems, feel such desperate weariness, a weariness from which nothing remains to set us free except death.

"Pending that release, I know I have no place in the world of today; once I'd definitely refused to kill, I doomed myself to an exile that can never end. I leave it to others to make history. I know, too, that I'm not qualified to pass judgment on those others. There's something lacking in my mental make-up, and its lack prevents me from

being a rational murderer. So it's a deficiency, not a superiority. But as things are, I'm willing to be as I am; I've learned modesty.

All I maintain is that on this earth there are pestilences and there are victims, and it's up to us, so far as possible, not to join forces with the pestilences. That may sound simple to the point of childishness; I can't judge if it's simple, but I know it's true. You see, I'd heard such quantities of arguments, which very nearly turned my head, and turned other people's heads enough to make them approve of murder; and I'd come to realize that all our troubles spring from our failure to use plain, clean-cut language. So I resolved always to speak, and to act, quite clearly, as this was the only way of setting myself on the right track. That's why I say there are pestilences and there are victims; no more than that. If, by making that statement, I, too, become a carrier of "the plague-germ, at least I don't do it willfully. I try, in short, to be an innocent murderer. You see, I've no great ambitions. "I grant we should add a third category: that of the true healers. But it's a fact one doesn't come across many of them, and anyhow it must be a hard vocation. That's why I decided to take, in every predicament, the victims' side, so as to reduce the damage done. Among them I can at least try to discover how one attains to the third category; in other words, to peace."

Tarrou was swinging his leg, tapping the terrace lightly with his heel, as he concluded. After a short silence the doctor raised himself a little in his chair and asked if Tarrou had an idea of the path to follow for attaining peace.

"Yes," he replied. "The path of sympathy."

Two ambulances were clanging in the distance. The dispersed shouts they had been hearing off and on drew together on the outskirts of the town, near the stony hill, and presently there was a sound like a gunshot. Then silence fell again.

Rieux counted two flashes of the revolving light. The breeze freshened and a gust coming from the sea filled the air for a moment with the smell of brine.

And at the same time they clearly heard the low sound of waves lapping the foot of the cliffs.

"It comes to this," Tarrou said almost casually; "what interests me is learning how to become a saint."

"But you don't believe in God."

"Exactly! Can one be a saint without God?, that's the problem, in fact the only problem, I'm up against today."

A sudden blaze sprang up above the place the shouts had come from and, stemming the wind-stream, a rumor of many voices came to their ears. The blaze died down almost at once, leaving behind it only a dull red glow. Then in a break of the wind they distinctly heard some strident yells and the discharge of a gun, followed by the roar of an angry crowd. Tarrou stood up and listened, but nothing more could be heard.

"Another skirmish at the gates, I suppose."

"Well, it's over now," Rieux said.

Tarrou said in a low voice that it was never over, and there would be more victims, because that was in the order of things.

"Perhaps," the doctor answered. "But, you know, I feel more fellowship with the defeated than with saints. Heroism and sanctity don't really appeal to me, I imagine. What interests me is being a man."

"Yes, we're both after the same thing, but I'm less ambitious."

Rieux supposed Tarrou was jesting and turned to him with a smile. But, faintly lit by the dim radiance falling from the sky, the face he saw was sad and earnest. There was another gust of wind and Rieux felt it warm on his skin. Tarrou gave himself a little shake.

"Do you know," he said, "what we now should do for friendship's sake?"

"Anything you like, Tarrou."

"Go for a swim. It's one of these harmless pleasures that even a saint-to-be can indulge in, don't you agree?" Rieux smiled again, and Tarrou continued: "With our passes, we can get out on the pier. Really, it's too damn silly living only in and for the plague. Of course, a man should fight for the victims, but if he ceases caring for anything outside that, what's the use of his fighting?"

"Right," Rieux said. "Let's go."

Some minutes later the car drew up at the harbor gates. The moon had risen and a milk-white radiance, dappled with shadows, lay around them. Behind them rose the town, tier on tier, and from it came warm, fetid breaths of air that urged them toward the sea. After showing their passes to a guard, who inspected them minutely, they crossed some open ground littered with casks, and headed toward the pier. The air here reeked of stale wine and fish. Just before they reached the pier a smell of iodine and seaweed announced the nearness of the sea and they clearly heard the sound of waves breaking gently on the big stone blocks.

Once they were on the pier they saw the sea spread out before them, a gently heaving expanse of deep-piled velvet, supple and sleek as a creature of the wild. They sat down on a boulder facing the open. Slowly the waters rose and sank, and with their tranquil breathing sudden oily glints formed and flickered over the surface in a haze of broken lights. Before them the darkness stretched out into infinity. Rieux could feel under his hand the gnarled, weather-worn visage of the rocks, and a strange happiness possessed him. Turning to Tarrou, he caught a glimpse on his friend's face of the same happiness, a happiness that forgot nothing, not even murder.

They undressed, and Rieux dived in first. After the first shock of cold had passed and he came back to the surface the water seemed tepid. When he had taken a few strokes he found that the sea was warm that night with the warmth of autumn seas that borrow from the shore the accumulated heat of the long days of summer. The movement of his feet left a foaming wake as he swam steadily ahead, and the water slipped along his arms to close in tightly on his legs. A loud splash told him that Tarrou had dived. Rieux lay on his back and stayed motionless, gazing up at the dome of sky lit by the stars and moon. He drew a deep breath. Then he heard a sound of beaten water, louder and louder, amazingly clear in the hollow silence of the night. Tarrou was coming up with him, he now could hear his breathing.

Rieux turned and swam level with his friend, timing his stroke to Tarrou's. But Tarrou was the stronger swimmer and Rieux had to put on speed to keep up with him. For some minutes they swam side by side, with the same zest, in the same rhythm, isolated from the world, at last free of the town and of the plague.

Rieux was the first to stop and they swam back slowly, except at one point, where unexpectedly they found themselves caught in an ice-cold current. Their energy whipped up by this trap the sea had sprung on them, both struck out more vigorously.

They dressed and started back. Neither had said a word, but they were conscious of being perfectly at one, and the memory of this night would be cherished by them both. When they caught sight of the plague watchman, Rieux guessed that Tarrou, like himself, was thinking that the disease had given them a respite, and this was good, but now they must set their shoulders to the wheel again.

Yes, the plague gave short shrift indeed, and they must set their shoulders to the wheel again. Throughout December it smoldered in the chests of our townsfolk, fed the fires in the crematorium, and peopled the camps with human jetsam. In short, it never ceased progressing with its characteristically jerky but unfaltering stride. The authorities had optimistically reckoned on the coming of winter to halt its progress, but it lasted through the first cold spells without the least remission. So the only thing for us to do was to go on waiting, and since after a too long waiting one gives up waiting, the whole town lived as if it had no future.

As for Dr. Rieux, that brief hour of peace and friendship which had been granted him was not, and could not be, repeated. Yet another hospital had been opened, and his only converse was with his patients. However, he noticed a change at this stage of the epidemic, now that the plague was assuming more and more the pneumonic form; the patients seemed, after their fashion, to be seconding the doctor. Instead of giving way to the prostration or the frenzies of the early period, they appeared to have a clearer idea of where their interests lay and on their own initiative asked for what might be most beneficial. Thus they were always clamoring for something to drink and insisted on being kept as warm as possible. And though the demands on him were as exhausting as before, Rieux no longer had the impression of putting up a solitary fight; the patients were co-operating. Toward the end of December he received a letter from M. Othon, who was still in quarantine. The magistrate stated that his quarantine period was over; unfortunately the date of his admission to camp seemed to have been mislaid by the secretariat, and if he was still detained it was certainly due to a mistake.

His wife, recently released from quarantine, had gone to the Prefect's office to protest and had been rudely treated; they had told her that the office never made mistakes. Rieux asked Rambert to look into the matter, and a few days later M. Othon called on him. There had, in fact, been a mistake, and Rieux showed some indignation. But M. Othon, who had grown thinner, raised a limp, deprecating hand; weighing his words, he said that everyone could make mistakes. And the doctor thought to himself that decidedly something had changed.

"What will you do now, Monsieur Othon?" Rieux asked. "I suppose you have a pile of work awaiting you."

"Well, as a matter of fact, I'm putting in for some leave."

"I quite understand. You need a rest."

"It's not that. I want to go back to the camp."

Rieux couldn't believe his ears. "But you've only just come out of it!"

"I'm afraid I did not make myself clear. I'm told there are some voluntary workers from government offices in that camp." The magistrate rolled his round eyes a little and tried to smooth down a tuft of hair. "It would keep me busy, you see. And also, I know it may sound absurd, but I'd feel less separated from my little boy."

Rieux stared at him. Could it be that a sudden gentleness showed in those hard, inexpressive eyes? Yes, they had grown misted, lost their steely glitter.

"Certainly," Rieux said. "Since that's your wish, I'll fix it up for you."

The doctor kept his word; and the life of the plague-ridden town resumed its course until Christmas. Tarrou continued to bring his quiet efficiency to bear on every problem. Rambert confided in the doctor that, with the connivance of the two young guards, he was sending letters to his wife and now and then receiving an answer. He suggested to Rieux that he should avail himself of this clandestine channel, and Rieux agreed to do so. For the first time for many months he sat down to write a letter. He found it a laborious business, as if he were manipulating a language that he had forgotten. The letter was dispatched.

The reply was slow in coming. As for Cottard, he was prospering, making money hand over fist in small, somewhat shady transactions. With Grand, however, it was otherwise; the Christmas season did not seem to agree with him.

Indeed, Christmas that year had none of its old-time associations; it smacked of hell rather than of heaven. Empty, unlighted shops, dummy chocolates or empty boxes in the confectioners' windows, streetcars laden with listless, dispirited passengers, all was as unlike previous Christmastides as it well could be. In the past all the townspeople, rich and poor alike, indulged in seasonable festivity; now only a privileged few, those with money to burn, could do so, and they caroused in shamefast solitude in a dingy back shop or a private room. In the churches there were more supplications than carols.

You saw a few children, too young to realize what threatened them, playing in the frosty, cheerless streets. But no one dared to bid them welcome-in the God of former days, bringer of gifts, and old as human sorrow, yet new as the hopes of youth. There was no room in any heart but for a very old, gray hope, that hope which keeps men from letting themselves drift into death and is nothing but a dogged will to live.

Grand had failed to show up as usual on the previous evening. Feeling somewhat anxious, Rieux called at his place early in the morning, but he wasn't at home.

His friends were asked to keep a lookout for him. At about eleven Rambert came to the hospital with the news that he'd had a distant glimpse of Grand, who seemed to be wandering aimlessly, "looking very queer." Unfortunately he had lost sight of him almost at once. Tarrou and the doctor set out in the car to hunt for Grand.

At noon Rieux stepped out of his car into the frozen air; he had just caught sight of Grand some distance away, his face glued to a shop-window full of crudely carved wooden toys. Tears were steadily flowing down the old fellow's cheeks, and they wrung the doctor's heart, for he could understand them, and he felt his own tears welling up in sympathy. A picture rose before him of that scene of long ago, the youngster standing in front of another shop-window, like this one dressed for Christmas, and Jeanne turning toward him in a sudden access of emotion and saying how happy she was. He could guess that through the mists of the past years, from the depth of his fond despair, Jeanne's young voice was rising, echoing in Grand's ears. And he knew, also, what the old man was thinking as his tears flowed, and he, Rieux, thought it too: that a loveless world is a dead world, and always there comes an hour when one is weary of prisons, of one's work, and of devotion to duty, and all one craves for is a loved face, the warmth and wonder of a loving heart.

Grand saw the doctor's reflection in the window. Still weeping, he turned and, leaning against the shop-front, watched Rieux approach.

"Oh, doctor, doctor!" He could say no more.

Rieux, too, couldn't speak; he made a vague, understanding gesture. At this moment he suffered with Grand's sorrow, and what filled his breast was the passionate indignation we feel when confronted by the anguish all men share.

"Yes, Grand," he murmured.

"Oh, if only I could have time to write to her! To let her know... and to let her be happy without remorse!"

Almost roughly Rieux took Grand's arm and drew him forward. Grand did not resist and went on muttering broken phrases.

"Too long! It's lasted too long. All the time one's wanting to let oneself go, and then one day one has to. Oh, doctor, I know I look a quiet sort, just like anybody else. But it's always been a terrible effort only to be, just normal. And now, well, even that's too much for me."

He stopped dead. He was trembling violently, his eyes were fever-bright. Rieux took his hand; it was burning hot.

"You must go home."

But Grand wrenched himself free and started running. After a few steps he halted and stretched out his arms, swaying to and fro.

Then he spun round on himself and fell flat on the pavement, his face stained with the tears that went on flowing. Some people who were approaching stopped abruptly and watched the scene from a little way off, not daring to come nearer. Rieux had to carry the old man to the car.

Grand lay in bed, gasping for breath; his lungs were congested. Rieux pondered. The old fellow hadn't any family. What would be the point of having him evacuated? He and Tarrou could look after him.

Grand's head was buried in the pillow, his cheeks were a greenish gray, his eyes had gone dull, opaque. He seemed to be gazing fixedly at the scanty fire Tarrou was kindling with the remains of an old packing-case. "I'm in a bad way," he muttered. A queer crackling sound came from his flame-seared lungs whenever he tried to speak. Rieux told him not to talk and promised to come back. The sick man's lips parted in a curious smile, and a look of humorous complicity flickered across the haggard face. "If I pull through, doctor, hats off!" A moment later he sank into extreme prostration.

Visiting him again some hours later, they found him half sitting up in bed, and Rieux was horrified by the rapid change that had come over his face, ravaged by the fires of the disease consuming him. However, he seemed more lucid and almost immediately asked them to get his manuscript from the drawer where he always kept it. When Tarrou handed him the sheets, he pressed them to his chest without looking at them, then held them out to the doctor, indicating by a gesture that he was to read them. There were some fifty pages of manuscript. Glancing through them, Rieux saw that the bulk of the writing consisted of the same sentence written again and again with small variants, simplifications or elaborations.

Persistently the month of May, the lady on horseback, the avenues of the Bois recurred, regrouped in different patterns. There were, besides, explanatory notes, some exceedingly long, and lists of alternatives. But at the foot of the last page was written in a studiously clear hand: "My dearest Jeanne, Today is Christmas Day and..." Eight words only. Above it, in copperplate script, was the latest version of the famous phrase. "Read it," Grand whispered. And Rieux read:

"One fine morning in May, a slim young horsewoman might have been seen riding a glossy sorrel mare along the avenues of the Bois, among the flowers...."

"Is that it?" There was a feverish quaver in the old voice. Rieux refrained from looking at him, and he began to toss about in the bed. "Yes, I know. I know what you're thinking. 'Fine' isn't the word. It's?"

Rieux clasped his hand under the coverlet.

"No, doctor. It's too late, no time..." His breast heaved painfully, then suddenly he said in a loud, shrill voice: "Burn it!"

The doctor hesitated, but Grand repeated his injunction in so violent a tone and with such agony in his voice that Rieux walked across to the fireplace and dropped the sheets on the dying fire. It blazed up, and there was a sudden flood of light, a fleeting warmth, in the room. When the doctor came back to the bed, Grand had his back turned, his face almost touching the wall. After injecting the serum Rieux whispered to his friend that Grand wouldn't last the night, and Tarrou volunteered to stay with him. The doctor approved.

All night Rieux was haunted by the idea of Grand's death. But next morning he found his patient sitting up in bed, talking to Tarrou. His temperature was down to normal and there were no symptoms other than a generalized prostration.

"Yes, doctor," Grand said. "I was overhasty. But I'll make another start. You'll see, I can remember every word."

Rieux looked at Tarrou dubiously. "We must wait," he said.

But at noon there was no change. By nightfall Grand could be considered out of danger. Rieux was completely baffled by this "resurrection."

Other surprises were in store for him. About the same time there was brought to the hospital a girl whose case Rieux diagnosed as hopeless, and he had her sent immediately to the isolation ward.

She was delirious' and had all the symptoms of pneumonic plague. Next morning, however, the temperature had fallen. As in Grand's case the doctor assumed this was the ordinary morning fall that his experience had taught him to regard as a bad sign. But at noon her temperature still showed no rise and at night it went up only a few degrees.

Next morning it was down to normal. Though very exhausted, the girl was breathing freely. Rieux remarked to Tarrou that her recovery was "against all the rules!" But in the course of the next week four similar cases came to his notice.

The old asthma patient was bubbling over with excitement when Rieux and Tarrou visited him at the end of the week.

"Would you ever have believed it! They're coming out again," he said.

"Who?"

"Why, the rats!"

Not one dead or living rat had been seen in the town since April.

"Does that mean it's starting all over again?" Tarrou asked Rieux.

The old man was rubbing his hands.

"You should see 'em running, doctor! It's a treat, it is!"

He himself had seen two rats slipping into the house by the street door, and some neighbors, too, had told him they'd seen rats in their basements. In some houses people had heard those, once familiar scratchings and rustlings behind the woodwork. Rieux awaited with much interest the mortality figures that were announced every Monday. They showed a decrease.

PART V

Though this sudden setback of the plague was as welcome as it was unlooked-for, our townsfolk were in no hurry to jubilate. While intensifying their desire to be set free, the terrible months they had lived through had taught them prudence, and they had come to count less and less on a speedy end of the epidemic. All the same, this new development was the talk of the town, and people began to nurse hopes none the less heartfelt for being unavowed. All else took a back place; that daily there were new victims counted for little beside that staggering fact: the weekly total showed a decrease. One of the signs that a return to the golden age of health was secretly awaited was that our fellow citizens, careful though they were not to voice their hope, now began to talk, in, it is true, a carefully detached tone, of the new order of life that would set in after the plague.

All agreed that the amenities of the past couldn't be restored at once; destruction is an easier, speedier process than reconstruction. However, it was thought that a slight improvement in the food-supply could safely be counted on, and this would relieve what was just now the acutest worry of every household.

But in reality behind these mild aspirations lurked wild, extravagant hopes, and often one of us, becoming aware of this, would hastily add that, even on the rosiest view, you couldn't expect the plague to stop from one day to another.

Actually, while the epidemic did not stop "from one day to another," it declined more rapidly than we could reasonably have expected. With the first week of January an unusually persistent spell of very cold weather settled in and seemed to crystallize above the town. Yet never before had the sky been so blue; day after day its icy radiance flooded the town with brilliant light, and in the frost-cleansed air the epidemic seemed to lose its virulence, and in each of three consecutive weeks a big drop in the death-roll was announced. Thus over a relatively brief period the disease lost practically all the gains piled up over many months. Its setbacks with seemingly predestined victims, like Grand and Rieux's girl patient, its bursts of activity for two or three days in some districts synchronizing with its total disappearance from others, its new practice of multiplying its victims on, say, a Monday, and on Wednesday letting almost all escape, in short, its accesses of violence followed by spells of complete inactivity, all these gave an impression that its energy was flagging, out of exhaustion and exasperation, and it was losing, with its self-command, the ruthless, almost mathematical efficiency that had been its trump card hitherto. Of a sudden Castel's anti-plague injections scored frequent successes, denied it until now. Indeed, all the treatments the doctors had tentatively employed, without definite results, now seemed almost uniformly efficacious. It was as if the plague had been hounded down and cornered, and its sudden weakness lent new strength to the blunted weapons so far used against it. Only at rare moments did the disease brace itself and make as it were a blind and fatal leap at three or four patients whose recovery had been expected, a truly ill-starred few, killed off when hope ran highest. Such was the case of M. Othon, the magistrate, evacuated from the quarantine camp; Tarrou said of him that "he'd had no luck," but one couldn't tell if he had in mind

the life or the death of M. Othon. But, generally speaking, the epidemic was in retreat all along the line; the official communiques, which had at first encouraged no more than shadowy, half-hearted hopes, now confirmed the popular belief that the victory was won and the enemy abandoning his positions. Really, however, it is doubtful if this could be called a victory. All that could be said was that the disease seemed to be leaving as unaccountably as it had come. Our strategy had not changed, but whereas yesterday it had obviously failed, today it seemed triumphant. Indeed, one's chief impression was that the epidemic had called a retreat after reaching all its objectives; it had, so to speak, achieved its purpose.

Nevertheless, it seemed as if nothing had changed in the town. Silent as ever by day, the streets filled up at nightfall with the usual crowds of people, now wearing overcoats and scarves. Cafes and picture-houses did as much business as before. But on a closer view you might notice that people looked less strained, and they occasionally smiled. And this brought home the fact that since the outbreak of plague no one had hitherto been seen to smile in public. The truth was that for many months the town had been stifling under an airless shroud, in which a rent had now been made, and every Monday when he turned on the radio, each of us learned that the rift was widening; soon he would be able to breathe freely. It was at best a negative solace, with no immediate impact on men's lives. Still, had anyone been told a month earlier that a train had just left or a boat put in, or that cars were to be allowed on the streets again, the news would have been received with looks of incredulity; whereas in mid-January an announcement of this kind would have caused no surprise. The change, no doubt, was slight. Yet, however slight, it proved what a vast forward stride our townsfolk had made in the way of hope. And indeed it could be said that once the faintest stirring of hope became possible, the dominion of the plague was ended.

It must, however, be admitted that our fellow citizens' reactions during that month were diverse to the point of incoherence. More precisely, they fluctuated between high optimism and extreme depression. Hence the odd circumstance that several more attempts to escape took place at the very moment when the statistics were most encouraging. This took the authorities by surprise, and, apparently, the sentries too, since most of the "escapists" brought it off. But, looking into it, one saw that people who tried to escape at this time were prompted by quite understandable motives. Some of them plague had imbued with a scepticism so thorough that it was now a second nature; they had become allergic to hope in any form. Thus even when the plague had run its course, they went on living by its standards. They were, in short, behind the times. In the case of others, chiefly those who had been living until now in forced separation from those they loved, the rising wind of hope, after all these months of durance and depression, had fanned impatience to a blaze and swept away their self-control. They were seized with a sort of panic at the thought that they might die so near the goal and never see again the ones they loved, and their long privation have no recompense. Thus, though for weary months and months they had endured their long ordeal with dogged perseverance, the first thrill of hope had been enough to shatter what fear and hopelessness had failed to impair. And in the frenzy of their haste they tried to outstrip the plague, incapable of keeping pace with it up to the end.

Meanwhile, there were various symptoms of the growing optimism. Prices, for instance, fell sharply. This fall was unaccountable from the purely economic viewpoint.

Our difficulties were as great as ever, the gates were kept rigorously closed, and the food situation was far from showing any improvement. Thus it was a purely psychological reaction, as if the dwindling of the plague must have repercussions in all fields. Others to profit by the spread of optimism were those who used to live in groups and had been forced to live apart. The two convents reopened and their communal life was resumed. The troops, too, were regrouped in such barracks as had not been requisitioned, and settled down to the garrison life of the past.

Minor details, but significant.

This state of subdued yet active ferment prevailed until January 25, when the weekly total showed so striking a decline that, after consulting the medical board, the authorities announced that the epidemic could be regarded as definitely stemmed. True, the communique went on to say that, acting with a prudence of which the population would certainly approve, the Prefect had decided that the gates of the town were to remain closed for two weeks more, and the prophylactic measures to remain in force for another month. During this period, at the least sign of danger the standing orders would be strictly enforced and, if necessary, prolonged thereafter for such a period as might be deemed desirable."

All, however, concurred in regarding these phrases as mere official verbiage, and the night of January 25 was the occasion of much festivity. To associate himself with the popular rejoicings, the Prefect gave orders for the street lighting to be resumed as in the past. And the townspeople paraded the brilliantly lighted streets in boisterous groups, laughing and singing.

True, in some houses the shutters remained closed, and those within listened in silence to the joyful shouts outside. Yet even in these houses of mourning a feeling of deep relief prevailed; whether because at last the fear of seeing other members of the household taken from them was calmed or because the shadow of personal anxiety was lifted from their hearts. The families that perforce withdrew themselves the most from the general jubilation were those who at this hour had one of their members down with plague in hospital and, whether in a quarantine camp or at home, waited in enforced seclusion for the epidemic to have done with them as it had done with the others. No doubt these families had hopes, but they hoarded them and forbade themselves to draw on them before feeling quite sure they were justified. And this time of waiting in silence and exile, in a limbo between joy and grief, seemed still crueler for the gladness all around them.

But these exceptions did not diminish the satisfaction of the great majority. No doubt the plague was not yet ended, a fact of which they were to be reminded; still, in imagination they could already hear, weeks in advance, trains whistling on their way to an outside world that had no limit, and steamers hooting as they put out from the harbor across shining seas. Next day these fancies would have passed and qualms of doubt returned. But for the moment the whole town was on the move, quitting the dark, lugubrious confines where it had struck its roots of stone, and setting forth at last, like a shipload of survivors, toward a land of promise.

That night Tarrou, Rieux, Rambert, and their colleagues joined for a while the marching crowds and they, too, felt as if they trod on air. Long after they had turned off the main streets, even when in empty byways they walked past shuttered houses, the joyful clamor followed them up, and because of their fatigue somehow they could not disassociate the sorrow behind those closed shutters from the joy filling the central streets. Thus the coming liberation had a twofold aspect, of happiness and tears.

At one moment, when the cries of exultation in the distance were swelling to a roar, Tarrou stopped abruptly. A small, sleek form was scampering along the roadway: a cat, the first cat any of them had seen since the spring. It stopped in the middle of the road, hesitated, licked a paw and quickly passed it behind its right ear; then it started forward again and vanished into the darkness.

Tarrou smiled to himself; the little old man on the balcony, too, would be pleased.

BUT in those days when the plague seemed to be retreating, slinking back to the obscure lair from which it had stealthily emerged, at least one person in the town viewed this retreat with consternation, if Tarrou's notes are to be trusted; and that man was Cottard.

To tell the truth, these diary notes take a rather curious turn from the date on which the death returns began to drop. The handwriting becomes much harder to read, this may have been due to fatigue, and the diarist jumps from one topic to another without transition. What is more, these later notes lack the objectivity of the earlier ones; personal considerations creep in. Thus, sandwiched between long passages dealing with the case of Cottard, we find a brief account of the old man and the cats. Tarrou conveys to us that the plague had in no wise lessened his appreciation of the old fellow, who continued equally to interest him after the epidemic had run its course; unfortunately, he could not go on interesting him, and this through no lack of good intentions on Tarrou's part.

He had done his best to see him again. Some days after that memorable 25th of January he stationed himself at the corner of the little street. The cats were back at their usual places, basking in the patches of sunlight. But at the ritual hour the shutters stayed closed. And never once did Tarrou see them open on the following days. He drew the rather odd conclusion that the old fellow was either dead or vexed, if vexed, the reason being that he had thought that he was right and the plague had put him in the wrong; if dead, the question was (as in the case of the old asthmatic) had he been a saint? Tarrou hardly thought so, but he found in the old man's case "a pointer."

"Perhaps," he wrote, "we can only reach approximations of sainthood. In which case we must make shift with a mild, benevolent diabolism."

Interspersed with observations relating to Cottard are remarks, scattered here and there, about Grand, he was now convalescent and had gone back to work as if nothing had happened, and about Rieux's mother. The occasional conversations he had with her, when living under the same roof, the old lady's attitudes, her opinions on the plague, are all recorded in detail in the diary. Tarrou lays stress above all on Mme Rieux's self-effacement, her way of explaining things in the simplest possible words, her predilection for a special window at which she always sat in the early evening, holding herself rather straight, her hands at rest, her eyes fixed on the quiet street below, until twilight filled the room and she showed among the gathering shadows as a motionless black form which gradually merged into the invading darkness. He remarks on the "lightness" with which she moved from one room to the other; on her kindness, though no precise instances had come to his notice he discerned its gentle glow in all she said and did; on the gift she had of knowing everything without (apparently) taking thought; and lastly that, dim and silent though she was, she quailed before no light, even the garish light of the plague. At this point Tarrou's handwriting began to fall off oddly; indeed, the following lines were almost illegible. And, as if in confirmation of this loss of grip upon himself, the last lines of the entry deal, for the first time in the diary, with his personal life. "She reminds me of my mother; what I loved most in Mother was her self-effacement, her 'dimness,' as they say, and it's she I've always wanted to get back to. It happened eight years ago; but I can't say she died. She only effaced herself a trifle more than usual, and when I looked round she was no longer there."

But to return to Cottard. When the weekly totals began to show a decline, he visited Rieux several times on various pretexts. But obviously what he really wanted was to get from Rieux his opinion on the probable course of the epidemic.

"Do you really think it can stop like that, all of a sudden?" He was skeptical about this, or anyhow professed to be. But the fact that he kept on asking the question seemed to imply he was less sure than he professed to be. From the middle of January Rieux gave him fairly optimistic answers. But these were not to Cottard's liking, and his reactions varied on each occasion, from mere petulance to great despondency. One day the doctor was moved to tell him that, though the statistics were highly promising, it was too soon to say definitely that we were out of the wood.

"In other words," Cottard said promptly, "there's no knowing. It may start again at any moment."

"Quite so. Just as it's equally possible the improvement may speed up."

Distressing to everyone else, this state of uncertainty seemed to agree with Cottard. Tarrou observed that he would enter into conversations with shopkeepers in his part of the town, with the obvious desire of propagating the opinion expressed by Rieux. Indeed, he had no trouble in doing this. After the first exhilaration following the announcement of the plague's decline had worn off, doubts had returned to many minds. And the sight of their anxiety reassured Cottard. Just as at other times he yielded to discouragement. "Yes," he said gloomily to Tarrou, "one of these days the gates will be opened. And then, you'll see, they'll drop me like a live coal!"

Everyone was struck by his abrupt changes of mood during the first three weeks of January. Though normally he spared no pains to make himself liked by neighbors and acquaintances, now, for whole days, he deliberately cold-shouldered them. On these occasions, so Tarrou gathered, he abruptly cut off outside contacts and retired morosely into his shell. He was no more to be seen in restaurants or at the theater or in his favorite cafes. However, he seemed unable to resume the obscure, humdrum life he had led before the epidemic. He stayed in his room and had his meals sent up from a near-by restaurant. Only at nightfall did he venture forth to make some small purchases, and on leaving the shop he would furtively roam the darker, less-frequented streets. Once or twice Tarrou ran into him on these occasions, but failed to elicit more than a few gruff monosyllables. Then, from one day to another, he became sociable again, talked volubly about the plague, asking everyone for his views on it, and mingled in the crowd with evident pleasure.

On January 25, the day of the official announcement, Cottard went to cover again. Two days later Tarrou came across him loitering in a side-street. When Cottard suggested he should accompany him home, Tarrou demurred; he'd had a particularly tiring day. But

Cottard wouldn't hear of a refusal. He seemed much agitated, gesticulated freely, spoke

very rapidly and in a very loud tone. He began by asking Tarrou if he really thought the official communique meant an end of the plague. Tarrou replied that obviously a mere official announcement couldn't stop an epidemic, but it certainly looked as if, barring accidents, it would shortly cease.

"Yes," Cottard said. "Barring accidents. And accidents will happen, won't they?"

Tarrou pointed out that the authorities had allowed for that possibility by refusing to open the gates for another fortnight.

"And very wise they were!" Cottard exclaimed in the same excited tone. "By the way things are going, I should say they'll have to eat their words."

Tarrou agreed this might be so; still, he thought it wiser to count on the opening of the gates and a return to normal life in the near future.

"Granted!" Cottard rejoined. "But what do you mean by 'a return to normal life'?"

Tarrou smiled. "New films at the picture-houses."

But Cottard didn't smile. Was it supposed, he asked, that the plague wouldn't have changed anything and the life of the town would go on as before, exactly as if nothing had happened? Tarrou thought that the plague would have changed things and not changed them; naturally our fellow citizens' strongest desire was, and would be, to behave as if nothing had changed and for that reason nothing would be changed, in a sense. But, to look at it from another angle, one can't forget everything, however great one's wish to do so; the plague was bound to leave traces, anyhow, in people's hearts.

To this Cottard rejoined curtly that he wasn't interested in hearts; indeed, they were the last thing he bothered about. What interested him was knowing whether the whole administration wouldn't be changed, lock, stock, and barrel; whether, for instance, the public services would function as before. Tarrou had to admit he had no inside knowledge on the matter; his personal theory was that after the upheaval caused by the epidemic, there would be some delay in getting these services under way again. Also, it seemed likely that all sorts of new problems would arise and necessitate at least some reorganization of the administrative system.

Cottard nodded. "Yes, that's quite on the cards; in fact everyone will have to make a fresh start."

They were nearing Cottard's house. He now seemed more cheerful, determined to take a rosier view of the future. Obviously he was picturing the town entering on a new lease of life, blotting out its past and starting again with a clean sheet.

"So that's that," Tarrou smiled. "Quite likely things will pan out all right for you, too, who can say? It'll be a new life for all of us, in a manner of speaking."

They were shaking hands at the door of the apartment house where Cottard lived.

"Quite right!" Cottard was growing more and more excited. "That would be a great idea, starting again with a clean sheet."

Suddenly from the lightless hall two men emerged. Tarrou had hardly time to hear his companion mutter: "Now, what do those birds want?" when the men in question, who looked like subordinate government employees in their best clothes, cut in with an inquiry if his name was Cottard. With a stifled exclamation Cottard swung round and dashed off into the darkness. Taken by surprise, Tarrou and the two men gazed blankly at each other for some moments.

Then Tarrou asked them what they wanted. In noncommittal tones they informed him that they wanted "some information," and walked away, unhurrying, in the direction Cottard had taken.

On his return home Tarrou wrote out an account of this peculiar incident, following it up with a "Feeling very tired tonight", which is confirmed by his handwriting in this entry. He added that he had still much to do, but that was no reason for not "holding himself in readiness," and he questioned if he were ready. As a sort of postscript, and, in fact, it is here that Tarrou's diary ends, he noted that there is always a certain hour of the day and of the night when a man's courage is at its lowest ebb, and it was that hour only that he feared.

When next day, a few days before the date fixed for the opening of the gates, Dr. Rieux came home at noon, he was wondering if the telegram he was expecting had arrived. Though his days were no less strenuous than at the height of the epidemic, the prospect of imminent release had obliterated his fatigue. Hope had returned and with it a new zest for life. No man can live on the stretch all the time, with his energy and willpower strained to the breaking-point, and it is a joy to be able to relax at last and loosen nerves and muscles that were braced for the struggle. If the telegram, too, that he awaited brought good news, Rieux would be able to make a fresh start. Indeed, he had a feeling that everyone in those days was making a fresh start.

He walked past the concierge's room in the hall. The new man, old Michel's successor, his face pressed to the window looking on the hall, gave him a smile.

As he went up the stairs, the man's face, pale with exhaustion and privation, but smiling, hovered before his eyes.

Yes, he'd make a fresh start, once the period of "abstractions" was over, and with any luck? He was opening the door with these thoughts in his mind when he saw his mother coming down the hall to meet him. M. Tarrou, she told him, wasn't well. He had risen at the usual time, but did not feel up to going out and had returned to bed. Mme Rieux felt worried about him.

"Quite likely it's nothing serious," her son said.

Tarrou was lying on his back, his heavy head deeply indenting the pillow, the coverlet bulging above his massive chest. His head was aching and his temperature up. The symptoms weren't very definite, he told Rieux, but they might well be those of plague.

After examining him Rieux said: "No, there's nothing definite as yet."

But Tarrou also suffered from a raging thirst, and in the hallway the doctor told his mother that it might be plague.

"Oh!" she exclaimed. "Surely that's not possible, not now!" And after a moment added: "Let's keep him here, Bernard."

Rieux pondered. "Strictly speaking, I've no right to do that," he said doubtfully. "Still, the gates will be opened quite soon. If you weren't here, I think I'd take it on myself."

"Bernard, let him stay, and let me stay too. You know, I've just had another inoculation."

The doctor pointed out that Tarrou, too, had had inoculations, though it was possible, tired as he was, he'd overlooked the last one or omitted to take the necessary precautions.

Rieux was going to the surgery as he spoke, and when he returned to the bedroom Tarrou noticed that he had a box of the big ampoules containing the serum.

"Ah, so it is that," he said.

"Not necessarily; but we mustn't run any risks."

Without replying Tarrou extended his arm and submitted to the prolonged injections he himself had so often administered to others.

"We'll judge better this evening." Rieux looked Tarrou in the eyes.

"But what about isolating me, Rieux?"

"It's by no means certain that you have plague."

Tarrou smiled with an effort.

"Well, it's the first time I've known you do the injection without ordering the patient off to the isolation ward."

Rieux looked away.

"You'll be better here. My mother and I will look after you."

Tarrou said nothing and the doctor, who was putting away the ampoules in the box, waited for him to speak before looking round. But still Tarrou said nothing, and finally Rieux went up to the bed. The sick man was gazing at him steadily, and though his face was drawn, the gray eyes were calm. Rieux smiled down on him.

"Now try to sleep. I'll be back soon."

As he was going out he heard Tarrou calling, and turned back. Tarrou's manner had an odd effect, as though he were at once trying to keep back what he had to say and forcing himself to say it.

"Rieux," he said at last, "you must tell me the whole truth. I count on that."

"I promise it."

Tarrou's heavy face relaxed in a brief smile.

"Thanks. I don't want to die, and I shall put up a fight. But if I lose the match, I want to make a good end of it."

Bending forward, Rieux pressed his shoulder.

"No. To become a saint, you need to live. So fight away!"

In the course of that day the weather, which after being very cold had grown slightly milder, broke in a series of violent hailstorms followed by rain. At sunset the sky cleared a little, and it was bitterly cold again. Rieux came home in the evening. His overcoat still on, he entered his friend's bedroom. Tarrou did not seem to have moved, but his set lips, drained white by fever, told of the effort he he was keeping up.

"Well?" Rieux asked.

Tarrou raised his broad shoulders a little out of the bedclothes.

"Well," he said, "I'm losing the match."

The doctor bent over him. Ganglia had formed under the burning skin and there was a rumbling in his chest, like the sound of a hidden forge. The strange thing was that Tarrou showed symptoms of both varieties of plague at once.

Rieux straightened up and said the serum hadn't yet had time to take effect. An uprush of fever in his throat drowned the few words that Tarrou tried to utter.

After dinner Rieux and his mother took up their posts at the sick man's bedside.

The night began with a struggle, and Rieux knew that this grim wrestling with the angel of plague was to last until dawn. In this struggle Tarrou's robust shoulders and chest were not his greatest assets; rather, the blood that had spurted under Rieux's needle and, in this blood, that something more vital than the soul, which no human skill can bring to light. The doctor's task could be only to watch his friend's struggle. As to what he was about to do, the stimulants to inject, the abscesses to stimulate? many months' repeated failures had taught him to appreciate such expedients at their true value. Indeed, the only way in which he might help was to provide opportunities for the beneficence of chance, which too often stays dormant unless roused to action. Luck was an ally he could not dispense with. For Rieux was confronted by an aspect of the plague that baffled him. Yet again it was doing all it could to confound the tactics used against it; it launched attacks in unexpected places and retreated from those where it seemed definitely lodged. Once more it was out to darken counsel.

Tarrou struggled without moving. Not once in the course of the night did he counter the enemy's attacks by restless agitation; only with all his stolid bulk, with silence, did he carry on the fight. Nor did he even try to speak, thus intimating, after his fashion, that he could no longer let his attention stray. Rieux could follow the vicissitudes of the struggle only in his friend's eyes, now open and now shut; in the eyelids, now more closely welded to the eyeball, now distended; and in his gaze fixed on some object in the room or brought back to the doctor and his mother. And each time it met the doctor's gaze, with a great effort Tarrou smiled.

At one moment there came a sound of hurrying footsteps in the street. They were in flight before a distant throbbing which gradually approached until the street was loud with the clamor of the downpour; another rain-squall was sweeping the town, mingled presently with hailstones that clattered on the sidewalk. Window awnings were flapping wildly. Rieux, whose attention had been diverted momentarily by the noises of the squall, looked again across the shadows at Tarrou's face, on which fell the light of a small bedside lamp. His mother was knitting, raising her eyes now and then from her work to gaze at the sick man.

The doctor had done everything that could be done. When the squall had passed, the silence in the room grew denser, filled only by the silent turmoil of the unseen battle. His nerves overwrought by sleeplessness, the doctor fancied he could hear, on the edge of the silence, that faint eerie sibilance which had haunted his ears ever since the beginning of the epidemic. He made a sign to his mother, indicating she should go to bed. She shook her head, and her eyes grew brighter; then she examined carefully, at her needle-tips, a stitch of which she was unsure. Rieux got up, gave the sick man a drink, and sat down again.

Footsteps rang on the pavement, nearing, then receding; people were taking advantage of the lull to hurry home. For the first time the doctor realized that this night, without the clang of ambulances and full of belated wayfarers, was just like a night of the past, a plague-free night. It was as if the pestilence, hounded away by cold, the street-lamps, and the crowd, had fled from the depths of the town and taken shelter in this warm room and was launching its last offensive at Tarrou's inert body. No longer did it thresh the air above the houses with its flail. But it was whistling softly in the stagnant air of the sickroom, and this it was that Rieux had been hearing since the long vigil began. And now it was for him to wait and watch until that strange sound ceased here too, and here as well the plague confessed defeat.

A little before dawn Rieux leaned toward his mother and whispered:

"You'd better have some rest now, as you'll have to relieve rne at eight. Mind you take your drops before going to bed."

Mme Rieux rose, folded her knitting, and went to the bedside. Tarrou had had his eyes shut for some time. Sweat had plastered his hair on his stubborn forehead.

Mme Rieux sighed, and he opened his eyes. He saw the gentle face bent over him and, athwart the surge of fever, that steadfast smile took form again. But at once the eyes closed. Left to himself, Rieux moved into the chair his mother had just left. The street was silent and no sound came from the sleeping town. The chill of daybreak was beginning to make itself felt.

The doctor dozed off, but very soon an early cart rattling down the street awaked him. Shivering a little, he looked at Tarrou and saw that a lull had come; he, too, was sleeping. The iron-shod wheels rumbled away into the distance. Darkness still was pressing on the windowpanes. When the doctor came beside the bed, Tarrou gazed at him with expressionless eyes, like a man still on the frontier of sleep.

"You slept, didn't you?" Rieux asked.

"Yes."

"Breathing better?"

"A bit. Does that mean anything?"

Rieux kept silent for some moments; then he said:

"No, Tarrou, it doesn't mean anything. You know as well as I that there's often a remission in the morning."

"Thanks." Tarrou nodded his approval. "Always tell me the exact truth."

Rieux was sitting on the side of the bed. Beside him he could feel the sick man's legs, stiff and hard as the limbs of an effigy on a tomb. Tarrou was breathing with more difficulty.

"The fever'll come back, won't it, Rieux?" he gasped.

"Yes. But at noon we shall know where we stand."

Tarrou shut his eyes; he seemed to be mustering up his strength. There was a look of utter weariness on his face. He was waiting for the fever to rise and already it was stirring somewhat in the depths of his being. When he opened his eyes, his gaze was misted. It brightened only when he saw Rieux bending over him, a tumbler in his hand.

'Drink '

Tarrou drank, then slowly lowered his head on to the pillow.

"It's a long business," he murmured.

Rieux clasped his arm, but Tarrou, whose head was averted, showed no reaction.

Then suddenly, as if some inner dike had given way without warning, the fever surged back, dyeing his cheeks and forehead. Tarrou's eyes came back to the doctor, who, bending again, gave him a look of affectionate encouragement.

Tarrou tried to shape a smile, but it could not force its way through the set jaws and lips welded by dry saliva. In the rigid face only the eyes lived still, glowing with courage.

At seven Mme Rieux returned to the bedroom. The doctor went to the surgery to ring up the hospital and arrange for a substitute. He also decided to postpone his consultations; then lay down for some moments on the surgery couch. Five minutes later he went back to the bedroom. Tarrou's face was turned toward Mme Rieux, who was sitting close beside the bed, her hands folded on her lap; in the dim light of the room she seemed no more than a darker patch of shadow. Tarrou was gazing at her so intently that, putting a finger to her lips, Mme Rieux rose and switched off the bedside lamp. Behind the curtains the light was growing, and presently, when the sick man's face grew visible, Mme Rieux could see his eyes still intent on her. Bending above the bed, she smoothed out the bolster and, as she straightened up, laid her hand for a moment on his moist, tangled hair. Then she heard a muffled voice, which seemed to come from very far away, murmur: "Thank you," and that all was well now. By the time she was back in her chair Tarrou had shut his eyes, and, despite the sealed mouth, a faint smile seemed to hover on the wasted face.

At noon the fever reached its climax. A visceral cough racked the sick man's body and he now was spitting blood. The ganglia had ceased swelling, but they were still there, like lumps of iron embedded in the joints. Rieux decided that lancing them was impracticable. Now and then, in the intervals between bouts of fever and coughing fits, Tarrou still gazed at his friends. But soon his eyes opened less and less often and the glow that shone out from the ravaged face in the brief moments of recognition grew steadily fainter. The storm, lashing his body into convulsive movement, lit it up with ever rarer flashes, and in the heart of the tempest he was slowly drifting, derelict. And now Rieux had before him only a masklike face, inert, from which the smile had gone forever. This human form, his friend's, lacerated by the spear-thrusts of the plague, consumed by searing, superhuman fires, buffeted by all the raging winds of heaven, was foundering under his eyes in the dark flood of the pestilence, and he could do nothing to avert the wreck. He could only stand, unavailing, on the shore, empty-handed and sick at heart, unarmed and helpless yet again under the onset of calamity. And thus, when the end came, the tears that blinded Rieux's eyes were tears of impotence; and he did not see

Tarrou roll over, face to the wall, and die with a short, hollow groan as if somewhere within him an essential chord had snapped.

The next night was not one of struggle but of silence. In the tranquil death-chamber, beside the dead body now in everyday clothing, here, too, Rieux felt it brooding, that elemental peace which, when he was sitting many nights before on the terrace high above the plague, had followed the brief foray at the gates. Then, already, it had brought to his mind the silence brooding over the beds in which he had let men die. There as here it was the same solemn pause, the lull that follows battle; it was the silence of defeat. But the silence now enveloping his dead friend, so dense, so much akin to the nocturnal silence of the streets and of the town set free at last, made Rieux cruelly aware that this defeat was final, the last disastrous battle that ends a war and makes peace itself an ill beyond all remedy. The doctor could not tell if Tarrou had found peace, now that all was over, but for himself he had a feeling that no peace was possible to him henceforth, any more than there can be an armistice for a mother bereaved of her son or for a man who buries his friend.

The night was cold again, with frosty stars sparkling in a clear, wintry sky.

And in the dimly lit room they felt the cold pressing itself to the windowpanes and heard the long, silvery suspiration of a polar night. Mme Rieux sat near the bed in her usual attitude, her right side lit up by the bedside lamp. In the center of the room, outside the little zone of light, Rieux sat, waiting. Now and then thoughts of his wife waylaid him, but he brushed them aside each time.

When the night began, the heels of passers-by had rung briskly in the frozen air.

"Have you attended to everything?" Mme Rieux had asked.

"Yes, I've telephoned."

Then they had resumed their silent vigil. From time to time Mme Rieux stole a glance at her son, and whenever he caught her doing this, he smiled. Out in the street the usual night-time sounds bridged the long silences. A good many cars were on the road again, though officially this was not yet permitted; they sped past with a long hiss of tires on the pavement, receded, and returned. Voices, distant calls silence again, a clatter of horse hoofs, the squeal of streetcars rounding a curve, vague murmurs, then once more the quiet breathing of the night.

"Bernard?"

"Yes?"

"Not too tired?"

"No."

At that moment he knew what his mother was thinking, and that she loved him. But he knew, too, that to love someone means relatively little; or, rather, that love is never strong enough to find the words befitting it. Thus he and his mother would always love each other silently. And one day she, or he, would die, without ever, all their lives long, having gone farther than this by way of making their affection known. Thus, too, he had lived at Tarrou's side, and Tarrou had died this evening without their friendship's having had time to enter fully into the life of either. Tarrou had "lost the match," as he put it. But what had he, Rieux, won? No more than the experience of having known plague and remembering it, of having known friendship and remembering it, of knowing affection and being destined one day to remember it. So all a man could win in the conflict between plague and life was knowledge and memories. But Tarrou, perhaps, would have called that winning the match.

Another car passed, and Mme Rieux stirred slightly. Rieux smiled toward her. She assured him she wasn't tired and immediately added:

"You must go and have a good long rest in the mountains, over there."

"Yes, Mother."

Certainly he'd take a rest "over there." It, too, would be a pretext for memory.

But if that was what it meant, winning the match, how hard it must be to live only with what one knows and what one remembers, cut off from what one hopes for! It was thus, most probably, that Tarrou had lived, and he realized the bleak sterility of a life without illusions. There can be no peace without hope, and Tarrou, denying as he did the right to condemn anyone whomsoever, though he knew well that no one can help condemning and it befalls even the victim sometimes to turn executioner, Tarrou had lived a life riddled with contradictions and had never known hope's solace. Did that explain his aspiration toward saintliness, his quest of peace by service in the cause of others? Actually Rieux had no idea of the answer to that question, and it mattered little. The only picture of Tarrou he would always have would be the picture of a man who firmly gripped the steering-wheel of his car when driving, or else the picture of that stalwart body, now lying motionless. Knowing meant that: a living warmth, and a picture of death.

That, no doubt, explains Dr. Rieux's composure on receiving next morning the news of his wife's death. He was in the surgery. His mother came in, almost running, and handed him a telegram; then went back to the hall to give the telegraph-boy a tip. When she returned, her son was holding the telegram open in his hand. She looked at him, but his eyes were resolutely fixed on the window; it was flooded with the effulgence of the morning sun rising above the harbor.

"Bernard," she said gently.

The doctor turned and looked at her almost as if she were a stranger.

"The telegram?"

"Yes," he said, "that's it. A week ago."

Mme Rieux turned her face toward the window. Rieux kept silent for a while. Then he told his mother not to cry, he'd been expecting it, but it was hard all the same. And he knew, in saying this, that this suffering was nothing new. For many months, and for the last two days, it was the selfsame suffering going on and on.

AT last, at daybreak on a fine February morning, the ceremonial opening of the gates took place, acclaimed by the populace, the newspapers, the radio, and official communiques. It only remains for the narrator to give what account he can of the rejoicings that followed, though he himself was one of those debarred from sharing in them wholeheartedly.

Elaborate day and night fetes were organized, and at the same time smoke began to rise from locomotives in the station, and ships were already heading for our harbour, reminders in their divers ways that this was the long-awaited day of reuniting, and the end of tears for all who had been parted.

We can easily picture, at this stage, the consequences of that feeling of separation which had so long rankled in the hearts of so many of our townsfolk.

Trains coming in were as crowded as those that left the town in the course of the day. Every passenger had reserved his seat long in advance and had been on tenterhooks during the past fortnight lest at the last moment the authorities should go back on their decision. Some of these incoming travelers were still somewhat nervous; though as a rule they knew the lot of those nearest and dearest to them, they were still in the dark about others and the town itself, of which their imagination painted a grim and terrifying picture. But this applies only to people who had not been eating their hearts out during the long months of exile, and not to parted lovers.

The lovers, indeed, were wholly wrapped up in their fixed idea, and for them one thing only had changed.

Whereas during those months of separation time had never gone quickly enough for their liking and they were always wanting to speed its flight, now that they were in sight of the town they would have liked to slow it down and hold each moment in suspense, once the brakes went on and the train was entering the station. For the sensation, confused perhaps, but none the less poignant for that, of all those days and weeks and months of life lost to their love made them vaguely feel they were entitled to some compensation; this present hour of joy should run at half the speed of those long hours of waiting. And the people who awaited them at home or on the platform, among the latter Rambert, whose wife, warned in good time, had got busy at once and was coming by the first train, were likewise fretting with impatience and quivering with anxiety. For even Rambert felt a nervous tremor at the thought that soon he would have

to confront a love and a devotion that the plague months had slowly refined to a pale abstraction, with the flesh-and-blood woman who had given rise to them.

If only he could put the clock back and be once more the man who, at the outbreak of the epidemic, had had only one thought and one desire: to escape and return to the woman he loved! But that, he knew, was out of the question now; he had changed too greatly. The plague had forced on him a detachment which, try as he might, he couldn't think away, and which like a formless fear haunted his mind. Almost he thought the plague had ended too abruptly, he hadn't had time to pull himself together. Happiness was bearing down on him full speed, the event outrunning expectation. Rambert understood that all would be restored to him in a flash, and joy break on him like a flame with which there is no dallying.

Everyone indeed, more or less consciously, felt as he did, and it is of all those people on the platform that we wish to speak. Each was returning to his personal life, yet the sense of comradeship persisted and they were exchanging smiles and cheerful glances among themselves. But the moment they saw the smoke of the approaching engine, the feeling of exile vanished before an uprush of overpowering, bewildering joy. And when the train stopped, all those interminable-seeming separations which often had begun on this same platform came to an end in one ecstatic moment, when arms closed with hungry possessiveness on bodies whose living shape they had forgotten. As for Rambert, he hadn't time to see that form running toward him; already she had flung herself upon his breast. And with his arms locked around her, pressing to his shoulder the head of which he saw only the familiar hair, he let his tears flow freely, unknowing if they rose from present joy or from sorrow too long repressed; aware only that they would prevent his making sure if the face buried in the hollow of his shoulder were the face of which he had dreamed so often or, instead, a stranger's face. For the moment he wished to behave like all those others around him who believed, or made believe, that plague can come and go without changing anything in men's hearts.

Nestling to one another, they went to their homes, blind to the outside world and seemingly triumphant over the plague, forgetting every sadness and the plight of those who had come by the same train and found no one awaiting them, and were bracing themselves to hear in their homes a confirmation of the fear that the long silence had already implanted in their hearts. For these last, who had now for company only their new-born grief, for those who at this moment were dedicating themselves to a lifelong memory of bereavement, for these unhappy people matters were very different, the pangs of separation had touched their climax. For the mothers, husbands, wives, and lovers who had lost all joy, now that the loved one lay under a layer of quicklime in a death-pit or was a mere handful of indistinctive ashes in a gray mound, the plague had not yet ended.

But who gave a thought to these lonely mourners? Routing the cold flaws that had been threshing the air since early-morning, the sun was pouring on the town a steady flood of tranquil light. In the forts on the hills, under the sky of pure, unwavering blue, guns were thundering without a break. And everyone was out and about to celebrate those crowded moments when the time of ordeal ended and the time of forgetting had not yet begun.

In streets and squares people were dancing. Within twenty-four hours the motor traffic had doubled and the ever more numerous cars were held up at every turn by merry-making crowds. Every church bell was in full peal throughout the afternoon, and the bells filled the blue and gold sky with their reverberations.

Indeed, in all the churches thanksgiving services were being held. But at the same time the places of entertainment were packed, and the cafes, caring nothing for the morrow, were producing their last bottles of liquor. A noisy concourse surged round every bar, including loving couples who fondled each other without a thought for appearances. All were laughing or shouting. The reserves of emotion pent up during those many months when for everybody the flame of life burned low were being recklessly squandered to celebrate this, the red-letter day of their survival. Tomorrow real life would begin again, with its restrictions. But for the moment people in very different walks of life were rubbing shoulders, fraternizing. The leveling-out that death's imminence had failed in practice to accomplish was realized at last, for a few gay hours, in the rapture of escape.

But this rather tawdry exuberance was only one aspect of the town that day; not a few of those filling the streets at sundown, among them Rambert and his wife, hid under an air of calm satisfaction subtler forms of happiness. Many couples, indeed, and many families, looked like people out for a casual stroll, no more than that; in reality most of them were making sentimental pilgrimages to places where they had gone to school with suffering. The newcomers were being shown the striking or obscurer tokens of the plague, relics of its passage. In some cases the survivor merely played the part of guide, the eyewitness who has "been through it," and talked freely of the danger without mentioning his fear. These were the milder forms of pleasure, little more than recreation. In other cases, however, there was more emotion to these walks about the town, as when a man, pointing to some place charged for him with sad yet tender associations, would say to the girl or woman beside him: "This is where, one evening just like this, I longed for you so desperately, and you weren't there!" These passionate pilgrims could readily be distinguished; they formed oases of whispers, aloof, self-centered, in the turbulence of the crowd. Far more effectively than the bands playing in the squares they vouched for the vast joy of liberation. These ecstatic couples, locked together, hardly speaking, proclaimed in the midst of the tumult of rejoicing, with the proud egoism and injustice of happy people, that the plague was over, the reign of terror ended. Calmly they denied, in the teeth of the evidence, that we had ever known a crazy world in which men were killed off like flies, or that precise savagery, that calculated frenzy of the plague, which instilled an odious freedom as to all that was not the here and now; or those charnel-house stenches which stupefied whom they did not kill. In short, they denied that we had ever been that hag-ridden populace a part of which was daily fed into a furnace and went up in oily fumes, while the rest, in shackled impotence, waited their turn.

That, anyhow, was what seemed evident to Rieux when towards the close of the afternoon, on his way to the outskirts of the town, he walked alone in an uproar of bells, guns, bands, and deafening shouts. There was no question of his taking a day off; sick men have no holidays. Through the cool, clear light bathing the town rose the familiar smells of roasting meat and anise-flavored liquor. All around him happy faces were turned toward the shining sky, men and women with flushed cheeks embraced one another with low, tense cries of desire. Yes, the plague had ended with the terror, and those passionately straining arms told what it had meant: exile and deprivation in the profoundest meaning of the words.

For the first time Rieux found that he could give a name to the family likeness that for several months he had detected in the faces in the streets. He had only to look around him now. At the end of the plague, with its misery and privations, these men and women had come to wear the aspect of the part they had been playing for so long, the part of emigrants whose faces first, and now their clothes, told of long banishment from a distant homeland. Once plague had shut the gates of the town, they had settled down to a life of separation, debarred from the living warmth that gives forgetfulness of all. In different degrees, in every part of the town, men and women had been yearning for a reunion, not of the same kind for all, but for all alike ruled out. Most of them had longed intensely for an absent one, for the warmth of a body, for love, or merely for a life that habit had endeared. Some, often without knowing it, suffered from being deprived of the company of friends and from their inability to get in touch with them through the usual channels of friendship, letters, trains, and boats. Others, fewer these, Tarrou may have been one of them, had desired reunion with something they couldn't have defined, but which seemed to them the only desirable thing on earth. For want of a better name, they sometimes called it peace.

Rieux walked on. As he progressed, the crowds grew thicker, the din multiplied, and he had a feeling that his destination was receding as he advanced. Gradually he found himself drawn into the seething, clamorous mass and understanding more and more the cry that went up from it, a cry that, for some part at least, was his. Yes, they had suffered together, in body no less than in soul, from a cruel leisure, exile without redress, thirst that was never slaked. Among the heaps of corpses, the clanging bells of ambulances, the warnings of what goes by the name of fate, among unremitting waves of fear and agonized revolt, the horror that such things could be, always a great voice had been ringing in the ears of these forlorn, panicked people, a voice calling them back to the land of their desire, a homeland.

It lay outside the walls of the stifled, strangled town, in the fragrant brushwood of the hills, in the waves of the sea, under free skies, and in the custody of love. And it was to this, their lost home, toward happiness, they longed to return, turning their backs disgustedly on all else.

As to what that exile and that longing for reunion meant, Rieux had no idea. But as he walked ahead, jostled on all sides, accosted now and then, and gradually made his way into less crowded streets, he was thinking it has no importance whether such things have or have not a meaning; all we need consider is the answer given to men's hope.

Henceforth he knew the answer, and he perceived it better now he was in the outskirts of the town, in almost empty streets. Those who, clinging to their little own, had set their hearts solely on returning to the home of their love had sometimes their reward, though some of them were still walking the streets alone, without the one they had awaited. Then, again, those were happy who had not suffered a twofold separation, like some of us who, in the days before the epidemic, had failed to build their love on a solid basis at the outset, and had spent years blindly groping for the pact, so slow and hard to come by, that in the long run binds together ill-assorted lovers. Such people had had, like Rieux himself, the rashness of counting overmuch on time; and now they were parted forever. But others, like Rambert, to whom the doctor had said early that morning: "Courage! It's up to you now to prove you're right", had, without faltering, welcomed back the loved one who they thought was lost to them. And for some time, anyhow, they

would be happy. They knew now that if there is one thing one can always yearn for and sometimes attain, it is human love. But for those others who aspired beyond and above the human individual toward something they could not even imagine, there had been no answer. Tarrou might seem to have won through to that hardly-come-by peace of which he used to speak; but he had found it only in death, too late to turn it to account. If others, however, Rieux could see them in the doorways of houses, passionately embracing and gazing hungrily at one another in the failing sunset glow, had got what they wanted, this was because they had asked for the one thing that depended on them solely. And as he turned the corner of the street where Grand and Cottard lived, Rieux was thinking it was only right that those whose desires are limited to man and his humble yet formidable love should enter, if only now and then, into their reward.

THIS chronicle is drawing to an end, and this seems to be the moment for Dr. Bernard Rieux to confess that he is the narrator. But before describing the closing scenes, he would wish anyhow to justify his undertaking and to set it down that he expressly made a point of adopting the tone of an impartial observer. His profession put him in touch with a great many of our townspeople while plague was raging, and he had opportunities of hearing their various opinions. Thus he was well placed for giving a true account of all he saw and heard. But in so doing he has tried to keep within the limits that seemed desirable. For instance, in a general way he has confined himself to describing only such things as he was enabled to see for himself, and has refrained from attributing to his fellow sufferers thoughts that, when all is said and done, they were not bound to have.

And as for documents, he has used only such as chance, or mischance, put in his way.

Summoned to give evidence regarding what was a sort of crime, he has exercised the restraint that behooves a conscientious witness. All the same, following the dictates of his heart, he has deliberately taken the victims' side and tried to share with his fellow citizens the only certitudes they had in common, love, exile, and suffering. Thus he can truly say there was not one of their anxieties in which he did not share, no predicament of theirs that was not his.

To be an honest witness, it was for him to confine himself mainly to what people did or said and what could be gleaned from documents. Regarding his personal troubles and his long suspense, his duty was to hold his peace. When now and then he refers to such matters, it is only for the light they may throw on his fellow citizens and in order to give a picture, as well defined as possible, of what most of the time they felt confusedly. Actually, this self-imposed reticence cost him little effort. Whenever tempted to add his personal note to the myriad voices of the plague-stricken, he was deterred by the thought that not one of his sufferings but was common to all the others and that in a world where sorrow is so often lonely, this was an advantage. Thus, decidedly, it was up to him to speak for all.

But there was at least one of our townsfolk for whom Dr. Rieux could not speak, the man of whom Tarrou said one day to Rieux: "His only real crime is that of having in his heart approved of something that killed off men, women, and children. I can understand the rest, but for that I am obliged to pardon him."

It is fitting that this chronicle should end with some reference to that man, who had an ignorant, that is to say lonely, heart.

On turning out of the main thoroughfares where the rejoicings were in full swing, and entering the street where Grand and Cottard lived, Dr. Rieux was held up by a police cordon. Nothing could have surprised him more. This quiet part of the town seemed all the quieter for the sounds of festivity in the distance, and the doctor pictured it as deserted as it was tranquil.

"Sorry, doctor," a policeman said, "but I can't let you through. There's a crazy fellow with a gun, shooting at everybody. But you'd better stay; we may need you."

Just then Rieux saw Grand coming toward him. Grand, too, had no idea what was happening and the police had stopped him, too. He had been told that the shots came from the house where he lived. They could see, some way down the street, the front of the house, bathed in cool evening light. Farther down the street was another line of policemen like the one that had prevented Rieux and Grand from advancing, and behind the line some of the local residents could be seen crossing and recrossing the street hastily. The street immediately in front of the house was quite empty and in the middle of the hollow square lay a hat and a piece of dirty cloth. Looking more carefully, they saw more policemen, revolver in hand, sheltering in doorways facing the house. All the shutters in Grand's house were closed, except one on the third floor that seemed to be hanging loose on one hinge only. Not a sound could be heard in the street but for occasional snatches of music coming from the center of the town.

Suddenly two revolver-shots rang out; they came from one of the buildings opposite and some splinters flew off the dismantled shutter. Then silence came again. Seen from a distance, after the tumult of the day, the whole business seemed to Rieux fantastically unreal, like something in a dream.

"That's Cottard's window," Grand suddenly exclaimed. "I can't make it out. I thought he'd disappeared."

"Why are they shooting?" Rieux asked the policeman.

"Oh, just to keep him busy. We're waiting for a car to come with the stuff that's needed. He fires at anyone who tries to get in by the front door. He got one of our men just now."

"But why did he fire?"

"Ask me another! Some folks were having fun in the street, and he let off at them. They couldn't make it out at first. When he fired again, they started yelling, one man was wounded, and the rest took to their heels. Some fellow out of his head, I should say."

The minutes seemed interminable in the silence that had returned. Then they noticed a dog, the first dog Rieux had seen for many months, emerging on the other side of the street, a draggled-looking spaniel that its owners had, presumably, kept in hiding. It ambled along the wall, stopped in the doorway, sat down, and began to dig at its fleas. Some of the policemen whistled for it to come away.

It raised its head, then walked out into the road and was sniffing at the hat when a revolver barked from the third-floor window. The dog did a somersault like a tossed pancake, lashed the air with its legs, and floundered on to its side, its body writhing in long convulsions. As if by way of reprisal five or six shots from the opposite house knocked more splinters off the shutter. Then silence fell again. The sun had moved a little

and the shadow-line was nearing Cottard's window. There was a low squeal of brakes in the street, behind the doctor.

"Here they are," the policeman said.

A number of police officers jumped out of the car and unloaded coils of rope, a ladder, and two big oblong packages wrapped in oilcloth. Then they turned into a street behind the row of houses facing Grand's. A minute or so later there were signs of movement, though little could be seen, in the doorways of the houses.

Then came a short spell of waiting. The dog had ceased moving; it now was lying in a small, dark, glistening pool.

Suddenly from the window of one of the houses that the police officers had entered from behind there came a burst of machine-gun fire. They were still aiming at the shutter, which literally shredded itself away, disclosing a dark gap into which neither Grand nor Rieux could see from where they stood. When the first machine-gun stopped firing, another opened up from a different angle, in a house a little farther up the street. The shots were evidently directed into the window space, and a fragment of the brickwork clattered down upon the pavement.

At the same moment three police officers charged across the road and disappeared into the doorway. The machine-gun ceased fire. Then came another wait. Two muffled detonations sounded inside the house, followed by a confused hubbub growing steadily louder until they saw a small man in his shirt-sleeves, screaming at the top of his voice, being carried more than dragged out by the doorway.

As if at an expected signal all the shutters in the street flew open and excited faces lined the windows, while people streamed out of the houses and jostled the lines of police. Rieux had a brief glimpse of the small man, on his feet now, in the middle of the road, his arms pinioned behind him by two police officers. He was still screaming. A policeman went up and dealt him two hard blows with his fists, quite calmly, with a sort of conscientious thoroughness.

"It's Cottard!" Grand's voice was shrill with excitement. "He's gone mad!"

Cottard had fallen backwards, and the policeman launched a vigorous kick into the crumpled mass sprawling on the ground. Then a small, surging group began to move toward the doctor and his old friend.

"Stand clear!" the policeman bawled.

Rieux looked away when the group, Cottard and his captors, passed him.

The dusk was thickening into night when Grand and the doctor made a move at last. The Cottard incident seemed to have shaken the neighborhood out of its normal lethargy and even these remote streets were becoming crowded with noisy merry-makers. On his doorstep Grand bade the doctor good night; he was going to put in an evening's work, he said. Just as he was starting up the stairs he added that he'd written to Jeanne and was feeling much happier. Also he'd made a fresh start with his phrase. "I've cut out all the adjectives."

And, with a twinkle in his eye, he took his hat off, bringing it low in a courtly sweep. But Rieux was thinking of Cottard, and the dull thud of fists belaboring the wretched man's face haunted him as he went to visit his old asthma patient. Perhaps it was more painful to think of a guilty man than of a dead man.

It was quite dark by the time he reached his patient's house. In the bedroom the distant clamor of a populace rejoicing in its new-won freedom could be faintly heard, and the old fellow was as usual transposing peas from one pan to another.

"They're quite right to amuse themselves," he said. "It takes all sorts to make a world, as they say. And your colleague, doctor, how's he getting on?"

"He's dead." Rieux was listening to his patient's rumbling chest.

"Ah, really?" The old fellow sounded embarrassed.

"Of plague," Rieux added.

"Yes," the old man said after a moment's silence, "it's always the best who go.

That's how life is. But he was a man who knew what he wanted."

"Why do you say that?" The doctor was putting back his stethoscope.

"Oh, for no particular reason. Only, well, he never talked just for talking's sake. I'd rather cottoned to him. But there you are! All those folks are saying:

'It was plague. We've had the plague here.' You'd almost think they expected to be given medals for it. But what does that mean, 'plague'? Just life, no more than that."

"Do your inhalations regularly."

"Don't worry about me, doctor! There's lots of life in me yet, and I'll see 'em all into their graves. I know how to live."

A burst of joyful shouts in the distance seemed an echo of his boast. Halfway across the room the doctor halted.

"Would you mind if I go up on the terrace?"

"Of course not. You'd like to have a look at 'em, that it? But they're just the same as ever, really." When Rieux was leaving the room, a new thought crossed his mind. "I say, doctor. Is it a fact they're going to put up a memorial to the people who died of plague?"

"So the papers say. A monument, or just a tablet."

"I could have sworn it! And there'll be speeches." He chuckled throatily. "I can almost hear them saying: 'Our dear departed...' And then they'll go off and have a good snack."

Rieux was already halfway up the stairs. Cold, fathomless depths of sky glimmered overhead, and near the hilltops stars shone hard as flint. It was much like the night when he and Tarrou had come to the terrace to forget the plague.

Only, tonight the sea was breaking on the cliffs more loudly and the air was calm and limpid, free of the tang of brine the autumn wind had brought. The noises of the town were still beating like waves at the foot of the long line of terraces, but tonight they told not of revolt, but of deliverance. In the distance a reddish glow hung above the big central streets and squares. In this night of new-born freedom desires knew no limits, and it was their clamor that reached Rieux's ears.

From the dark harbor soared the first rocket of the firework display organized by the municipality, and the town acclaimed it with a long-drawn sigh of delight. Cottard.

Tarrou, the men and the woman Rieux had loved and lost, all alike, dead or guilty, were forgotten. Yes, the old fellow had been right; these people were "just the same as ever." But this was at once their strength and their innocence, and it was on this level, beyond all grief, that Rieux could feel himself at one with them. And it was in the midst of shouts rolling against the terrace wall in massive waves that waxed in volume and duration, while cataracts of colored fire fell thicker through the darkness, that Dr. Rieux

resolved to compile this chronicle, so that he should not be one of those who hold their peace but should bear witness in favor of those plague-stricken people; so that some memorial of the injustice and outrage done them might endure; and to state quite simply what we learn in a time of pestilence: that there are more things to admire in men than to despise.

None the less, he knew that the tale he had to tell could not be one of a final victory. It could be only the record of what had had to be done, and what assuredly would have to be done again in the never ending fight against terror and its relentless onslaughts, despite their personal afflictions, by all who, while unable to be saints but refusing to bow down to pestilences, strive their utmost to be healers.

And, indeed, as he listened to the cries of joy rising from the town, Rieux remembered that such joy is always imperiled. He knew what those jubilant crowds did not know but could have learned from books: that the plague bacillus never dies or disappears for good; that it can lie dormant for years and years in furniture and linen-chests; that it bides its time in bedrooms, cellars, trunks, and bookshelves; and that perhaps the day would come when, for the bane and the enlightening of men, it would rouse up its rats again and send them forth to die in a happy city.